Mac and His Problem

Enrique Vila-Matas

Mac and His Problem

Translated from the Spanish
by Margaret Jull Costa & Sophie Hughes

Harvill *Secker*

LONDON

1 3 5 7 9 10 8 6 4 2

Harvill Secker, an imprint of Vintage,
20 Vauxhall Bridge Road,
London SW1V 2SA

Harvill Secker is part of the Penguin Random House group of companies
whose addresses can be found at global.penguinrandomhouse.com

Penguin
Random House
UK

First published by Harvill Secker in 2019
First published with the title *Mac y su contratiempo* in Spain by Seix Barral in 2017

A CIP catalogue record for this book is available from the British Library

penguin.co.uk/vintage

ISBN 9781787300453

Co-funded by the
Creative Europe Programme
of the European Union

*The European Commission support for the production of this publication does not constitute an
endorsement of the contents which reflects the views only of the authors, and the Commission
cannot be held responsible for any use which may be made of the information contained therein.*

Extract from the poem beginning 'Me he quedado aquí' from
Obra completa by Luís Pimentel, translated by Margaret Jull Costa and
Sophie Hughes; extract from the poem 'Notes Toward a Supreme Fiction'
from *The Collected Poems* by Wallace Stevens; lyrics quoted from the
Beatles song 'Yesterday' written by Paul McCartney and John Lennon.

Printed and bound in Great Britain by Clays Ltd, Elcograf S.p.A.

Penguin Random House is committed to a sustainable future
for our business, our readers and our planet. This book is made
from Forest Stewardship Council® certified paper.

MIX
Paper from
responsible sources
FSC® C018179

For Paula de Parma

I remember that I almost always went dressed as a hobo or a ghost.
Once I went as a skeleton.

Joe Brainard, *I Remember*

Mac and His Problem

I'm fascinated by the current vogue for posthumous books, and I'm thinking of writing a fake one that could appear to be "posthumous" *and* "unfinished" when it would, in fact, be perfectly complete. Were I to die during the writing process, the book really would be my "final, interrupted work," and that would, among other things, ruin my great dream of becoming a falsifier. Then again, a beginner must be prepared for anything, and I am just that, a debutant. My name is Mac. Perhaps because I am only a beginner, the best and most sensible thing would be to wait a while before attempting anything as challenging as a fake "posthumous" book. Given my status as a writing novice, my priority will be not to launch straight into that "last" book or to create some other kind of fake, but simply to put pen to paper every day and see what happens. And then there might come a time when, feeling more prepared, I decide to make a stab at that book falsely interrupted by my death, disappearance, or suicide. For the moment, I will content myself with writing this diary, which I am starting today, feeling utterly terrified, not even daring to look in the mirror for fear of catching sight of my head hunched down inside my shirt collar.

As I said, my name is Mac. I live here in the Coyote district. I'm sitting in my usual room, as if I'd been sitting here forever. I'm listening to Kate Bush, and Bowie's lined up next. Outside, the summer looks set to do its worst, and Barcelona is preparing—so the weathermen say—for a sharp rise in temperatures.

I'm called Mac after a famous scene in John Ford's *My Darling*

Clementine. My parents saw the movie shortly before I was born and particularly liked the part when Sheriff Wyatt asks the old barman in the saloon:

"Mac, you ever been in love?"

"No, I been a bartender all my life."

They loved the bartender's response and ever since then, since the day in April in the late 1940s when I was born, I've been Mac.

Mac here, there, and everywhere. I'm Mac to everyone. In recent years, on more than one occasion, I've been mistaken for a Macintosh computer. And that always tickles me, perhaps because, as far as I'm concerned, it's far better to be known as Mac than by my real name, which is just awful, a tyrannical imposition by my paternal grandfather, and I refuse even to pronounce it, still less write it.

Everything I say in this diary I'll be saying to myself, because no one else is going to read it. I withdraw to this private space where, among other things, I'm trying to ascertain if—as Nathalie Sarraute once said—writing really is an attempt to find out what we would write if we wrote. This is a secret diary of initiation, which doesn't even know yet if it's showing signs of having been started. I, on the other hand, text certainly have started giving out signals that, at the age of sixty-plus, I'm embarking on a new path. I've waited too long for this moment to arrive to throw it all away now. The time is nigh, if it isn't already upon me.

"Mac, Mac, Mac."

Who's speaking?

It's the voice of a dead man who appears to be lodged inside my head. I assume he's trying to advise me not to rush things, but that's no reason to rein in my hopes and aspirations. That voice isn't going to frighten me, and so I'll proceed exactly as I intended to. Does the voice not realize that for two months and seven days, ever since the family construction business went bust, I've felt both demoralized and immensely liberated, as if the closure of all our offices and the abrupt suspension of payments has helped me find my place in the world?

I have my own reasons for feeling better than when I earned my living as a prosperous builder. However, that newfound happiness—yes, let's call it that—isn't exactly something I'm aching for other people to notice. I dislike all forms of ostentation. I've always felt a need to be as inconspicuous as possible, which is the origin of my tendency, whenever possible, to hide.

Lying low, hunkering down with these pages will keep me entertained; although I would just say that, if, for some reason, I should be discovered, that wouldn't be a catastrophe either. In the meantime, I prefer for this diary to remain secret, which gives me greater freedom to say what I like, to say now, for example, that you can spend years and years believing yourself to be a writer, safe in the knowledge that no one's going to bother telling you: "Quit kidding yourself, you're not." Now, if, one day, that same would-be writer decides to make his debut, to knuckle down and finally put pen to paper, that bold beginner will immediately notice, if he's honest with himself, that this activity has nothing to do with the vulgar idea of believing himself to be a writer, because—and I want to say this now with no more beating about the bush—in order to write one must cease to be *a writer*.

Although in the next few days I'll agree to accept the paltry sum from the sale of the apartment that, up until now, I've managed to hang on to after my economic ruin, I worry about ending up entirely dependent on Carmen's business. Or worse, having to ask for help from my children. Who would have thought that one day I would be at the mercy of my wife's furniture restoration workshop, when only a few short weeks ago, I was the owner of a rock-solid construction company? It worries me having to depend on Carmen, but even if I lost everything, I don't think I would be any worse off than when I was building houses, lining my pockets with gold, but also plagued with all manner of frustrations and neuroses.

Although life's mundane affairs have led me down unanticipated paths, and although I've never written anything of a literary nature before, I've always been passionate about reading and an aficionado of brevity. First it was poetry, then it was short stories. I love short stories. I don't, on the other hand, have much sympathy for novels, because they are, as Barthes said, a form of death, transforming life into Fate. If I were to write a novel, I'd like to lose it the way you might mislay an apple after buying a whole bagful from the local Pakistani convenience store. I'd like to lose it just to prove that I don't care one bit about novels and prefer other literary forms. I was deeply impressed by a very short story by Ana María Matute, in which she said that the story has an old vagabond heart that wanders into town, then disappears.... Matute concludes: "The story withdraws, but leaves its mark." I sometimes tell myself that I was saved from a great misfortune when, from a very early age, everything conspired to leave me without even a moment to discover that to write is to cease to write. If I'd had the necessary free time, I might now be oozing literary talent, or else be quite simply destroyed and finished as a writer, but in either case entirely unable to enjoy the marvelous beginnerish spirit I'm relishing at this precise moment, this perfect moment, on the dot of noon on the morning of June 29, just as I'm preparing to crack open a bottle of 1966 Vega Sicilia, experiencing, let's say, the joy of someone who knows he's still unpublished and is celebrating the start of this apprentice's diary, this secret diary, and looking around him in the silence of the morning, aware of a faintly luminous air, which may exist only inside his brain.

[WHOROSCOPE]

At the point when one can begin to call evening night, and when I was already slightly tipsy, I decided to dig out a 1970 Spanish edition of *Poems* by Samuel Beckett. The first section of the book is entitled *Whoroscope*. It's a meditation on time and was written and published in 1930. I understood it less than when I first read it, but, for whatever reason, perhaps precisely because I understood less, I liked it much more. Those hundred lines by Beckett on the passing of the days, dissipation, and hen's eggs sound distinctly Cartesian, or like Descartes's ventriloquized voice. The thing I least understood was that business about chickens and their eggs, but, boy, did I have fun not understanding it. Perfect.

&

I wonder why it is that today, knowing myself to be a mere novice, I worked my fingers to the bone trying in vain to begin this diary with a few impeccable opening paragraphs. The hours I spent on this absurd enterprise! To say that I have plenty of time and nothing else to do is no excuse. The fact is that I wrote everything in pencil on pages torn from my notebook, then went through it with a fine-tooth comb, typed it on my computer, printed it out, reread it, studied the corrected version, and edited it some more—which is when a writer really writes—then, after transferring this back onto my PC, I erased all trace of what I'd written by hand and gave final approval to my notes of the day, which have remained buried inside my computer's enigmatic innards.

I realize now that I behaved as if I didn't know that—ultimately—perfect paragraphs don't stand the test of time, because they are mere language, and can be destroyed by a sloppy typesetter, by changes in fashions and usage, in short, by life itself.

But, says the voice, since you're only a beginner, the gods of writing can still forgive you your mistakes.

2

Yesterday, the cheerful, fanatical lifelong reader in me looked down at my desk, at the small rectangle of wood positioned in one corner of my study, and made his writing debut.

I began my diary exercises without a plan, aware that in literature you don't start because you have something to write about and then write it. It's the writing process itself that allows the author to discover what it is he wants to say. That's how I began yesterday, with the intention of maintaining a readiness to learn slowly and steadily and perhaps, one day, achieve a depth of knowledge that might allow me to take on far greater challenges. That's how I began yesterday, and that's how I mean to go on, just being carried along and finding out as I go where my words will lead me.

Seeing myself, so modest and insignificant, seated at the small wooden structure that Carmen built for me years ago in her workshop—not for me to write at, but so that I could work on my thriving business from home—has made me think about how certain minor and even basic characters in books stay with you longer than other more spectacular heroes. I'm thinking of drab, unassuming Akaky Akakievich, Gogol's copyist in "The Overcoat," a bureaucrat destined to be—to put it plainly—an "insignificant fellow." Akakievich only appears in this one brief tale, but he is undoubtedly one of the most vivid and convincing characters in the history of world literature, perhaps because, in this short work, Gogol threw common sense to the wind and worked away gaily on the edge of his own private abyss.

I've always been fond of Akaky Akakievich, who needs a new overcoat to protect himself from the St. Petersburg winter, but, on acquiring one, notices that the cold persists—an unending, universal cold. It hasn't escaped me that Akakievich the copyist was brought into the world by Gogol in 1842, which leads me to believe that he has his direct descendants in all those characters who crop up in the literature of the day, the creatures we see painstakingly copying things out in schools and offices, transcribing documents around the clock under the dim light of an oil lamp; they copy texts mechanically and appear capable of repeating everything that's still to be repeated in the world, without ever expressing any personal opinions, or making attempts to modify anything. "I don't do change," I think I recall one of those characters saying. "I don't want any changes," said another.

Another person who doesn't want any changes is "the repeater" (better known at school as "34"), a character from one of the stories in *My Documents* by Alejandro Zambra. 34 has repeater syndrome.

He's a specialist in repeating the school year, without this constituting, for him, any kind of setback. Quite the opposite. Zambra's
repeater is strangely unresentful; he's a perfectly laid-back young
man: "Sometimes we'd see him talking to teachers we didn't know.
They were animated conversations.... He liked to remain on
friendly terms with the teachers who had failed him."

The last time I saw Ana Turner—one of the booksellers at La
Súbita, the only bookstore in the Coyote neighborhood, and a very
happy one, too—she told me that she'd sent an email to her friend
Zambra asking him about 34 and received this reply: "It seems to
me that we poets and storytellers are the real repeaters. The poet is
a repeater. Those who needed to write only one book—some not
even that—in order to pass the year aren't like the rest of us, who
are obliged to keep on trying."

To me, Ana Turner is a constant source of surprise and admiration: I have no idea how, working at La Súbita, she managed to
contact a writer like Zambra. Equally intriguing is how she manages to grow more attractive by the day. Every time I see her I'm
bowled over. I try to play it cool, but there's always some new—not
necessarily physical—detail about Ana that I wasn't expecting.
The afternoon when I last saw her I discovered, thanks to Zambra's
words—"it seems to me that we poets and storytellers are the real
repeaters"—that Ana was quite possibly a poet. I do write poems,
she confessed rather diffidently. But really they're just attempts, she
added. And her words seemed to echo Zambra, saying that writers
are "obliged to keep on trying."

Hearing this from the mouth of someone like Ana, I first thought
how lovely life can be, but then my mind flitted to other, darker
thoughts, like the back row in a school classroom, and the students
condemned to write two hundred lines, all in the name of improving their handwriting.

I also thought about a novelist who was once asked by a lady at
a conference when he was going to stop writing about people who
murdered women. He replied:

"I assure you that as soon as I get it right, I'll stop."

At several points this morning, as I recalled those repeaters-cum-calligraphers about whom I'm now writing, I had the feeling that I was glimpsing the dark parasite of repetition that lies at the core of all literary creation. A parasite in the form of the solitary gray droplet that exists in the midst of every rain shower or storm and also at the very center of the universe, where, as we know, the same routines, always the same, are repeated over and over, because everything there gets ceaselessly, crushingly repeated.

[WHOROSCOPE 2]

A little early-evening prose. I've had my three customary afternoon nips and consulted the horoscope in my favorite newspaper. I was astonished when I read this in the box for my sign: "For Aries, the Sun in conjunction with Mercury suggests brilliant intuitions that will lead you to believe this prediction and think it's meant especially for you."

Whoroscope! This time the prediction really did seem to be meant especially for me, as if Peggy Day—the pseudonym of the lady responsible for the horoscope—had somehow gotten wind of my mistake last week when, in front of more people than I'd care to remember, I mentioned that, at the end of each day, I like to read the horoscope in my favorite newspaper and that, even when the prediction has no relevance to my life at all, in the end, my experience as a seasoned reader leads me to interpret the text so that whatever it says seems to fit perfectly with whatever has happened to me that day.

You just have to know how to read, I said on that occasion, and I even spoke to them about the seers and sibyls of old and how their ravings would be interpreted by one of the many priests with which antiquity was teeming at the time. For the true art of those sibyls lay in those interpretations. I even spoke to them about Lídia, that native of Cadaqués, who, according to Dalí, possessed the most magnificently paranoid mind he'd ever known. In 1904, Lídia briefly saw Eugeni d'Ors and was so struck by him that, ten years later, in the local social club, she would interpret the articles that d'Ors published in a Barcelona newspaper as responses to the letters she sent him and to which he never replied.

I also told them that I intend to go on interpreting prophecies until the day I die. The thing is, everything I said at that friendly gathering could perfectly well have reached the ears of Peggy Day, because there were people there who work for the same paper. I haven't seen her for forty years and, to tell the truth, I don't think she's a real astrologer at all. I met Peggy in my youth, one summer in S'Agaró. Back then, she was called Juanita Lopesbaño, and I suspect that she won't have very fond memories of me.

You consider yourself a modest sort, and then, one day, without thinking, you start blowing your own trumpet about how good you are at interpreting newspaper horoscopes—an unthinkable mistake after so many years of discretion—and suddenly your life, most unfairly, becomes terribly complicated. Yes, life becomes incredibly complicated all because of one moment of vanity in the middle of a party.

Is it simply my remorse at having made this mistake that whipped up all this paranoia at the thought that Peggy Day knows about my blunder?

3

Stupidity isn't my strong suit, said Monsieur Teste. I've always liked that line and I would repeat it over and over right now were it not for the fact that I'm hoping to write something similar, only different; saying, for example, that repetition is my strong suit. Or perhaps: repetition is my theme. Or else: I like to repeat things, but in modified form. That last phrase best suits my personality, because I'm a tireless modifier. I see, I read, I listen, and it seems to me that everything could benefit from a little editing. And I edit everything. I never stop.

My vocation is as a modifier of things.

And as a repeater of things, too. But that vocation is more commonplace. Essentially we are all repeaters. Repetition, that most human of gestures, is one I would like to analyze, research, and then I would modify the conclusions other people have reached. Do any of us come into this life to do anything that's not the repetition of something already tried and tested by those who came before us? Basically, repetition is such a vast subject that any attempt to pin it down risks seeming ridiculous. My fear, too, is that the subject of repetition might conceal within its very nature something deeply troubling. And yet researching it is sure to have its interesting side, because repetition could be seen as something that looks to the future. Kierkegaard was referring to this attractive aspect of repetition when he said that repetition and recollection were the same movement, only in opposite directions, since "what is recollected is repeated backward, whereas repetition properly so-called is recollected forward. Therefore repetition, if it is possible, makes a man happy, whereas recollection makes him unhappy...."

As a modifier of things, I would now modify what Kierkegaard said, but I don't know how. And so I'll allow a few hours to pass and see if my modifying instinct improves. Meanwhile, I'll record only that the afternoon is light, anodyne, provincial, elemental, perfect. I'm in an extraordinarily good mood, which is, perhaps, why I find even the anodyne nature of this afternoon so immensely pleasing. This afternoon is, in fact, no different from any other.

I'm sitting here quite still, my vigilant gaze fixed beyond my study on the spacious living room, that room where light and shade do not meet. The hours, sometimes with quite inconceivable regularity, ring out from the church clock here in the neighborhood where I've lived for forty years. I tell myself that, perhaps, as regards the clock, there is no repetition, just the exact same hour chiming every time: life seen as a single afternoon, as an elemental, anodyne afternoon; very occasionally glorious, but never without a grayish undertone.

I've always worked in the business set up by my grandfather, and which has shown me both the splendid and—in recent years—the catastrophic side of the building sector. I worked very hard in that tumultuous family business, and as a meager compensation for such crazy—truly crazy—work, in my free time I've been a compulsive reader, eavesdropping as much as I could—sometimes with astonishment and at others with pity—on writers from all ages, but especially contemporary writers.

When not being consumed by that demanding and, ultimately, failed business, my preferred activities were reading and intense family life. Let me be clear, I'm no stranger to misfortune. For example, when I was forty years old and had everything I could possibly want, I remember feeling utterly miserable, because my one wish was to escape from that business and, instead, return to my studies and become, say, a lawyer; but my cruel paternal grandfather (he who cannot be named) wouldn't allow it.

I sometimes think I would love to have been like lawyer and poet Wallace Stevens. It seems to me that, as a general rule, we always want to be what we are not. I would love to have been capable of writing these lines to the editor of a literary review, as Stevens did in 1922: "Do, please, excuse me from the biographical note. I am a lawyer and live in Hartford. But such facts are neither gay nor instructive."

I've always found it hard to look back, but I'm going to do so now in order to recall the very first time I heard the word "repetition."

Cronos is a god unknown to the extremely young. Then, one day, while we are drifting, happily supine on our lake of ignorance, our first experience of repetition plunges us into time, perhaps almost as if it were a mirage.

I had my first experience of repetition when I was four years old, when, at school, someone told me that the boy I shared my desk with, little Soteras, was going to repeat his preschool year. That verb "repeat" dropped like a bomb into my young, busily expanding mind and plunged me suddenly into the circle of Time, because then I understood—it hadn't even occurred to me before—that such things as years existed and that one school year would be followed by another school year and that we were all trapped in that nightmarish network of days, weeks, months, and "kilometers" (as a child, I thought the years were called kilometers and perhaps I wasn't far wrong).

I entered the circle of Time in September 1952, shortly after my parents had enrolled me in a Catholic school. In the early 1950s, so-called Primary Education consisted of four stages: Preschool, Elementary, Middle Grade, and Senior Grade. You started school at four or five and could leave, en route to university, when you were sixteen or seventeen. Preschool lasted only one year and was very like a children's playground, what, today, we call kindergarten, except that the children were all seated at desks, as if they were already expected to study seriously.

It was a time when children seemed very old, and the old seemed virtually dead. My clearest memory of that preschool year is of little Soteras's sad face. I call him "little" because there was something about him, quite what we didn't know, that made him appear younger than the rest of us, for, with each passing day, we seemed to become older than our years, and continued to do so at a rate of knots. The country needed us, one teacher told us, doubtless pleased to see how we were growing.

I remember Soteras would sometimes play with an inflatable ball that was, quite literally, *his* and which he would allow us all to play with during recess. The fact of actually owning something was the only thing that made Soteras seem older, like us. As soon as we went back to our desks, Soteras became younger again. I'll never forget the gray cape he wore in winter, and, for a long time, I was fascinated by his status as a repeater.

I'm giving him a false name because I would prefer to treat him as a character, and also because, even though I'm not expecting anyone to read this, I cannot summon him up without imagining some possible future reader. What explanation can I give for that strange contradiction? None. But if I were obliged to find at least one, I would resort to this Hasidic saying: "The man who thinks he can live without others is mistaken; the one who thinks others can't live without him is even more deluded."

For many years, Soteras having to repeat the preschool year remained a great enigma to me. Then, one afternoon, when he was studying architecture and I'd abandoned my university studies to work in the family business, we bumped into each other on the No. 7 bus on Avenida Diagonal in Barcelona, and I couldn't resist asking him, straight out, why he had repeated the year that no one ever repeats, namely, the preschool year.

Not only was Soteras entirely unsurprised by my question, he looked at me and smiled, and seemed really glad to be able to answer it, as if he had spent years preparing himself for that day.

"You won't believe it," he said, "but I asked my parents to let me stay down a year because I was afraid of moving up to the next one."

I did believe him, because I found that perfectly plausible. And it seemed even more plausible when he added that he had seen what the next year was like and realized how hard pupils had to study, and that it appeared to be an environment deliberately created to be cold. In those days, I thought to myself, we were afraid of change, afraid of studying, afraid of the coldness of life, afraid of everything; there was an awful lot of fear around then. And I was still thinking this when Soteras asked if I'd ever heard of someone going to see a movie twice, and entirely failing to understand it the second time around. I stood rooted to the spot, dumbstruck, in the middle of that crowded bus.

"Well," he said, "that's what happened to me after spending two years in preschool: the first time I understood everything, the second time nothing at all."

[WHOROSCOPE 3]

"Problems with the kids in the morning. In the afternoon, you will discover that the world is so perfect that it lacks for nothing."

This time, Peggy wasn't addressing me directly; presumably having done so yesterday was enough. However, as usual, this didn't stop me from giving her oracle a personal interpretation. She seems to be warning me not to continue writing, not to add anything to the world, because I would simply be repeating and repeating. Or are there things that have yet to be written? As for those "problems with the kids," they surely didn't apply to my three children, who are all grown up now and leading their own lives, but, rather, to the complicated technical difficulties I've had to resolve this morning while writing. The children she mentions are the paragraphs that have caused me so many problems and anxieties.

As for that "In the afternoon, you will discover" business, this clearly refers to what I learned a couple of hours ago from Ander Sánchez and what he said to Ana Turner and me when I went out to buy some cigarettes and met him outside the bookstore, enjoying a laugh with Ana. Our famous neighbor Sánchez, the "celebrated Barcelona writer," greeted me with unusual warmth. He rarely does so, but then, we weren't both hurrying off down the street, as has tended to be the case whenever we've met over the years. Instead, he was standing outside the bookstore, an easy target for anyone wishing to assail him with a few admiring or merely courteous words. There he was, making no attempt to conceal the fact that he was in thrall to the charms of the marvelous Ana, something that made me feel unexpectedly jealous.

Who doesn't know Sánchez in an area that, in part, owes its name—Coyote—to his existence, because, by the most coincidental of coincidences, the apartment where Sánchez has lived for some decades—in the building next to mine—once belonged to José Mallorquí, the most popular Barcelona writer of the 1940s. Or it might be that Sánchez bought it unaware that Mallorquí had been its former occupant; however, word on the street is that he bought it precisely because he thought it might help him to become, like that former occupant, the most widely sold author in Spain. For, from 1943 on, in what is now Sánchez's apartment, José Mallorquí wrote the two hundred novels in the series *El Coyote*, pulp novels that were huge bestsellers in postwar Spain.

When I came to live in this neighborhood all those years ago, this part of the Eixample had no name, then we and some other neighbors, half-joking, decided to call it the Coyote district. The name caught on, and now almost everyone calls it that, although in the vast majority of cases, they have no idea where the name comes from. It's a neighborhood that extends, with no very definite borders, as far as Plaza de Francesc Macià, formerly called Calvo Sotelo, and before that, during the civil war, Plaza Hermanos Badía.

Anyway, today, Sánchez—who has no idea that I was among those who participated in the naming of this neighborhood—deigned to say hello to me. More than that, he spoke to me with such exquisite, elaborate politeness that I was obliged, unaccustomed as I am, to reciprocate in rather clumsy fashion.

And in the middle of all this, he began—more, I thought, in order to impress Ana than anything else—to talk brilliantly about all kinds of things, and, without the least encouragement from either of us, he ended up revealing the difficulties he had in recalling the years of his youth, and one year in particular, when he had doubtless drunk even more than usual, he said, because he wrote a novel about a ventriloquist and a sunshade from Java (which concealed a deadly weapon) and about a miserable barber from Seville.

"But I can't remember much more than that," he said, "except that it contained a few passages that were completely incomprehensible, or, rather, opaque, dense, how can I put it, verging on the deeply stupid…."

He was clearly very good at laughing at himself. And it occurred to me that perhaps I should attempt to follow his lead, although if I were to try out my self-ridicule on Ana, I'd do such a bad job of it that I'd just end up making a complete fool of myself.

What most intrigued Sánchez, he said, was how he could have written a book full of such utter nonsense. He was probably talking about the novel from his early period, *Walter and His Problem*. He was amazed he'd managed to write the book at all, given that he was permanently drunk at the time, and even more amazed that the novel was blithely accepted by his publisher, who published it without a murmur, perhaps because he was paying Sánchez so little and so couldn't really afford to be too demanding.

It was, he said, a book full of inconsistencies and mistakes, the occasional absurd change in pace, and all kinds of twaddle, al-though—and here he chose to brag—it did also contain the oc-casional brilliant idea, which, oddly enough, sprang directly out of all the other nonsense. He could only partially remember the novel, his memory being somewhat watered down, as if he could only re-member the tonic from the G&Ts that he drank incessantly while writing his ventriloquist's deliberately partial memoirs.

Having told us this whole saga, he suddenly fell silent. Ana seemed more and more captivated by him, and this so irritated me that I had to remind myself that, according to recent statements straight from the horse's mouth, Sánchez was currently planning a total of four autobiographical novels in the style of the Norwegian writer Knausgaard. And I screamed under my breath:

"You cannot be serious!"

The other two looked at me uncomprehendingly, but, at the same time, entirely unfazed by their failure to comprehend, which only confirmed that I was completely incidental to the goings-on there. I thought about *Walter and His Problem*, because it was a book not entirely unfamiliar to me. I remembered that it was strangely beauti-ful in places, and, in others, uneven and quite deranged, and I was pretty sure that I hadn't actually read it to the end. Yes, I remember now, I abandoned it about halfway through, having begun to grow bored with the inclusion in every story or chapter of one or two paragraphs that had nothing to do with anything else; unbearable paragraphs, which, if I'm not mistaken, Sánchez had justified later on, in interviews after the book came out, saying that he had delib-erately made them confusing "because the plot demanded it."

Because the plot demanded it! It was hardly the most cast-iron of plots. The book was supposedly the memoirs of a ventriloquist, but that plot or lifeline consisted—again if I remember rightly—of a few "biographical sketches." It resembled a life of which we were given only the bare bones: a few significant moments, alongside other more tangential episodes, and still others that had barely any connection with Walter's world at all, as if they were part of some-one else's memoirs.

"I was very young when I wrote it," he said, "and I think now that it was a misuse of my talent. Actually, I really regret having let that novel get away. It was sheer stupidity on my part. But what can you do? You can't turn back the clock. Luckily for me, no one remembers it now."

He bowed his head for a moment, then glanced up again to say:

"There are days when I even wonder if someone else wrote it for me."

And he seemed about to look at me.

Oh hell, I thought with a shudder, I hope he doesn't think I wrote it.

4

I spent the morning half asleep, just as a certain poor beginner was at last discovering what it was he wanted to write about and had embarked on an investigation into repetition, which was, without a doubt, the subject to which his first three days of writing exercises had led him. Hadn't this debutant predicted that it was the writing process itself that would help him discover what it was he wanted to say?

What's more, a voice was saying: "Repetition is my strong suit."

Anyway. On realizing, still half asleep, that this poor beginner might in fact be me, I had even more of a ridiculous shock than Stan Laurel gets in the scene where a thief slips his hand over the back of the bench where he is napping, and Stan, in his sleepy reverie, with his own hands clasped together, mistakes the stranger's hand for one of his.

A little later, as I sat pondering the theme of repetition, it occurred to me that, even supposing that you triumph in your first battle as a writer and produce something amazing—they say it's rare to carve out such a path, to find your voice—such a victory can end up being something of a problem, containing, as it does, the seed that sooner or later will inevitably lead the author to repeat himself. Which isn't to say that this rare victory—finding the unique tone or register—isn't still highly desirable, for no one can deny the gulf that exists between the writer who has found his own voice and the bleating literary chorus from the mass grave of the talentless, even if, ultimately, at the end of the long road, there is but one icy plain for all of us.

Of course, you could also look at things another way and see, for example, that we wouldn't be anything without imitation or other similar activities, which means that repetition isn't quite the beast it's made out to be: "I say, too, that when a painter wishes to gain fame with his art, he attempts to imitate the works of the great masters he knows, and this same rule applies to all other crafts and professions that serve to enrich the nation" (*Don Quixote*, chapter XXV).

Put another way: in and of itself, repetition is far from being a harmful thing. Where would we be without it? And, while we're on the subject, where does that deep-rooted belief come from, so dear to all self-deprecating authors, that repeating yourself is the slippery slope to ruin? I can't understand where this notion comes from, when really there isn't a soul on the planet who doesn't repeat himself. You need look no further than Stanley Kubrick, who was consistently praised for switching genres, styles, and themes. People were always saying how much he changed from movie to movie, but if you look carefully at the work of this great director you'll be amazed to discover that, really, it's all built around the same closed circle of obsessive repetitions.

The fear of repeating oneself. This morning, still half asleep, I was filled by that same panic—and I've only been writing this diary for three days!... I can only say that women have an admirable ability to rise above such problems, which I suspect have been thought up by envious types with the intention of paralyzing the most creative minds.

Women seem better able to quash all those absurd concerns that haunt and devastate us poor men; we are always more foolish and tormented than our female counterparts, who seem to have a sixth sense that allows them to simplify problems intelligently. I'm thinking, for example, of Hebe Uhart, the Argentinian writer. Asked whether she worried about repeating herself she said no, not at all, because she always wrote about journeys and no two journeys were ever the same; she always discovered something new on her trips, and the particular circumstances of each one obliged her to write different things....

Isak Dinesen, to give another example, was equally quick to solve this problem: "The fear of repeating yourself is offset by the joy of knowing that you're making your way forward in the company of stories from the past." Dinesen saw the wisdom in building out of the past. In *I've Been Here Before*, the writers Jordi Balló and Xavier Pérez talk about the pleasure of repetition, which shouldn't prevent creators from making new or unforeseen discoveries. They also write about how the cultural sector has for years depended on the fallacy that novelty is all that matters, a publishing myth that has been embraced by the public and taken to ludicrous extremes, precisely because the cult now aims to conceal the original sources of its stories: "When it comes to fiction that repeats itself, on the other hand, we acknowledge that a connection with the past is essential to its narrative. And it is this awareness that leads these fictions into experimental territory, because they try to be original not by harking back to their own 'pilot episode,' but by exploiting the potential of that initial experiment to open out into new universes."

&

As evening fell, and I sat thinking about what Sánchez had said yesterday about his novel full of tiresome twaddle and ponderous digressions, I recalled a day, about three months ago, when I sat down at a table on the terrace of the Baltimore, very close to a group of graying forty-somethings with a bohemian, almost vagrant look about them—it was hard to know exactly which of these two groups they belonged to, although in the end one suspected the former: some very second-rate bohemians—and whom I'd never seen before. Having exhausted, successively and at the tops of their voices, the subjects of women, soft drugs, and soccer, they ended up telling long-winded stories about dogs.

And who should be sitting with these café conversationalists, the most sparkling and vocal among them, but a nephew of Sánchez, about whom I knew nothing, mainly because he didn't live locally, or at least I'd never seen him around. And I would have remembered seeing him, because his physique—his powerful broad shoulders—stood out a mile. You really couldn't miss him.

Listening to their doggy anecdotes—through strained ears, because their tone became suddenly hushed and secretive as if they were trying to prevent me from eavesdropping on their barbarous tales—I ended up hearing—sometimes only partially, sometimes perfectly clearly—the quite incredible story of an author's dog. Someone asked which author they were talking about, and the nephew replied:

"Sánchez. Sánchez's dog."

This declaration was followed by a foul stream of calculated insults all directed at his uncle, to whom he referred several times as "the family idiot."

It was immediately clear to me from his extreme aggression that the nephew was highly dependent on the supposed glory of his famous relative. In fact, to say he was highly dependent would be an understatement. For the entire time I spent observing him, he never stopped mocking Sánchez or describing alleged acts of stupidity on his part, above all tearing into his literary style with vile jibes and cruel send-ups, showing no mercy to either the slighted uncle or his dog.

It was clear that the nephew had let his uncontrollable vanity run away with him, for he boasted nonstop about his own talent, as if he truly believed it was far superior to Sánchez's. And yet, every now and then, he would come out with something that revealed him to be a great powder keg of envy.

"To think that I've given up on reams of poems and novellas, which, had I published them, would have been read and loved by future generations...."

Future generations!

What a way to talk, and yet nothing suggested he was anything but deadly serious. According to this nephew, successful writers—he was incapable of making any other kind of value judgment—owed their success to their having adapted better than others to the market, to the book industry. It made no difference if they were talented, or even brimming with genius: all successful authors, by the mere fact of having secured a readership, were nobodies. The truly, seriously good ones were a handful of marginal and marginalized authors, a few unknown types existing entirely outside the system. To count yourself among these heroes you had to have been lauded by one specific critic from Benimagrell, whose name I hadn't heard of, just as the town, Benimagrell, didn't ring any bells either. Nonetheless, on my return home I was able to look it up online and confirm that the town does indeed exist, somewhere in the Alicante region, although I found no reference to any critic hailing from there, at least not one with even minimal standing.

To be honest—because the last thing I'd do here is deceive myself—that day it also occurred to me that I might actually agree with some of the things the antagonistic nephew was saying if it weren't for the disproportionately angry way in which he said them. He reminded me of "Rameau's nephew," the character through whom, whether intentionally or not, Diderot foresaw a time when there would be no ethical distinctions between great men and those who ridiculed them. Again, to be honest, I must say that, putting aside for a moment his surly tone and foul mouth, I began to see that the nephew had his appeal, a rare kind of wit, especially when it came to his most vicious lines. I hate to admit it, because that monster really was a monster, but he clearly had the makings of a writer....

I pretended that I needed something from the bar so that, on my return, I could get a better view of his face and the rest of him, hitherto out of eyeshot.

I ordered a Cherry Coke (a now-forgotten variety of Coca-Cola), and, as I should have known, they neither had it nor knew what I was talking about.

"Right," I said, "well, in that case I think I'll forget it."

I made my way back to my table, but not without snatching a head-on glance at the monster, and what I saw was a puffed-up giant with a ghastly beard, which looked—perhaps to rival those wastes-of-space beside him—as if swallows had nested in it....

It's strange, but yesterday, when I bumped into Sánchez standing outside La Súbita, I didn't recall either his nephew or the critic from Benimagrell. Today, on the other hand, I haven't stopped thinking about the broad-shouldered giant, because I've begun to associate my meeting with Sánchez yesterday with my chance encounter, about three months ago now, with that antagonistic nephew whom I haven't laid eyes on since. And I've noticed that these two sequences together form a very slight novelistic plot: as if, all of a sudden, certain autobiographical incidents had decided to piece together for me a single story, and one with literary overtones to boot; as if certain chapters of my daily life were colluding and crying out to be told, and, what's more, demanding to be turned into fragments of a novel.

But this is a diary! I shout out these words to no one and tell myself in passing that nobody can make another person write a novel, least of all me, who so loves his short stories. And besides, what I'm writing here is strictly a diary, this is a diary, I don't even know why I need to remind myself of that. I am experiencing literature as a secret, private activity. This is a daily exercise that allows me to try my hand at writing—preliminary literary scraps with my sights set on the future—while saving me from losing all hope in the depths I've been left in by my financial and professional ruin.

This is a diary, it's a diary, a diary! It's also a secret vindication of the "writing of literature." I don't really approve of everyday life conspiring to lend a novelistic tone to my writings, although I should really thank it for providing me with some writing material. Without it, I might very well have none. But no. Try as I might, I can't look favorably on this meddling on the part of everyday life, especially while this awkward tension between novel and diary persists, entirely unnecessarily.

5

Yesterday, I wrote about works of fiction trying to be original not by harking back to their "pilot episode," but by exploiting the potential of that initial experiment to open out onto new universes. And now I'm wondering if, basing myself on the potential of an original like *Walter and His Problem*, I could set about repeating the book that Sánchez claims to have more or less forgotten.

First, I would have to work long and hard as a beginner and not stray from that path, but, later, I could take up that challenge, even, perhaps, in this very diary. After all, these pages are what led me onto the theme of repetition, a theme that I see now as being more relevant to myself than I thought.

A second phase of my life as a beginner could be spent rewriting *Walter and His Problem*. Why not? If I can reach that point with plenty of writing practice behind me, I might even go so far as to modify any parts of the original that I felt needed changing. For example, when repeating the book, I would probably, at the very least, do away with Sánchez's most irritatingly unreadable paragraphs, the confusing ones written when he was boozed.

[WHOROSCOPE 5]

A little early-evening prose. There's barely enough daylight left to read my horoscope: "The Mercury-Sun conjunction for Aries indicates that it doesn't matter what you do; but remember that, ultimately, what you do only exists so you can discover what you really want to do."

Is this really a daily horoscope? Horoscopes, in my experience, usually aren't written in those terms. Today's predictions for the other signs are perfectly normal and not in the least philosophical, which means she's treated Aries quite differently from the others. It really is as if she were writing it knowing that I'd be reading it. Even if she weren't, I can't help interpreting today's message. She seems to be saying that everything I've been doing in this diary will lead me to discover what I really want to do. It's as if what she really meant is: "The Mercury-Sun conjunction for Aries indicates that only the book matters, but that, ultimately, the book is there only to lead you on in your search for the book."

And that's not the end of it either, because if that is what she meant—and I know it's improbable, but I like to think it's true—then I would make a further modification so that it reads: "The Mercury-Sun conjunction for Aries indicates that your free repetition of *Walter and His Problem* could end up becoming the search for your own book."

Given that this possibility has just occurred to me, I won't write it off. If that search began and, as would be only logical, continued, then Peggy's supposed "horoscopal" suggestion would be ushering in the shade of the great Macedonio Fernández, the writer who devoted years of his life to *The Museum of Eterna's Novel*, a book that didn't get beyond the project stage, because he never actually began the story, and the preamble was a series of searches described in multiple prologues. Macedonio was a kind of literary Marcel Duchamp. Just as the latter played chess in a bar in Cadaqués, Macedonio Fernández played guitar around a campfire; strumming was his distinguishing feature, the hallmark of his prose going nowhere.

The Museum of Eterna's Novel is the unfinished book par excellence, but it never pretends to have been left incomplete. It's incomplete because that is its very nature. If it had also been a "posthumous" book, it would have been closer to the kind of text I might one day attempt to write: a book that would appear to have been interrupted, but that would, in fact, be perfectly complete.

The other day, I read that a museum in New York was putting on an exhibition of unfinished works. It included pieces by Turner, none of which had been shown during the artist's lifetime: these were sketches for other paintings, but without the harbors, the ships, and the mythological references. There was also a Rubens battle scene, in which the upper half of the canvas had been painted with great virtuosity, while the lower half was only sketched in, revealing the skeleton of what was to be, like the Pompidou Museum in Paris, which, instead of a traditional façade, reveals the actual internal structure of the building, pure and simple. Entirely unwittingly, Rubens was appearing in that exhibition in ultramodern form—almost as part of the contemporary avant-garde—because he was giving us a comment on his own work, showing us a battlefield and how to paint it.

The person writing the article commented that contemporary art doesn't offer us finished works, but only inconclusive ones for the viewer to complete in his or her imagination. This exhibition of unfinished works, he went on, actually described the way we look at art now, when the works themselves aren't enough and we, the viewers, need a space, a fissure, a crack in order to complete them.

That fissure or crack has, I think, something of the secret sign about it. I remember one of Walter Benjamin's aphorisms in *Short Shadows*: "Every piece of knowledge contains a dash of nonsense, just as in ancient carpet patterns or ornamental friezes it is always possible to find somewhere or other a minute deviation from the regular pattern. In other words, what really matters is not the progression from one piece of knowledge to the next, but the leap or crack inherent in any one piece of knowledge." That crack allows us to add details of our own to the unfinished masterpiece. Today, without those cracks opening up paths and setting our imaginations working—which is the hallmark of the incomplete artwork—we would probably be unable to take a step or possibly, even, to breathe.

&

Perhaps the thing I remember best about my neighbor's novel is that it purported to be the memoirs of the ventriloquist Walter, memoirs subtly interspersed with certain elements: a sunshade from Java, a barber from Seville, the city of Lisbon, a thwarted love affair.... Those memoirs, if I remember correctly, centered on Walter's main problem, a very grave one for a person in his profession, namely, that he had only one voice, *the* voice that writers so yearn to find, but which, for him, for obvious reasons, was highly problematic. However, he finally overcame this by splitting into as many voices as there are stories or slices of life contained in the memoirs.

That is what I remember best about *Walter and His Problem*, which I intend to reread over the next few days. At that time, on that first reading, I didn't get beyond the first half of the book, although I did glance at the final chapter—something I often do when I don't want to finish a book, but do want to know how it ends—and I discovered that the ventriloquist fled from Lisbon and, after traveling through various countries, threw himself into a canal in which there was a kind of whirlpool that went deep down into the Earth's core, and, just when it seemed that our man was completely lost in that endless darkness, the whirlpool whisked him back up to the surface again and deposited him in a strange, remote region of the world, where, far from feeling disoriented, he began to work as a storyteller in the historic heart of that source of all stories: the fortunate land of ancient Arabia.

Basically—or so I felt on the day that I flicked through that final chapter—the book was a journey back to the origins of the story, to its oral past.

6

What wouldn't I give, debutant that I am, stooped over this rectangle of wood, to have that one voice which, for the ventriloquist, represents such a tremendous occupational problem?

Nothing. I wouldn't give anything, because I don't even see it as a problem that concerns me. Because I'm not a ventriloquist, nor am I a proper writer; just an apprentice diarist who paces about his study deliberating over what form that insect, the dark parasite of repetition, might take, constantly sapping the leaves of their lush green, eating away at the written page, and hiding itself among life's many twists and turns.

I was thinking along these lines—rehearsing what I might finally transpose onto the computer—when, right in the middle of Avenida Diagonal, I spotted a woman who had caught my and Carmen's eye when our Cisalpino train broke down at Kirchbach station on a trip we made years ago. It seemed so implausible, not to say impossible, that this was the same woman we'd watched elegantly smoking a cigarette against that snowy backdrop and about whom we knew not even her name, that I wondered whether, in my eagerness to record run-of-the-mill episodes in my diary and distance myself from the threat of the novel, I might be looking for things that weren't there.

I moved closer and, as one would expect, it wasn't the woman from Kirchbach. In that exact same spot on Avenida Diagonal—a pedestrian crossing leading to Calle Calvet—only some months earlier, another woman had had the same troubling effect on me. And no doubt it was this coincidence that led me to think that this particular spot had something peculiar about it, which I ought not to lose sight of. On that previous occasion, a few months ago—just days after my business went under—this young stranger, who was talking on her cell phone a few yards ahead of me, let out a sudden cry, breaking down in such sobs that she bent double and dropped to her knees.

So this is real life, I thought to myself that day. And that was my sole, cold reaction on seeing that young woman fall to the ground; a reaction in slow motion, perhaps because, since my business folded, I was spending much of my time distractedly roaming the streets, immersed in my own world, parallel to the real one.

Going over the events of that day—I later learned that the young woman had just been told of the death of a loved one—I've come to understand that that passing stranger existed in real life and had feelings, and that I, too, existed in the same reality, but with less capacity to feel, to truly feel. Perhaps I only knew how to feel with my imagination. And not only has that encounter led me to this conclusion, but I have also begun to admire or even envy that young woman, because she had just one life, just one, which is perhaps why she felt her pain so intensely, while I went around sketching

29

the hazy wisps of a parallel world that left me somewhat detached from real life.

To tell the truth, I literally stepped back, almost in fear, when it became clear that the woman on Avenida Diagonal was definitely not the woman from Kirchbach. But I really don't know what I'd expected. Did I honestly think she would be the very same woman I had in mind? I realize that, lately, there are days when I only have to think something and my whimsical side expects it to appear instantly, right there, wherever I might be, as if I believed myself capable of shaping reality.

A brief note: this sudden heightened attachment to reality might be the upshot of having now spent six days on these writing exercises. In any case, I've decided to include the incident with the woman from Kirchbach in the diary. I had the impression that it was the sort of episode I'd end up forgetting before I got home. And, indeed, I would have forgotten were it not for the fact that it became closely connected with the sudden appearance this morning of Sánchez in my field of vision. My illustrious neighbor was leaning against a wall beside a clothes-store window on Calle Calvet, smoking and staring vacantly into the distance.

As I approached, it didn't take me long to realize that he was waiting for Delia, his wife, who was inside the store browsing clothes. On seeing me, he forced a smile and made a show of flicking away his cigarette with a hint of disgust, as if to let me know that, although he smokes, he no longer takes any pleasure in it. I got the impression that he wasn't too happy about his wife leaving him waiting on the street, becoming, as he did, an easy target for any passersby who had read his books. Passersby like me, as it happens.

His scowling face and haughty air notwithstanding, he spoke to me with the same ease and openness he had displayed the other day outside La Súbita. He began by saying how awful Saturdays were. I immediately wanted to know why.

"Because they invariably involve having conversations," he said.

Initially, paranoid as I am, I thought his response was related to the fact that he'd bumped into me again and that perhaps he didn't feel as gracious today as he had last time and feared that I might lure him into a conversation. But that wasn't what he meant; it turned out that his Saturdays were dedicated to Delia, who only allowed him to work from nine to eleven, on his regular Sunday newspaper column. As per the terms of their agreement, come eleven it was time for a walk and to engage in social life, conversation, the gateway to the outside world. He rather blurted all of this out and thus, in a way—and as if we'd known each other our whole lives—he opened his heart to me.

He knew, he said, that he simply wasn't cut out for weekends. And yet, he recognized that those two days of freedom must represent a real luxury for normal people. (He looked at me as if, although I belonged to that class of normal people, he was letting me off.) In fact, Sánchez went on, he had always envied other people their weekends. For him, Saturday and Sunday were a torment of tedium and frustration, to which was added the painful struggle to pass for a human being. When he wasn't sitting at his desk, he felt empty, "like a piece of boneless flesh," he said. And I believed him, even though it seemed to me that no one, not even he, could really believe that.

I asked him what tomorrow's column would be about.

"Fascination," he said.

A laconic, mysterious answer.

"Fascination in general?"

"The fascination we feel for the parts of books and films that we don't understand. For example, tomorrow's column is about *The Big Sleep*. There's one scene in particular where Lauren Bacall sings in a casino lounge, and it's never been clear why. It's about things that happen in movies and books that don't make the least sense because they're entirely extraneous to the context."

Just then, Delia came out of the store; she seemed very happy, radiant, and she wanted to know what we were laughing about. Since neither of us was laughing, we didn't know how to reply, and both of us stood there a little hesitant and ridiculous, saying nothing for a few long seconds. You could hear the sound of water falling in one of those little Barcelona fountains nearby; an unmusical sound, the sound of splashing or dripping.

"We were just saying, Delia, that your name is straight out of a crime series," Sánchez said, clearly making it up on the spot.

She then wanted to know if we were thinking of *The Black Dahlia*, and all I could think of doing was to turn to Sánchez and tell him that Saturdays truly are awful. I said this in an attempt to take my relationship with him—or rather with both of them—to the next level, but I realized at once that I'd put my foot in it, because it was he who'd said Saturdays are awful, going on to explain that the reason for this was that his wife would always drag him out shopping. I stood glumly rooted to the spot for a few moments, and it seemed that Delia was asking me, not her husband, for an explanation.

Saying the first thing that came into my head to cover my gaffe, I asked—as if I were an admirer of his work—which was the best time of year to write. Summer, Delia said. Summer is the least favorable period, Sánchez said, since he tended to get out more, whereas October to February was the time to hunker down, ideal for letting one's intellectual energies roam free.

Without wiping the dim-witted look from my face, I thought—perversely, because I like to give the impression that I've read very little—of a line by Mallarmé.

"Winter, clear winter, season of serene art."

&

I had no idea where we were heading, but for a few minutes we strolled together up Calle Calvet. A pleasant breeze tempered the already powerful early July sun and I would say, without exaggeration, that it was a perfect morning, although the situation—walking uphill with that married couple with whom I'd never before gone for a walk—made it all rather complicated, not least because I wasn't entirely sure what I was doing there, walking and talking so casually beside them, having, at no point, been invited along.

It suddenly seemed the ideal moment to tell Sánchez that I was thinking about rewriting his all-but-forgotten novel. Telling him might provide some reason for my strolling along with them. But I quickly remembered that I'd already decided not to tell him and that, besides, I didn't have to find a reason for our walk; it was enough to put one foot in front of the other and carry on.

Aware that telling him I planned to rewrite *Walter and His Problem* would land me in a colossal mess, in the end, I didn't dare. I didn't even hint at the idea. I also needed to remind myself that our relationship has never been exactly easy or chummy, despite the many years we've spent as neighbors. In fact, it's always been stonily cordial: the relationship of two people who might make small talk one day and the next avoid each other's eye so as not to have to say hello. The fact that we were now walking and talking as if we'd known each other all our lives made me feel faintly uncomfortable, perhaps because the whole situation was so out of the ordinary. But I was under no illusions. Sánchez had a significantly vain side to him, and probably believed himself to be superior to me in all respects. I knew very little about him really, or, indeed, about my other neighbors in Coyote, all of whom were perfect strangers; the majority unapproachable, cordial but distant—and sometimes not even cordial.

So, in the end, I opted not to tell him that one day, when I felt suitably prepared, I was going to rewrite his old novel. Instead, I told him that, ever since he'd opened up to me about it a few days ago, I'd thought about finding the time to dig out *Walter and His Problem* from my library and give it a read.

His face seemed to drain of all color.

"Give it a read? But no one reads that book anymore!" he said, and I think this roundabout recommendation that I leave his flawed work in peace came straight from the heart.

In fact, in telling him that I was going to find the time to search out his old novel, I was telling a lie, since I had found it last night and refreshed my memory by reading the back cover.

Of the ten stories told in the book, nine had been written in each of the ventriloquist's different voices. Having overcome, in the very first chapter, the problem of having just one voice—clearly an absolutely overwhelming and paralyzing dilemma—Walter then cut loose in as many voices—nine—as there were chapters left for his biased memoirs. The chapters were stories, and the stories were chapters. And what the reader found in this book were Walter's memoirs, but also a novel which was, at the same time, a short-story collection. At least, that is what was written on the back of the book, and, despite having abandoned it halfway through, I'd had a clear view of the novel as a whole at the time and still did.

Behind the different voices corresponding to each of the stories lay, camouflaged, "imitations, sometimes satirical and at other times not, of the voices of the masters of the short story." And so, behind the narrator in the first story—the first chapter of the novel—we find a voice and style reminiscent of John Cheever; behind the narrator of the second story, a voice that appears to have fallen under the influence of Djuna Barnes; behind the third, someone trying to evoke the inimitable style of Borges; behind "Something in Mind," the fourth story, a narrator who takes Hemingway's very characteristic narrative approach; while in "An Old Married Couple," one can trace the footprints of Raymond Carver's rugged style....

To return to the point, I didn't dare tell Sánchez that last night, albeit very superficially, I had revisited his thirty-year-old book and was thus reminded that the stories were all headed with an epigraph by the corresponding "master of the short story," giving each chapter a definite hallmark. And since I didn't want to tell him that I'd merely flicked through *Walter and His Problem*, neither did I care to bring up the matter of the ghastly, exhausting, insufferable (when not just drunkenly rambling) paragraphs, which he had justified at the time, saying that they were excruciating because the plot demanded it.

I might be a novice when it comes to writing, but I have many years as an experienced reader under my belt, and it hasn't escaped my notice that Sánchez should simply have erased those paragraphs altogether. Especially when you consider that there were at least one or two—and sometimes as many as three—such confused passages per chapter. During each one, the narrator—usually the ventriloquist himself, who was the one organizing his memoirs—would become particularly slow and confused, cloying and extremely ponderous, with absolutely no redeeming features, as if his head were about to burst, as if his writing talent had completely lost its way: the sort of prose you might expect to have been written by someone in a lazy, hungover state.

Nor did I wish to tell him that *Walter and His Problem* reminded me of those times, particularly in France at the end of the nineteenth century, when, for certain writers, the short story represented a genre that somehow worked against the novel, which overtook or sidestepped it; the sign of a new aesthetic.

I didn't intend to say any of this, so I don't know how I ended up telling him that the thing I remembered most clearly from *Walter and His Problem* was the strange matter of those dense, muddled passages. Did he remember them? I waited for his reply, but he remained silent for a long time, as if it pained him to be reminded of precisely that detail.

"Luckily for me, no one remembers it now," he'd said to Ana Turner just recently. And now I had almost certainly wounded him deeply. I looked at him to confirm his discomfort, and it seemed to me as if Sánchez might even be downright furious. I thought: it's one thing someone badmouthing one of his books, and quite another if that someone is his neighbor.

&

Turning down Calle Rector Ubach, Sánchez broke his silence to tell me, in a friendly voice almost certainly intended to mask his deep unease, that, back in the day, a critic had described those passages as "dizzy spells," and that perhaps he'd been right on the money. Obviously, he went on, it was never true that he'd included those dense passages on purpose.

And at this point he began to stumble over his words. I think it had dawned on him that he was paying a high price for having said, in my presence, during his flirtation with Ana Turner the other day, that he had once written a bad novel.

Each one of these "dizzy spells," he began saying, was, without exception, the product of one of his alcoholic binges the night before. By publishing the book in such a crazy way, without correcting a single word, he'd subsequently had to make up something to justify those "dizzy spells," which could be found in every chapter, and that's when he'd told the press that they were intentional errors, put there to show the world that even "the great masters of the short story"—that's how he described his selection of ten narrators—had their sticky patches. After all, they weren't gods, but people. The dizzy spells were deliberate imperfections, he told journalists, intended to help readers see that the major works from the last two centuries were flawed masterpieces, since the best authors dealt, within the very structures of their narrative, with the chaos of the world and the difficulty of understanding and expressing it.... That's what he told those journalists, but he was merely bluffing to keep them from focusing on those ridiculously convoluted passages. Of course, he could have corrected those sections, but in those days he didn't have time to go to such trouble, driven as he was by a boundless desire to publish, an incredible sense of urgency (which he described as ill-advised), a need for money and fame; he thought that by publishing books, he would be displayed in bookstore windows, and find more writing jobs, and thus keep his head above water.

"I was just bluffing," he said candidly. "You can't imagine the feeling of peace it gives you, after publishing a book, to put it out there that your stories contain strange passages on purpose, in order to demonstrate that not only are the masters of the short story imperfect, they can also be very tedious. The best thing was, it worked. Most people believed that I'd pulled off an intriguing, albeit rather labored, experimental exercise, and no one could take that away from me."

"Repent, you bastard," Delia suddenly blurted out.

It took me a second to realize that she was joking. Sánchez froze and very slowly lit a cigarette, as if this might calm her down.

"On your knees, sinner," Delia said, glaring at him with such hatred that I could only assume she was acting, although it wasn't at all clear.

The whole time I was thinking: not a bad idea, you publish the book and waste no time in finding an excuse for why you haven't written something at the level of, say, John Cheever. Or even at the level of Djuna Barnes, or of any of those others who, for you, represent "the masters of the short story." That way, you're one step ahead of all the pains-in-the-neck primed to screw you over with their bad reviews. And come nighttime, you might even sleep more soundly.

I also thought about how, all things considered, it was absolutely true that the great masters were indeed flawed.

Delia was now wearing an enigmatic smile on her face.

Why that smile and why so mysterious? Perhaps Delia was simply an enigmatic person and her smile held no mysteries at all.

What did I care about Delia, or any of that? I wasn't in the mood for enigmas. But, thinking about it, I came to realize that I did care, especially about the extremely tense atmosphere of that encounter, and Sánchez's somewhat overwrought language, his agitation, the banal small change of his repeated excuses, the awkwardness of the situation.

Had they invited me to walk with them up Calle Calvet and back down along Rector Ubach? No, I'd gotten myself into that fix by wanting to play along, and, who knows, perhaps out of an eagerness to learn how to write, and get to know the man whose forgotten novel I would one day copy, with the aim of improving it.

I parted company with the couple when we reached Calle Aribau. I was worried that, at any moment, Sánchez would ask me to explain myself and tell me to leave his things well alone. And I knew that if this happened I'd feel like a ridiculous snoop, a meddler, and that my head would, quite literally, hang in shame.

"Goodbye, Mac," he said as if he'd known me all his life, as if we'd always been on first-name terms.

"See you around," Delia said.

And I walked away from them thinking how little I knew that more northerly part of Coyote, a place I'd secretly reinvented in my head over the previous few years, transforming it into a terrifying place. I don't know why, since it wasn't very different from the southern part of the neighborhood.

[WHOROSCOPE 6]

"Try to cultivate relationships relating to a project which, though slow to get off the ground, shows great promise."

Peggy is referring, perhaps, to the great promise of my secretly repeating Sánchez's novel, and also to the fact that tonight, Saturday, I have cultivated an important relationship.

Since the newspaper provides an email address alongside Peggy Day's column, I had a sudden burst of daring and, in a moment of restless impatience, of curiosity to know if she had caught wind of what I'd said about her not long ago in public—a moment of gin-soaked weakness—I wrote this to her:

"My name is Mac Vives, perhaps you remember me. S'Agaró, some forty years ago. When it rained, we would listen to the rain. And to the thunder. When it wasn't raining, we would show up barefoot at the Flamingo Club and dance as if there were no tomorrow. I wanted so much to protect you from the world when you probably didn't need protecting. I walked out of your life like someone walking out of a sentence. Forgive the idiot that I was. And know that today you correctly predicted what was about to happen to me. Because it's true, I've just begun to cultivate a relationship that will lead to great things for me. Yours, Mac."

After sending the email, it dawned on me that I might well have avoided such madness, but it was too late. And so I began pacing the house, half asleep, as if the error of having sent the email had left me much more than just disoriented. In an effort to fend off my growing unease, I decided to go to bed without turning off the house lights—that is, wasting energy, and not just squandering it willy-nilly, but because it seemed to me that excess itself can feel like life and, in a strange way, make us feel more alive.

&

I wake up and get out of bed to note down a detail I remember from the end of my nightmare. Someone was saying to me over and again:

"The thing is, it's just really weird wanting to write your neighbor's novel."

7

Carmen has had to rush off to her furniture restoration workshop, which, though extremely buoyant, can also be a bit of an annoyance, because she seems to have to work ever longer hours, often at a moment's notice. And as if that weren't enough, she now has too many *new* customers, which could end up being a problem, because, at this rate, she'll have to work on Sundays as well. I asked if she'd be back soon and discovered—because she told me so—that I have a rare ability to irritate her. Despite years of married life and bringing up three children who have all now flown the nest and are doing very well for themselves, I had no idea I possessed the rare skill of irritating her simply by asking her what time she'd be home.

I went down to the garage with her and, cautiously, given how touchy she was, got into her car and asked if she could drop me off at the newsstand.

"But it's just around the corner," she protested.

I didn't even respond, fearing another explosion of that dangerously bad temper of hers.

Once at the newsstand, I was annoyed to find that there was a line, as there is every Sunday, and I had to wait my turn. I was particularly annoyed because most of those who buy a Sunday paper never read any other paper all week. They go to the newsstand on Sundays in the same way we used to go to the bakery—at least I did as an adolescent—where there were often equally interminable lines. In Coyote, of course, there is an added incentive to buy the Sunday papers: that is, the opportunity to ogle the news vendor's breasts.

Every district has its specialty.

Sitting in Black Bar, I kept thinking about how, since I can see no imminent end to my status as a beginner, I would fit very comfortably into the same niche as Macedonio, the Duchamp of literature.

I had three newspapers to read, but, instead, I passed the time pondering that thought and also something else I've been noticing lately: how so many writers think they have it in them to write a novel; they feel so utterly confident of this that, in their inexhaustible vanity, they're convinced that they *will* write one and will do it very well too, because they've spent years training to do just that, because they're intelligent and well-read, because they've studied contemporary literature, and, having noticed where other novelists fall short, they feel ready for anything, especially now that they've invested in the perfect home computer and a really good chair that won't do their back in.

Later, when they fail to write the novel of which they had so platonically dreamed, some go mad. For the essayist Dora Rester, writing a novel means writing the fragments of an attempt at a novel, not the whole obelisk: "The art lies in the attempt, and understanding what's outside us by using only what we have inside us is one of the hardest emotional and intellectual tasks anyone can undertake."

I wouldn't go that far. Or would I? I'm not sure, but it is true that when approaching this business of writing a novel, it's best to go step-by-step, to move with extreme caution; after all, I'm only aspiring to rewrite Sánchez's novel....

When I went to pick up Carmen from work at lunchtime, I found her still in a foul mood, although she did make some effort to lighten the atmosphere that she herself had created between us. This effort, however, proved short-lived, and battle soon recommenced. I did my best to give way on everything and to put an end to the argument as quickly as possible, but she wouldn't even let me do that, which then led me to try and get her to recognize that since she is prone to these sudden fits of depression, she should take steps to deal with it. I also tried to make her see that if she continued moaning on about the apartment and proposing alterations (a new kitchen, etc.), she should also bear in mind that, as she well knows, while I may not be flat broke, nor am I in a position to fund such refurbishments.

As you would expect, this only made matters worse, and she continued screaming at me all the way down the street. Finally, when we reached Bar Tender, and just when I was considering separation as a real possibility—I'd be left with no financial support, of course, which is why, although I do sometimes fantasize about leaving her, I nearly always almost instantly abandon the idea—a massive summer storm broke, and, in my agitated state, it seemed to me that the wind had changed direction twice.

The rain invaded everything, and I have, perhaps, never felt so emotionally trapped as I did today. Worst of all, I was far from my study and from my diary, which made me realize that, in the space of just one week, both have become indispensable to me.

I was suddenly overwhelmed by a very simple anxiety: was I becoming another version of that "piece of boneless flesh" that Sánchez said he became when he was away from his study? Or perhaps I was starting to inhabit the skin of John Cheever, the writer whose presence—although his talent is sometimes buried in the darkest of thickets—can be felt in the first story in *Walter and His Problem*, "I Had an Enemy."

In that first chapter of my neighbor's book, the narrator adopts a voice very similar to that of Cheever in his fraught diaries, where he holds forth about mundane matters and, after each potent sip of gin, considers getting a divorce.

Lately, when I think about separating from Carmen, I wonder why I don't just drop round to see Ana Turner at her bookstore. Yes, just go for broke and stride in, throw caution and reserve to the winds, and suggest to her that we run away together. It would end badly, I know, because she's not in the least bit interested in me, and besides, I can't afford to run away or whatever, but I do like to entertain the idea so that, just for a moment, I can forget about my latest row with Carmen and feel a little more at peace with myself.

In "I Had an Enemy"—in which the narrator does a very good imitation of Cheever's voice—the ventriloquist himself begins his partial memoirs by telling us that, for some time now, he has been stalked by someone named Pedro, a kind of "gratuitous antagonist" who, very persistently and sometimes successfully, tries to eat away at his morale, like a kind of homespun Moriarty.

Since the stalker is at the root of all his problems, Walter ends up blaming this entirely gratuitous enemy for the sad fact that he has only one voice, which is making work with his dummies, with his puppets, extremely difficult. Misfortune follows misfortune with astonishing regularity until one amazing night when, not only does his enemy suddenly disappear—setting off for the South Seas beneath a perfectly full moon, never to return—but the ventriloquist also loses his voice completely.

Walter doesn't just lose his voice, he is literally struck dumb, and believes, moreover, that this is the end of everything, that he'll never speak again and won't be able to earn his living at all. A few days later, though, his aphonia begins to wane and the ability to form words gradually comes back, and he finds, to his surprise, that, with the slow return of the power of speech, he also retrieves the great variety of voices he once had and which he'd lost because of that tenacious dissident, that obstinate personal enemy, that tedious gratuitous antagonist, that braggart Pedro.

Having overcome this particular obstacle—the enemy who obliged him to have only one voice, "the voice that writers so yearn to find"—the ventriloquist with Cheever-like stylistic airs concludes the story thus:

"The disappearance of my enemy allowed me to recover all my voices, which is why I hope he stays in the South Seas for a very long time and never ever comes back; that Pedro fellow is doubtless living on some remote, grubby Pacific isle, in a thatched hut with four fawning Marist Brothers for company, and he keeps *my voice* stashed away in one of those little silver boxes of which collectors of baseless loathings are said to be so proud."

While I was pondering all this, I had the feeling that there, in Bar Tender, the wind had changed direction for a third time. Then, almost miraculously, the rain stopped, just like that. The intense heat began creeping back, confirming that this is the hottest summer in Barcelona for a hundred years.

Tempers cooled, especially mine. And so as not to continue the argument with Carmen, I devoted myself to the absorbing but impossible task of capturing all the different shades of green in each of the raindrops lingering on the leaves of the trees.

"So you admit defeat, do you?" Carmen asked.

"Of course, I never like to win."

I said this while thinking about something quite different: getting the hell out of there and going somewhere, anywhere; anywhere but here.

"To what was once Arabia Felix," said the voice.

It was the voice of the dead man inside my head, suddenly reappearing.

"Hell, no," I said. "These days it's just one big minefield."

Because my neighbor's novel—written thirty years ago—ends in the Yemen, when it was a country you could still quite happily visit, when it still had certain idyllic touches, and where, according to friends who traveled there at the time, you could spend a few days in the extraordinary city of Sana'a and feel as if you were living in a place that still retained a few luminous traces of Arabia Felix, the ancient paradise where, in the age of the classical Greeks, they exported coffee and incense from the port of Mocha.

"This is a difficult period economically, especially as regards matrimonial finances."

Peggy Day really hit the nail on the head in today's oracle. She may as well have written—a little birdie must have whispered as much in her ear—that while I may not be completely broke, in the long run, I might well end up having to live off Carmen, when I've always assumed that the opposite would be the case.

I'd like to believe that this is Peggy's chosen formula for responding to my email of yesterday. She replies with a double-edged message, very rudely in fact, because what she's really saying is that she knows I'm in some way dependent on my wife. It could also be that none of this bears any relation to what is going on, and Peggy may not even have read my email. Indeed, there was a moment this afternoon when I decided to think no more about the matter, to think about something else entirely and so I spent the evening reading reviews of Bob Dylan's performance last night in Barcelona. His first number was "Things Have Changed," a song he wrote for the movie *Wonder Boys*, and it seems that, as he sang it, he didn't move a muscle.

8

I went over to my sister Julia's for lunch, repeating one of my most routine outings. I've lost count of the number of times I've been for lunch at my sister's house. But today's visit was slightly different. First, because of this repetition syndrome dogging me that now seems to form part of my very nature, and which, once I was inside her house, made me feel the weight of all the gatherings that have taken place there over the years. And second, because I noticed something that had always escaped me in the past: my big sister doesn't write, nor does her husband, still less my other sister, Laura, or my three children—all of whom are too busy running thriving businesses—and my parents and grandparents never wrote either.

Indeed, not a single close relative of mine ever succumbed to any literary temptations.

And that made me realize that, having spent just one week on this diary, I've already begun to pick up on ideas that, before, would have meant nothing to me. For instance, it occurred to me that my repetition syndrome is closely linked to the genre we might call "the fiction of repetition."

This isn't the sort of thing I used to think about. I was already at Julia's house when I pictured her asking me what I devote my time to now that I'm a man of leisure, to which I would have answered:

"Fictions of repetition."

Julia would have been none the wiser, but in a way, nor would I, since I still didn't know exactly what this new genre consists of.

But my sister isn't the kind to ask "what do you do now that you don't do anything," so my thoughts quickly turned to something apparently more trivial, but which is actually very important: the extraordinary quality of the soups she has made for me over the years, even now, in the height of summer (like today, when gazpacho is on the menu). Never a truer word spoken: they really are very good. Delicious. They always have been. As the great Wisława Szymborska once said when speaking about her family (a family of nonwriters like mine), they are also "extraordinary soups, which one can eat safe in the knowledge that there is zero risk of them spilling onto some precious manuscript."

I drank too much in the house of the literatureless; that is, at Julia and her husband's place. By the end of my visit, I verged on the ridiculous, although, luckily, I didn't make a complete fool of myself and was able to bite my tongue and not tell Julia—in somewhat rambling terms, which I hope to be able to reproduce here now—that I saw her as a great river, and that this new condition of hers—as a powerful rushing stream and not as a sister—was transforming her, in my eyes, into the most fitting and precise image of the course of my own life. It was as if she and her waters encapsulated both my past and my destiny, so closely were both these impressions linked to our favorite childhood holidays: to our summers spent in the

Pyrenees, when we would row along the Garonne, in the days when I was so repelled by the mere sight of meat that even a few scraps left on a plate were almost enough to make me faint....

Luckily, I realized in time that saying all of this to Julia in an attempt to "literatize" my visit was as insane as it would be baffling. What's more, it betrayed both how unbalanced I am in the wake of losing the family business, and my increasingly excessive tendency to drink when I'm at her house, not to mention my tendency to spout long, rambling sentences which, for a few days now, I think I've been saying out loud in order to commit them to memory and record them in the diary, something which, fortunately, hasn't yet happened.

I contained myself, and our habitual sibling lunch passed peacefully, if a little eccentrically, because I really did drink an awful lot.

I can picture myself as I left: mute and stiff, saying a silent goodbye on the landing, then waiting for the metal doors of the elevator to close, and then, fueled by the vast amount of alcohol inside me, crying in silence as I tell myself: we're siblings, and yet my words will always be a kind of metaphysical phenomenon that she can never fully understand. And vice versa. It doesn't matter how many years pass, or how dearly we love each other, we are permanently confined to our respective selves. That's true for us, and we're siblings....

[WHOROSCOPE 8]

"Now is not a good moment to make proposals or establish important relations, for you will meet with obstacles," Peggy Day says.

Is she trying to discourage me from establishing relations with her so soon? Is she referring to that person with whom I began to cultivate "a relationship that will lead to great things?" Is Peggy trying to tell me to wait awhile before bothering her, and thus save myself a whole lot of problems?

In some ways, writing that email has left me more at the mercy of her projections than ever, and, of course, it's quite possible that I am turning into a kind of Lídia of Cadaqués, crazily interpreting Peggy's oracles as a daily response to the email I now wish I'd never sent.

I enjoy doing this, although, in the end, I always leave the party with an uneasy feeling in my stomach. A moment ago, I looked out of the window onto the street and, in my imagination, I observed the movements of the small handful of people who pass by our house at ten at night. I should think Carmen is now more than used to seeing me standing by the window at this hour, and to assuming that my visual sweeps of the outside world are one more consequence of the idleness and lack of direction to which she thinks I've become prey since I strayed from the speciously solid business path.

It's really quite unfair that she should think this. Gazing out of the window once too often makes me disoriented, does it? Fine, but it can happen to anyone. My mind might wander from time to time, at moments when I'm not sure what to do, but that's all. Besides, at other times of the day I couldn't be busier. Just a second ago, for instance, I couldn't have been busier as, standing at my window, I imagined bumping into Sánchez down on the street and asking him about the second story (or chapter) of his novel, "The Duel of Grimaces," and certain aspects of it that had intrigued me.

Before setting off for my sister's house, I spent this morning reading "The Duel of Grimaces," and saw that it really does have a Djuna Barnes feel to it. Barnes is barely read these days, but she was fashionable in Spain in the mideighties, and I still remember the polemics written against her in the weekend supplements, particularly in El País, where the critic Azancot branded her a lesbian and said she owed her unwarranted reputation to the support she had received from T. S. Eliot. That bilious review was a sign of things to come, the era of social media, in which, as Fernando Aramburu recently wrote, creative people are punished for aspiring to find happiness in the public exercise of the imagination and the written word.

But Sánchez can't have attached much weight to these reviews of Djuna Barnes because he happily included her in his book. I read Barnes in her day and have good memories of her work; she's an elegant stylist, combining archaic turns of phrase with innovative flourishes. When she swapped the night (which left her unwell and drunk) for the serenity of day, she became a perfectionist, working, so they say, up to eight hours a day, over three or four days on just two or three lines of poetry. She died, at age ninety, of starvation. Fietta Jarque, who wrote about her, said that no one ever knew if she just forgot to eat or if she deliberately starved herself. The point is, she clearly wanted to leave this life like one facing the dawn head on.

&

I would say that "The Duel of Grimaces" recalls one of Djuna Barnes's stories, the title of which I've forgotten, but it's one I think I read some time ago. In it, Barnes described a mother's horror at realizing that she has given birth to a son who, from an ethical point of view, is clearly going to grow up to be an immoral, malevolent type, as rotten to the core as herself. The epigraph that Sánchez borrows from Barnes for the start of "The Duel of Grimaces" doesn't concern these moral questions, but it does show complete contempt for sons in general. It might even be a line taken from that very story: "My son and heir has the character of a rat lost in a drop of water."

In "The Duel of Grimaces," the ventriloquist—it's clear from the outset that this is the narrator from the first story, which, in turn, suggests a certain continuity from story to story—visits one of his sons, whom he hasn't seen for twenty years. On discovering that he is an utterly abhorrent individual—"Why, in God's name, do we insist on perpetuating our sorely deficient human condition?"—the ventriloquist thinks how dreadful it is that, despite knowing full well what a shithole the world is, we carry on as if nothing were wrong; that is, we go on having children "who only increase the number of monsters inhabiting planet Earth." We go on "adding to the incessant line of useless beings, who, since time immemorial, have been born only to die, one after the other; and yet, on we go, unfazed, waiting for something, anything, fully aware that there is nothing to wait for...."

Dotted throughout "The Duel of Grimaces" are details that become gradually more pertinent to the subtle crime-novel element that runs throughout the book. One of them—which appears fleetingly, obliquely, in this story, without drawing attention to itself—is the Javan sunshade, that curious artifact with which the ventriloquist will go on to murder the barber from Seville.

At one point, the son turns on the father and tells him that he's had enough:

"You're really playing with my head, you know. I'm a poet, and you, on the other hand, are an out-of-work ventriloquist, a failure with a foul temper and, what's worse, full of resentment for all the successful ventriloquists, whom, I'm convinced, you would eat alive if you could."

The father's response displays a combination of calm wisdom and humor:

"Don't you worry, I'll propose a raise for both of us."

As replies go, this would appear to have nothing to do with what the son has just said, although in fact it does, because from it you learn that the son doesn't earn any money either; he, too, is penniless, following in the footsteps of his failure of a father.

Later on, beneath the deafening clatter of some helicopters on their way to put out a nearby forest fire, we see father and son sheltering—in tragicomic circumstances—in the attic of a neighbor's house. There they have turned into an impressive pair of grimacers.

The ventriloquist writes: "My son really liked both the idea of a duel, and the rules of the game: we were to use our most personal, individual, and intimate expressions and take them to their most offensive, devastating extremes, no holding back."

The father turns out to be the better grimacer, and his final winning grimace—pulling his mouth wide apart with his fingers and jutting out his teeth while simultaneously using his thumbs to make his eyes bulge—is so monstrous that his poor son, his poor opponent, can't outdo its gruesomeness and admits defeat. They're no longer two of a kind. The victor is the older monster, Walter.

That night, the son—the sad, lost loser, increasingly upset by his defeat—seems to slip into a black, very dark world, a place of fear and distrust, and becomes so terribly fixated on one particular line that he repeats it over and over again like a sick parrot. At the same time, it seems that, all of a sudden, the narrator has begun to spout gibberish, as if sleeptalking, or perhaps having drunk some kind of potion or strong liquor. But all that's happening is that we've found ourselves in the middle of a "dizzy spell." It's hard to miss these spells or tedious weak spots in Sánchez's novel, because, if I remember correctly, they all fall like lead balloons on the unsuspecting reader; these intermissions—lasting, mostly, for several sentences—are so mind-numbingly and painfully dull and ponderous that the reader cannot help but cringe.

Finally, having left behind Walter and Walter Jr.'s grimacing competition, and having waded through those "dizzy spells," we get to the final scene of the story, where we learn that the ventriloquist's univocal problem has been inherited by his miserable son, a specialist in, among other things, getting stuck on a single sentence.

I didn't recall that final scene from my previous reading of the story, and when I got to it I was surprised to come across that obsessive "episode of repetition"; that is, the anguished, sick-parrot-style phrase which the creepy son repeats so incessantly, and which made me think of that famous sequence in Stanley Kubrick's *The Shining*; the one where our suspicions about Jack Torrance's mental state are confirmed. It's a moment of sheer metaphysical terror. Wendy goes over to see what he's writing and discovers that her husband is compulsively typing out a set phrase on which he's become stuck, and which, insistently and disturbingly, he keeps repeating over and over: "All work and no play makes Jack a dull boy."

The line that the ventriloquist's son gets stuck on over and over, at one point repeating it up to four times in a row, is:

There would be no shadows if the sun weren't shining. There would be no shadows if the sun weren't shining. There would be no shadows if the sun weren't shining. There would be no shadows if the sun weren't shining.

9

There's nothing odder than a neighbor. For one neighbor to kill another is an almost daily item on the news, with a third neighbor invariably coming out to say of the unlikely criminal that he was a perfectly normal person. The other day, someone on television went still further and stated that the murderer on the same floor as him had always seemed "a natural neighbor." When I heard this, I asked myself—since dying is a law of nature—can anyone be said to have died of natural causes if killed by a natural neighbor?

The Vichy regime issued a law forbidding Jews to own a cat. The cat belonging to Christian Boltanski's parents one day peed on a rug on their neighbors' terrace. That night, those same neighbors, who were generally kind, genteel people, rang the doorbell and said that if Boltanski's parents didn't kill the cat, they would denounce them to the Gestapo, because they knew they were Jews.

Hell is other people, especially neighbors. I remember some friends from Bilbao, who, having happily moved into their first apartment together, as newlyweds, immediately began to hear strange noises coming through the wall. Every night, some bizarre ceremony took place in the adjoining apartment, what you might call "the constant repetition of the incomprehensible": they would hear spine-chilling laughter, the buzz of electric saws, the cawing of crows, horrific screams. Even when they found out that their neighbors, using the primitive special effects of the time, made their living recording horror stories for the radio, even then they didn't feel reassured. Neighbors always inspire fear, even when they have an explanation for everything.

[WHOROSCOPE 9]

Peggy Day's oracle for this date says that "a sense of guilt you've been dragging around for years could today cause you quite a few problems."

It's a surprising prediction. What will the other Aries think when they read that entry, which, dare I say, I suspect is addressed to me? I can't help thinking that Peggy, who must by now have received my email, is demanding an apology from me for having disappeared so abruptly at the end of that summer in S'Agaró.

I will never understand my behavior on that last day of August. Perhaps I wanted to emulate Mr. Invincible, the most admired member of our gang, who, without any explanation, also split up with his girlfriend at the end of that summer. He literally fled from her, and no one ever found out why. And I think I copied that strange impulse, seeing it, presumably, as a decision worthy of being imitated, because it seemed so macho. The point is that I didn't turn up for my final date of the summer with Juanita Lopesbaño and never saw her again. Once, I mistakenly thought I spotted her in front of a church in Módena. Her back, her figure, especially her behind, were very similar, but I felt horribly disappointed when, expecting to see the Marilynesque features of the Bombshell—as we used to call her—I instead found myself staring at the frigid, rather crazed face of a total stranger.

Sometimes, I look back on that sudden, senseless flight of mine and I find it impossible to comprehend. And because I know I never will understand it, I tell myself that it could well have been the gesture that began my relationship with the incomprehensible. I behaved in a way that was hard to explain. I fled, and deeply wounded a very nice young woman.

And yet, I am not to blame.

&

We come into this world in order to repeat what those who came before us also repeated. There have been supposedly significant technical advances, but as regards our human nature, we remain unchanged, with exactly the same defects and problems. We unwittingly imitate what those who preceded us tried to do. These add up to mere attempts with very few successes, which, when they do occur, are always second-rate. Every ten or fifteen years, people speak of new generations, but when you analyze those generations, which, on the face of it, do appear to be different, you see instead that they merely repeated, like a mantra, how urgent and vital it is to overturn the previous generation and, just to be safe, the one before the previous one, which, in its time, tried to erase the one before that. Oddly, though, no generation wants to position itself on the margins of that Great Path, but, rather, on the firm ground occupied by the previous generation. They must think there's nothing else beyond that firm ground, and this belief ultimately leads them to imitate and follow in the footsteps of those they started out despising. And so it goes on, not a single generation has placed itself on the margins or has said, almost as one voice: we don't like this, you can keep it. The young arrive, only to slink away the next day, no longer young, but old. In fleeing from the world, they're destroyed; and their memories are destroyed and they die, or they themselves die, so destroying their memories, which were born dead. This rule knows no exception. In this respect, everyone imitates everyone else. As an epitaph on a grave in a Cornish cemetery says: *Shall we all die. We shall die all. All die shall we. Die all we shall.*

10

We have to imagine a Borges completely adrift as a short-story writer, and also blind drunk—as far as I know, he didn't drink a drop—if we want to find even an echo of his voice in that of the narrator of "The Whole Theater Laughs," the third chapter in *Walter and His Problem* which, like all of the chapters in the book, can be read as a stand-alone story. That being said, it's also true that this is the chapter that least lends itself to being separated from the rest of the book, because, unlike the others, which are sometimes less integral to the memoirs, "The Whole Theater Laughs" contains the scene of the crime, an indispensable moment if the ventriloquist's partial autobiography is to make the slightest sense.

Without the Borges quote at the beginning—"I reach my center, my algebra and my key, my mirror. Soon I will learn who I am"—I don't think I would ever have worked out that the Argentinian was the inspiration behind "The Whole Theater Laughs." But the epigraph informed me that I would find Borges in the story. I can't really say that I did. In fact, I don't think there's anything of him in the narrator. I suppose, if I were to indulge Sánchez, I would say there is something of Borges in the way he subtly parodies certain dramatic stereotypes, and also in the way the narrative condenses a man's entire life into a single scene that defines his fate.

In this one scene, the artist Walter reaches his "center," the most crucial scene of his life, and he understands that he has to leave, that he must flee and go into hiding. This single scene, which takes place in a theater in Lisbon, is narrated by the ventriloquist himself, who, unless I'm mistaken, isn't the obvious narrator of all the other stories in the book. I seem to recall that in the fourth chapter, "Something in Mind," Walter isn't the narrator. I mean to verify this when I get to the story and reread it.

Anyway, in the case of "The Whole Theater Laughs," we're left in no doubt that it is the ventriloquist who, within the fragile framework of his memoirs, relates to us the brief story of his hasty departure from the stage; an unforeseen adieu for his followers, but one we sense that is justified, for Walter himself implies that if, after this final performance, he were to remain in the city of Lisbon, he would risk spending the rest of his life behind bars.

What crime could he have committed? It is half implied that something has happened that night, down one of the city's alleyways, to "the Scraper" (Walter's nickname for him). But at no point does Walter explicitly recount all of the details of the crime, which Lisbon's police are yet to uncover; the penny drops slowly, and we work it out from what he, as narrator, gradually reveals.

What the ventriloquist narrates—in the present tense—is the ridiculous way in which he simply goes to pieces in front of his public as he prepares—having reached his center, his "algebra"—to flee to some far-flung corner of the world in order to learn, at last, who he really is. This all takes place in a very tense, improvised scene in which, with the valuable help of his puppet Sansón, Walter relates the pathetic story of his passion for his assistant Francesca.

In one memorable scene, Walter actually weeps on stage for his lost love as he confesses everything apart from the fact that he has just killed the barber—his beloved's lover—which is the real reason he must leave the city that very night.

The whole story revels in the idea of saying goodbye in the most theatrical way possible. Walter's moving, terrifying farewell to the stage and to everything—he knows that the moment the performance ends, he'll be off like a shot—begins with an involuntary false note, his voice cracks the moment he opens his mouth to announce that he is going, that he is retiring from the stage.

It's an ominous sound, almost identical to that made by the stern professor in *The Blue Angel* in front of his students. Professor Unrat is on a steady path to ruin when the showgirl Lola Lola makes him fall in love with her just to strip him of his dignity. But that's where the similarity with Unrat ends, because Walter differs from the German professor in all other respects. Walter has Latin blood, which means that, despite never actually saying as much, he peppers his theatrical dialogue with Sansón with such emotive clues that we can't help but see, horrifying thought that this is, that he really has committed a crime that very night, killing—in some back alley of the city—the barber who stole Francesca from him.

In just a few hours, Walter will leave to travel very far away, not just because of those pressing reasons, but because he has lost interest in everything since Francesca, his beautiful Italian assistant, betrayed him with the dastardly Scraper. That betrayal has unhinged him and led him, during that final hour, to think that it is perfectly normal to talk and even argue—out loud in the dressing room and later on the stage—with Sansón the puppet.

Dramatically, but also obliquely, Walter continues telling his devoted audience the tale of a love cut short. And this is where he must rely on the help of his "good friend" Sansón, who, amidst riotous laughter from the stalls, pedantically corrects his owner on stage, doing what he can to get him to stick to the true version of events, something which Walter absolutely cannot do if he wants to avoid making a suicidal blunder.

A good portion of the public—a full house—still hasn't worked out what is really going on, but finally realizes what the other half of the stalls has: that the ventriloquist is acting out, live on stage, a highly dramatic and true fragment of his life—a fragment that is happening as it is being performed. At this point, this other half joins forces with the section of the audience that has already caught on to the unfolding drama, and the whole theater erupts in paroxysms of alternating, and even combined, laughter and tears.

"Your madness," Sansón reminds him in a very theatrical voice, "began back when you were kind and loving toward Francesca, back when you spoke to her in my voice, do you hear me? In *my* voice, not yours. Because whenever you spoke to her as *you*, it was in an artificial language which sounded unbearably aggressive."

"Aggressive? *Me?*" he replies in such a rage that the audience can't hold back its laughter.

"It was hard for Francesca to be treated so well by me and, on the other hand, to be so despised by you. That's why the relationship fell apart. Also, because you were constantly accusing her of neglecting the dressing room, your costumes, the boxes where you keep us, your puppets."

"That's not quite true, Sansón. You're upsetting the audience...."

"And then you blamed her for your own professional decline, which was totally unfair. That really was the limit. And she grew tired of it, Walter, she grew tired of it and she left you for another man. You lost her, which doesn't surprise me in the least. You with your whip and your crazy talk, telling her that we puppets were sleeping badly because she didn't look after us properly."

"Francesca didn't leave me, she didn't walk out," Walter tries to argue, ever more animated and desperate. "I sacked her! She was a lousy assistant. She realized it was better to go, go, GO! And in the end she slipped away among the spun-glass shadows of the dressing room."

"There were no spun-glass shadows in the dressing room," San-són corrects him.

The whole theater laughs.

And in a desperate, foolish attempt to turn his public's laughter into heartfelt sobs, Walter sings two verses of the song that he sang a few hours earlier to Francesca and the Scraper, having caught them in the middle of a performance in a cabaret in the south of Lisbon, and then learned that they were due to be married: "Don't marry her, she's already been kissed./Kissed by her lover, back when he loved her."

As he sings the song, visibly strained and upset, his voice cracks again, and everyone in the audience roars with laughter. It's neither a squeak nor quite a note, but rather a desperate, ridiculous warble, an anguished, deranged yelp, which sets part of the audience off again into uncontrollable fits of hysterics.

Not long afterward, and arguably motivated by his audience's cruelty, Walter decides to delay no longer and to bid farewell to his "distinguished public," on behalf of both himself and Sansón,

Sansón rebels, adding a few words of his own at the last minute, before he and his owner leave the stage:

"Pronounced murderous tendencies," he says, as if wanting to denounce his lord and master.

Just then, as he retreats, Walter gets the feeling that the small dagger tied to a band worn around his ankle—which, until a moment ago, had been concealed in the tip of the Javan sunshade—is peeping out from the folds of his tunic. But he is comforted by the thought that nobody in the audience, not even the most overactive imagination in the stalls, could suspect that the dagger contains traces of lethal cyanide.

11

I've noticed lately that the things that happen to me seem far more narratable than before I started writing this diary, when I was merely submerged in the eternal monotony of the real and, more specifically, in the tedious maelstrom of the construction world, in the day-to-day of business, always glumly marooned on the gray plains of the quotidian.

Today, for example, something happened to me which I knew at once would end up in this diary. It had nothing to do with the theme of repetition, which is perhaps why it pleased me even more, because it allowed me to distance myself from that obsessive topic and, for a few moments, to step outside and breathe, although the mere fact of breathing, of course, meant that I was repeating myself.

It occurred next to the newsstand where I buy my daily paper, and whose shining star, with her charm and physical exuberance, is its delightful owner. Things were jogging along with reassuring normality, when I was astonished to see someone heading straight toward me, hand outstretched, an individual with very square features—a Cubist pedestrian, I thought at once—a gentleman with motley-colored skin on his arms, and as ugly as sin.

I felt a slight shiver of disgust when I shook the monster's hand— his tattooed hand—but what else could I do; refusing to do so would have made things very awkward.

"I'm so pleased to meet you in the flesh at last," the square-featured pedestrian went on. "And I was equally pleased to see you on television yesterday."

As far as I know, I've never been on television, ever, and so it seemed to me that the man with the tattooed hand must be mistaken, or possibly crazy.

"You were very good," he insisted. "And I felt very proud. After all, we studied together with the Jesuits. The name's Boluda."

I was initially taken in by that surname, because I've been looking for a schoolfriend of mine by that name for the last forty years. Then I realized it was unlikely, not to say impossible, that this fellow—his physical appearance ruled him out—that he could possibly be the one I was looking for, although perhaps—there were a lot of Boludas at the school—he was his brother or his cousin.

The square-featured pedestrian began to list the more charismatic priests and teachers, which was proof that he really had studied alongside me and that his single—forgivable—error was to think that I had appeared on television.

I actually began to feel pleased to have bumped into him, realizing it was an opportunity—a rare one—to compare with someone else the real force of certain emotions from another time in my life.

Did I remember Father Corral? Boluda's question allowed me to expand on my own memories of that misunderstood teacher who used to recite medieval poems to us in class. And when, shortly afterward, the name of Father Guevara was mentioned, I immediately associated it with the priest who used to molest us boys and who committed suicide one misty morning by hurling himself into the playground from the roof of that sordid building.... There was much to be said about that murky episode, but Boluda preferred to turn the page on it as soon as possible and, somewhat nervously, recalled Father Benítez, the most human of our priests. He was the only one who had been a ladies' man before joining the staff, and was always very suntanned, as well as being a hard taskmaster in gym classes.

Of course I remembered him. I was becoming more and more animated, but Boluda didn't share in my excitement, and I soon found out the sad reason behind this: Father Benítez had always tried to ridicule and feminize him in front of the other boys, saying in one gym class that he looked like a boy straight out of a Murillo painting.

How odd, I said to myself, because it seemed to me that Boluda's features could never have been delicate enough for anyone to think he resembled one of Murillo's little angels.

Something wasn't right, and things took a turn for the worse when I discovered that the Cubist pedestrian had been a whole five years below me, and I had, therefore, never seen him before in my life, because I never took any notice of the younger boys at school.

I became indignant, although, at first, I said nothing. If he had told me this to start with, I wouldn't have wasted my time on him. I felt truly pissed off, furious, and, finally, could contain myself no longer—anything to do with my sacred memories of school has always been very close to my heart—and I reproached him with having been so ambiguous and allowing me to believe, falsely, that we had once been classmates. How dare he waste my time like that, especially when he was so ugly.

So *what?* he asked incredulously. So fat and so ugly, I said or repeated. Unperturbed, he asked if I considered myself to be exactly sylphlike—that's the word he used—and if I really believed that no one noticed that I had half my brain missing.

Half my brain? Was he really so upset that I'd called him "ugly?" "Yes, half your brain," he said, "it was blindingly obvious on television yesterday when you claimed that we had now emerged from the crisis."

"What television, and what crisis and what kind of Boluda are you?" I felt obliged to ask.

Impassive, yet persistent, he then asked if it didn't bother me to be caught lying on television. Because it seemed to him, he said, that he, too, had the right to introduce a few falsehoods into what he was telling me, which is why, for example, he had implied that I was fat when I wasn't, although it was true that I could hardly describe myself as skinny either.

"Do you genuinely think," he said, raising his voice, "that you are the only one who has the right to lie, you little rich kid?"

Little rich kid?

Had the class struggle finally reached Coyote?

"Do you remember," I said, "how we used to call Father Corral 'Chicken'?"

He was so enraged now, so angry, that he marched off, taking the rapid strides of a callow youth, leaving me with those words on my lips, feeling astonished, almost stunned, stranded somewhere beyond the newsstand and real life.

"Chicken!" I yelled after him, in a last-ditch attempt to wound and humiliate him.

But he had already turned the corner and left only a kind of trace in the air, the trace of a square-featured, I'd say Cubist man.

"An opportunity to speed up matters favorable to the family and the home, doubtless thanks to improved communication."

It's as if Peggy Day were telling me: "Turn your eyes homeward, to home sweet home, and leave me in peace, Mac."

Goddamned horoscope!

&

I discovered in La Súbita bookstore—or rather in the nightmare from which I've just awoken—that Peggy Day had published a personal diary of some seven thousand pages: philosophical notes, vivid descriptions of a day in the country, sketches of stories, descriptions of real people, details of her family circle, things that happened to her in the street, concerns about her health, growing anxieties about the future, the tormented prose of an insomniac, idle meanderings, all kinds of memories—none of which involved me—travel stories, even baseball commentaries (this last must have shocked me out of my slumbers).

12

"The Whole Theater Laughs" is a story I could read many times over without growing tired of it, because, apart from its obligatory "dizzy spell"—the one in this story, as dense as they come, is especially galling—it contains an appealing invitation to the reader to make a once-in-a-lifetime decision and run away.

Such escapes are always tempting and one never wants to give up on the idea entirely, even though, when it comes down to it, we always end up back where we started, having chosen the tranquility of the dull old city we've always called home. But if we can still find something to smile about, it's because we know that, however late in the game it might be, we do still have the option to drop every-thing and leave it all behind.

This doesn't mean that I myself wouldn't prefer an altogether less scandalous, very different kind of goodbye. I once read something about the tradition of the *sans adieu*, an expression which translates into eighteenth-century colloquial Spanish as "to take French leave" and which, to this day, is used to reproach someone who goes off without saying goodbye, without a word. It might seem that taking one's leave in this way is poor form, but, in fact, leaving a gathering without saying goodbye to anyone is far more refined and proper. Perhaps I see it this way because I still remember the days when, having drunk rather more than I should, I would do the rounds of the other guests, trying to say goodbye to absolutely everyone, when really I would have done far better to slip away and not let so many people witness me in that terrible state.

The *sans adieu* was fashionable throughout the eighteenth century in French high society, when, at soirées, it became customary to leave without bidding the salon farewell, without even saying good-night to one's hosts. Indeed, this habit came to be so accepted that actually saying goodbye was deemed ill-mannered. It was perfectly acceptable if, for example, a fellow guest began making it clear that he was impatient to leave, but much frowned upon if that same guest said goodnight when he did finally leave.

To "exit stage left" seems to me the most elegant way of leaving—just as Walter did in Lisbon, for example—because leaving without going through all the usual motions only speaks of our immense pleasure at being with our present companions, whom we fully intend to see again. To put it another way, we leave without saying a word, because to say goodbye would be a sign of displeasure and estrangement. All of this has led me, inevitably, to think about my abrupt disappearance from Juanita Lopesbaño's life. That was a very dirty trick to play on her. But there would be little point now, forty years after my sudden departure, in telling her that the reason I didn't bother to say goodbye was so that she wouldn't confuse my farewell with a sign of displeasure and estrangement. No, there wouldn't be much point in that. And besides, I'm sure she wouldn't believe me. Why would she when I scarcely believe it myself, fully aware as I am that, back then, I was completely oblivious to the subtleties of the *sans adieu*? I left with no idea why I was leaving, driven by a vague, impulsive instinct, perhaps by an overwhelming urge simply to leave.

"The Whole Theater Laughs" is, in effect, a story that I could read over and again without growing tired of it, because it also has the advantage of containing the whole of Lisbon. I love the tragic climate that Sánchez creates around Walter's great goodbye. And I also love how the story's climate of crime and fate is set in Lisbon, a city made for such things. I remember a friend saying that you had to see Lisbon in its entirety, at the first light of day, and then you would weep. And someone else, another friend, said the complete opposite: that you had to take in the whole of Lisbon in the time it takes for the faintest of smiles to fade, as you catch the sun's final fleeting glow on Rua da Prata.

It happened to me, and I know it's happened to others: the first time I went to Lisbon, I had the feeling that I'd lived there before; I didn't know when, and it made no sense, but I felt that I'd been in that city before ever having been there.

"Lisbon is for living, and for killing," the voice says.

I hardly need explain: it's the voice of the dead man lodged in my head.

[WHOROSCOPE 12]

A little early-evening prose: After a long stroll in and around the neighborhood—having gone beyond what you could reasonably call the Coyote district—I arrived home exhausted and, in keeping with an old habit, I mentally lit my pipe. In other words, as my mother would say, I "lit the fire in my mind," and I thought for a while about my old desire to leave one day and go somewhere far away, and also about my near-constant resolve to stop this diary from turning into a novel.

After this, I had a couple of drinks and began weighing the pros and cons of reading my horoscope. In the end, I decided to go and see what Juanita had written on that damn page of hers. But, just as I was about to do so, there appeared in my inbox a reply to my email of the other day. It goes without saying that I wasn't expecting it. And what I found was a rather cheery, frivolous, perhaps mocking, and certainly disconcerting postcard-style text: "Weather divine. Everything perfect. An awful lot of *far niente* and hula-hooping. And a little surfing. Ciao, stupid."

I understand it, but not entirely, why deny it? It upset me, offended me. I could have just laughed it off, but she caught me at a sensitive moment, and with a few drinks inside me.

Before collapsing onto the bed, I had just enough time to reply to Peggy and ask her, if she would be so kind, to tell me, in advance, what was going to happen to me tomorrow. My request was perfectly polite, but it's also true that I'm not quite myself at the moment, so now I'm very much afraid that …

(Figurative collapse)

&

Sometimes I picture myself leaving.

When this happens, in my mind's eye I become a seasoned traveler heading off to somewhere resembling the end of the world, a dapper sort in a well-cut jacket, the pockets of which, however, are wearing increasingly thin, perhaps because they hold his true identity: that of a vagabond.

This other I occasionally thinks about Sánchez's intriguing nephew, whom he hasn't seen since their last meeting, but who made a deep impression on him. And he comes to some unusual conclusions: it seems to him that if he were forced to choose between the resentful nephew and Sánchez himself, he would choose the former, because the former still hasn't written anything. What's more, of the two, the nephew—while hardly a paragon of virtue from a moral point of view—is clearly the only one who could, at this point, possibly reveal himself to be a literary genius, because his nonexistent career at least allows for this possibility, if only because he still hasn't written anything, whereas his uncle, while showing some merit, has already racked up a fair number of missteps and some impressive own goals.

The nephew, on the other hand, reminds him of Wittgenstein's nephew, who appears in a work by Thomas Bernhard. Bernhard himself follows the example of Diderot's satire *Rameau's Nephew*, dwelling on the possibility that Paul Wittgenstein was, in fact, a more important philosopher than his uncle, precisely because he never wrote anything on philosophy, and therefore didn't even come out with the famous line: "Whereof one cannot speak, thereof one must be silent."

"But Mac, Sánchez's nephew is nothing but a bum," says the voice in my head, as if now, on top of everything else, it wanted to show some common sense too.

13

The epigraph to the fourth story, "Something in Mind," comes from Hemingway's *A Moveable Feast*: "She was very pretty with a face as fresh as a newly minted coin if they minted coins in smooth flesh with rain-freshened skin...."

As far as I can remember, I've only ever seen a fresh face like that once in my life, and it was in Paris too, a real-life scene in the Bois de Boulogne: a woman who, moments before she plunged into the dense mist, turned round just enough to reveal, very fleetingly, a fresh face of imperfect but incredible beauty.

In my memory, that fragment, that glimpse of the unknown woman who turned slightly before vanishing into the mist, always appears in my mind as if it were a sequence from a movie that gets stuck and repeats itself over and over, never advancing. Whenever I evoke that scene, whenever I recall it, I see it on constant repeat, but

I have no way of knowing what happens after the woman plunges into the mist.

And always, perhaps because it frustrates me to see that I'll never know the outcome, perhaps because I can see that I'll never go beyond that interrupted sequence, a tragic, unresolvable doubt arises in me: what happened next? What did the unknown woman do after disappearing into that eternal mist?

Earlier on, while reading "Something in Mind"—a text that bears the Hemingway stamp from start to finish—I gave to the invisible young woman in that story the fleeting, beautiful face of the enigmatic creature glimpsed one day in the Bois de Boulogne. I was right to do so, because I could then give a face to the character, who is a silent presence throughout the whole of that fourth story. Unlike the three previous stories, it's clearly not told by the ventriloquist, but written in the voice of a stranger who gives us a plot that would seem to be entirely unconnected with Walter's memories were it not for the fact that the invisible girl, at least from the little we learn about her, is the very image of Francesca, Walter's great love.

"Something in Mind" merely appears to be a banal, insubstantial story: two teenage boys from Barcelona, after going on an idiotic all-nighter, turn up at the home of the grandmother of one of them, at seven o'clock in the morning, to ask her for money so that they can continue their private party in the full light of day. In the background, like a secret story that never fully surfaces, is the rivalry between the two boys for the favors of a very beautiful young girl who is never named, but who is there and whom neither of them forgets for a moment; an almost palpable *absence*, even though the story appears to do nothing more than reproduce the anodyne conversation between the two teens during their absurdly early morning visit.

The anonymous narrator, who employs what Hemingway called the Iceberg Theory, pours all his skill into the hermetic telling of that other secret story—two revelers in love with a young woman they never mention—and so skilled is he at the art of ellipsis that the reader becomes aware of that other, *absent* story of which the girl in question would be the protagonist. Indeed, the narrator writes the story as if the reader already knew that those two wild adolescents had spent the entire night quarreling over that same girl, who, given the epigraph, presumably has rain-freshened skin. But the conversation itself is just idle chitchat, except for one moment when the grandmother asks her grandson why his friend is so extremely timid. Even though the two friends are rivals in love, her grandson Juan denies that his friend is shy at all and, inventing a story on the spot, he tells his grandmother that his friend Luis isn't the least bit timid, but is merely distracted, that he is thinking about a story of love and death he's been writing and which was stolen from him just a short while ago.

The grandmother then wants to know where this theft took place.

"In a dance hall," Luis blurts out.

"Actually," Juan adds, "it wasn't really a love story, it was the memoir of a ventriloquist, and you could read it either as a novel or as a book of short stories."

"Actually," says Luis, "it was only a partial memoir."

Then the grandmother wants to know why *partial*. "Because he didn't tell you everything," Luis is quick to explain. And Juan adds: "The ventriloquist is one of those guys who's always thinking about dropping everything and running away, but, in his memoir, the real reason why he does finally run away never comes out."

The grandmother then wants to know what the real reason was.

"Because before leaving Lisbon," says Luis, "he'd done over the guy who had stolen his girlfriend."

"Done over?" asks the grandmother.

"Yes, and done him in too," says Luis.

Silence.

"Yes, Grandma," says Juan, "done him in good and proper. Now do you understand? He stabbed him with a dagger which he'd hidden inside a sunshade, but, obviously, the ventriloquist wasn't going to confess to that in his memoir and so he says something else, I guess to cover up what's really going on."

This fragment from that fourth story, "Something in Mind," nicely sums up the way in which the whole of *Walter and His Problem* is told. And so it's highly likely that Sánchez used this story with the anonymous narrator to explain that the whole novel, of which the story is a part, makes use of the Iceberg Theory. Because while a few relevant things do happen in the book, the secret story, the key story, the scene of the crime, is only ever suggested, it never actually appears; which is perfectly understandable if we put ourselves in Walter's shoes, because, if he did confess to his crime, he could land himself in big trouble.

Putting myself in Walter's shoes might be the first thing I have to do if, one day, I write a "remake" of the novel. Perhaps one way of seeing through the ventriloquist's eyes would be to transform myself into a jealous type—easy enough, since I already am—one capable of writing a memoir without revealing that he's killed a barber, but capable, too, of implying this strongly enough for the reader to figure out that he has in fact murdered him, which is why he has to get out and flee Lisbon.

But in order to experience intensely and authentically the, shall we say, "emotional storm" that might break over him following his crime in that city and his hasty withdrawal from the stage, I might have to find a way of fully identifying with that poor lost soul, Walter. Right now, the only method that occurs to me is the one used by that famous "painter of light," Turner, when he had himself lashed to a ship's mast for four whole hours in the midst of a violent storm, in the hope that this would help him get the full measure of nature's temperament.

[WHOROSCOPE 13]

Among my emails I found Peggy Day's answer to my request for an update on what would happen to me today: "Things couldn't be better. *Far niente* and hula-hoops. And a little surfing with a cool breeze behind you, my little sword-swallower."

I notice that this time she has omitted the offensive "stupid," but she's still clearly in a foul mood. As for that "cool breeze," she seems to be ordering me to take a running jump, with the coolest breeze possible behind me. She writes: "Things couldn't be better. *Far niente* and hula-hoops," and I notice her weakness for repetitions; not the kind of repetitions that appeal to me, but those that lack imagination and lead you down a road to nowhere.

In fact, if you stop to observe Peggy's own most repeated daily activity—her regular horoscopal rulings—you'll see that there, just as with the repetitive emails she's sent me, she has pretty much landed herself in a cul-de-sac. Because really Peggy uses a very limited vocabulary—"dream," "problems," "happiness," "family," "matters," "money," etc.—meaning that she quickly runs out of possible combinations. It's the kind of poetry of repetition that doesn't interest me in the least, because it leads one inevitably into a blind alley, a barren, bleak, and fatally dead end.

Nevertheless, I think that the failure of the investigatory path I opened up with Peggy has been an excellent experience for me as a beginner: it contains a lesson that could prove very useful to me from now on. As is usually the case, we learn from our mistakes. I wanted Peggy's oracles to work in tandem with my own forays into writing and to relate in some way to my sorties into the subject of repetition. And I did so because I thought that those two things—the oracles and my first literary ventures—would soon start to merge; but that isn't what happened at all. This business with the horoscopes has turned out to be another dead end, a spring that's dried up on me and which, at best, I'll learn to live with. It's clear that, in using those two things, I was trying to build something out of nothing, perhaps because I can't yet put it into words. As methods go, it's not bad at all; writers around the world combine subjects, which, at first glance, have nothing whatever to do with each other, in the hope that this will allow them access to something that exists in the realm of the *unsayable*. It's a trick that works in psychoanalysis, but not here in my diary. Or perhaps it does, and I simply haven't been able to see it. Whatever the case, I now know that opening up two distinct paths and trying to combine subjects which, on the surface, have nothing in common, doesn't always lead to a positive result.

14

This morning I was getting ready to reread "An Old Married Couple," the fifth story, when, as I listened to Big Bill Broonzy singing "Trouble in Mind," I gradually forgot what it was I'd set out to do and instead began thinking about how Borges always considered novels to be nonnarratives. They were, he said, too far removed from oral narratives, and, as a result, had lost the direct presence of an interlocutor, the presence of someone who could leave gaps for the reader to fill in, and had, therefore, lost the concision of short stories and folk tales. One had to remember, Borges went on to say, that although the presence of the listener, the presence of the person listening to the tale, is, indeed, a kind of strange hangover from the past, nonetheless, the short story has survived, in part, precisely thanks to that archaism, thanks to having preserved the figure of the listener, that ghost from the past.

I still don't know quite what made me think of all of this, but a diary exists as a lasting record of what we were thinking on any given day, just in case, in the future, on rereading whatever we told ourselves that morning, we discover that the things we wrote down without a second thought are now the only rocks we can cling to.

[OROSCOPE 14]

Yesterday, the Whoroscope lost its full name, and almost its raison d'être, because Peggy Day erased herself, to put it kindly. And now this is an Oroscope, in part a black ribbon to indicate a definitive goodbye, and, in part, an unremarkable and silent celebration to mark the end of the day. The Oroscope, just like its predecessor, the Whoroscope, is merely prose written as evening falls. While, up until now, I would normally make the most of this hour to focus on Peggy's oracle, now that I've put her astral pages behind me (and still further behind me, her unforgivably paltry and limited combination of words, that is, her dead-end language, doomed to extinction, at least where my diary is concerned), the Oroscope will live on, fulfilling one of its original functions: that of adding to the waning day anything that might be left to add.

Released from Peggy and her restricted vocabulary, I can now rest, perfectly relaxed, a glass of gin in my hand, not moving from the large red armchair in my room where I once worked as a building contractor and where I now work with my mind, which, frankly, I find infinitely more enjoyable.

15

Last night, there I was deep in all kinds of thoughts, and feeling, for some reason, half-engrossed and half-excited, when in through the half-open window flew a parakeet.

After colliding several times with the ceiling, the bird—green with a white breast—ended up getting trapped down a narrow gap (it's amazing there was room for it really), about four or five feet deep, where the two main bookshelves form an angle. I feel rather intrigued by this gap now, because, had it not been for what happened last night, I don't think I would ever have known of its existence, given that, in order to see it, I would, at some point during the many years I've lived in this apartment, have had to climb a ladder; but why would I climb a ladder when there was nothing of interest up there?

Finally, it was Carmen, thinking I was making it up, who scaled a ladder and got a terrible fright when she saw that there really was a parakeet lying at the bottom of the tiny gap she had never noticed either. At first, I thought we'd have to dismantle the two oak bookshelves; otherwise, given the depth and inaccessibility of the gap, the parakeet would remain irretrievable, lost down that unforeseen dark hole, invisible to the rest of the apartment. It would squawk for days and days, and I would sit there writing, unable to see it, but hearing it, and then, well, then the poor bird would die and its remains would begin to decompose, spreading its stench throughout the apartment, and filling up with maggots that would worm their way inside the books and end up eating everything, swallowing the entire history of world literature.

Rescuing that creature from the narrow depths of that four- or five-foot shaft seemed like an impossible task, but we clearly had to do something.

"You've got to do something," said Carmen, "and get it out of there."

I found the parakeet's squawks rather inspiring, but I couldn't say this to her, because it would only have made matters worse. The squawking was helping me to write, especially when the bird communicated—through the open window—with its brothers and sisters, the family of parakeets that appeared to be waiting for it outside. I sat writing in the middle of the imaginary flight path of those desperate cries, which traveled up from the depths and out onto the street, where they were greeted by the squawks of other parakeets who, from the tops of the trees, seemed to be asking my accidental pet where its anguished cries were coming from. And perhaps the worst thing was not being able to say any of this to my wife, because it would only prove to her that I was even crazier than she already thought I was.

Carmen was growing more and more agitated—she would have been even more so had she known that the bird's squawking was a source of inspiration to me and was helping me advance in my apprenticeship as a writer—and I was perhaps beginning to feel reluctant to take any action. In all the years of our marriage, I had never realized that she was terrified of birds. Finally, after fruitlessly summoning the local police (who came to the house, but had no idea what to do and washed their hands of what they said was a most unusual case), we called the fire brigade, and they, in turn, called the animal protection league (a free service provided by the city council), and, finally, a young protector of flying creatures—after an anxiety-filled ten-hour wait for him to come and a few painful, strained minutes, because, as we had foreseen, rescuing the bird was difficult in the extreme—he lowered a basket attached to a six-foot-long rope into the gap, and maneuvering the rope with exceptional ingenuity and skill, not to mention infinite patience, he managed to rescue the parakeet. And then, very gently, wearing gloves to protect himself from being pecked, he placed the bird on the highest shelf so that it could escape back out through the window and resume its life in flight. For a few moments, the now liberated parakeet appeared to hesitate, as if it didn't want to leave.

And I know this sounds crazy, and would seem strange if not laughable to anyone hearing it, but I'll burst if I don't say right here and now: I really miss that poor parakeet.

16

"An Old Married Couple" moves along at a cracking pace thanks to the constant back and forth of blows—or, rather, monologues—of a pair of cuckolds, Baresi and Pirelli, two strangers who have just met and who, perched precariously on their bar stools, begin to tell each other their respective (and almost identical) stories of doomed love.

Everything happens in the wee hours of the morning, in the bar of a hotel in the city of Basel, where the hopeless pair are drinking nonstop—hence their rather precarious position at the bar—and telling their tales of woe. The story begins with this monologue by Baresi, which I liked a lot. I think I might even learn a thing or two from it.

"You, sir, have led me to the bottle, or, rather, your confession that you like to hear other people's stories has driven me to drink (I said to an elegant Italian, an occasional drinking companion in the bar of a hotel in Basel), and now the truth is that I'm completely drunk and a little overemotional, or, to be more precise, I feel rather starry-eyed and in the mood to tell you this story, which you will recall I mentioned in passing when I said that, lately, I've noticed a certain propensity on my part to recount episodes from my life, episodes that I sometimes alter slightly so as not to be repetitive or to start to bore myself, Signor Pirelli, if you'll allow me to call you that, since here everyone seems to be called Pirelli, although nobody goes around wearing a monocle like yours—no, don't tell me your real surname, I'd have little use for it; for my sole interest is in telling you what happened to me with a compatriot of yours. You might enjoy hearing this story, Signor Pirelli."

We soon learn that Baresi lost his Italian bride soon after marrying her, having discovered that she belonged, at least in her heart, to another man. We also learn that, for his part, Pirelli discovered on the island of Java, after twenty years of peaceful marriage, that his wife still hadn't forgotten her first love, a young man who took his own life.

Baresi and Pirelli carry on sharing the details of their respective and almost identical sentimental failures, and you can see that, while Baresi delights in giving his monologue, embellishing his dreadful true story with fictional flourishes, Pirelli, narratively speaking, does the opposite, keeping strictly to the facts and inventing nothing. In other words, much as it pains him to do so, Pirelli tries to stay within the limits of what he deems to be the truth.

This turns the two lovelorn, jaded, and incurably lonely Italians into something more than two discarded old husbands. It means that one of them, Baresi, seems to embody the world of fiction writers—the world inhabited by those who believe that any work that tells a true story is an insult to both art and truth—and the other, Pirelli, represents those who think that reality can be reproduced exactly as it is, and that, as such, it should never be placed between quotation marks, given that there is only one truth.

Fiction and reality, an old married couple.

At the end of the story there's a scene which, under normal circumstances, would have made me raise an eyebrow and perhaps even look away, but that didn't happen because, deep down, the beauty of that perfect connection between the two bitter drunks propped up at the bar of that hotel in Basel seems to me just faultless. Baresi and Pirelli emerge as a single human subject in which fiction and reality fuse so intensely that, at certain moments, it seems impossible to separate them. In some way, for want of a closer comparison, Baresi and Pirelli remind us of the bull and the matador and how, when in the ring, and if the splendor of the bullfighting ritual is there in full force, they become a single, indivisible figure in which man and beast merge, making it hard to tell one from the other. Michel Leiris described the beautiful and tragic effect of this unity thus: "Insofar as the torero, slowly moving his red cape, manages to keep his feet still during a series of measured, fluid passes, he and the animal will form that prized configuration in which man, cape, and horned beast appear to be engaged in a game of reciprocal influences."

"And I, Signor Pirelli," we hear Baresi say between muffled sobs, "finally understood that whatever I did would be pointless, that I was going to lose her, and I also understood that, deep down, she had never been mine, that she belonged to another man, and that, with that other man, she formed an old married couple whose tense relationship dated back years, impossibly far back in time, or at least further back than the night when reality and fiction first paired up: an old married couple locked in an endless nightmare, with the same anguished obstinacy as a whore and her pimp. Do you understand now, Signor Pirelli?"

Pirelli does understand, but, somewhat mysteriously, he doesn't respond. And in the moments that follow he makes Baresi a proposal which, besides drawing their long conversation to a close, casts a shadow of doubt over their nocturnal meeting:

"And now, Signor Ventriloquist, allow me to invite you to my room. I would like you to believe in my story and for you to know that, from time to time, the dead man himself appears at my back. And in order for you to see that I really was in Java, allow me to give you some typical artifacts from the island. I keep them in my room. Come, come up with me. I want to offer you some souvenirs from Java. I would like to give you a special sunshade with a hidden spring that transforms it into a very sharp weapon, a kind of bayonet. Who knows, it might prove useful to you one day. And I would also like us to forget our woes by going to bed together. Don't you think we'd have more time then to put the world to rights à deux?"

So now we know where the Javan sunshade came from, which leads us to think that Baresi, who accepts the gift, might well be the person who gave Walter that murderous sunshade.

Special mention must be made of the inevitable "dizzy spell," to be found in every chapter of Sánchez's book, "An Old Married Couple" being no exception. This lumbering "dizzy spell" comes toward the end of the dialogue between the two drunks, in a section of the chapter which suddenly becomes incredibly dense. You can tell a mile off that the story is going belly up, as if the two interlocutors had suddenly come down with terrible headaches that reduced them to idiocy.

And yet, despite this brief, leaden, fizzing-aspirin section, this story in particular—because of its atmosphere and the way it conveys the metaphysics of marital angst—is perhaps the most accomplished of the first five. "The Whole Theater Laughs" is more moving, but "An Old Married Couple" feels more polished. Indeed, perhaps its worst defect is the epigraph, taken from Raymond Carver's book *Cathedral*: "But I made a point of getting him to mention his wife's name. 'Olla,' he said. Olla, I said to myself. Olla."

What's Carver got to do with all of this? What's Carver doing in a run-down hotel in Basel? It's also unclear why Sánchez chose such an inconsequential quote. Did he mean for the reader to read the marriage between reality and fiction as if it were an "*olla*," that is, a pressure cooker? Surely not. The story has a Carveresque feel, but it's much more sophisticated than the rough, everyday world Carver depicts. Now I'm the one with a head like a pressure cooker, and I really should call it a day. I ought to face facts: the booze I've been drinking has badly affected my intellectual faculties. I no longer even know if I'm Pirelli or Baresi.

Lou Reed is playing in the background.

Olla, I say to myself, and I repeat it until she hears me.... Who? Olla or Carmen? Why does Carmen pretend not to know that I'm writing this diary? What does she think I do in this study all day? Goof around online? She loathes the literary world, and I accept that. The sciences make her feel superior, even though she actually makes her living restoring furniture. Why does she feel the need to turn her nose up at books just to distance herself from me? Why that aggressive aversion to the printed page? She won't even let us keep the phone directory in the living room!

Oh well, tomorrow's another day.... Curse that gin.

In my head, only memories of past ravages. And this ebb and flow that lulls and dulls the mind.

17

At midday, I went out for a stroll and was pleasantly surprised when I bumped into Sánchez's nephew, who, despite having shaved off his beard, was even scruffier than before; he wore the look of someone who hasn't been to bed and he eyed me as if he were thinking: I know this guy from somewhere.

Although I had only observed him surreptitiously recently, he may have noticed me, which explains why he was staring at me like that. However, my pulse remained perfectly steady as I said to him:

"Excuse me, you're Sánchez's nephew, aren't you?"

"I will be tonight," he said. And with that he raced off, almost vanishing into thin air as he turned the corner.

The little creep.

&

The sad hero of the sixth story, "A Long Betrayal," is a gentleman by the name of Basi, about whom we are told in the second paragraph that "he had always been a late bloomer." The story starts off at a steady pace, suggesting that its writer must have been, at least that day—the day he began the story—perfectly sober and at no risk of suffering one of his frequent "dizzy spells":

"One night, woken by the sound of rain against the windows, Basi suddenly thought of his young wife lying in her damp grave.

This was a new experience for him, because he hadn't thought of his wife for so many years that remembering her now made him feel almost embarrassed. He imagined the open grave, the threads of water snaking in all directions, and his wife, whom he had married when there was a considerable age difference between them, lying alone in the midst of that ever-encroaching dampness. Not a single flower grew on the grave, even though he could have sworn he had paid for the grave to be maintained in perpetuity."

When I began rereading the story today, I realized that I wasn't, in fact, rereading it, for this was the story which, thirty years ago, I abandoned halfway through before promptly abandoning the entire book. I didn't continue the memoir—I remember this as if it were yesterday—because that same day I'd read in a review by Ricardo Ragú in *El País* that "A Long Betrayal" was an almost exact copy of a short story by Malamud. When I read this, I realized, among other things, that there was, therefore, nothing odd about the fact that Sánchez had chosen as the epigraph for this sixth story a quote from Bernard Malamud: "What's next isn't the point." And I also remember that, perhaps influenced by that epigraph, but also by what Ragú had said, I decided not to read on.

Today, on the other hand, I did read on.

The story describes how old Basi wakes one night to the sound of heavy rain beating on his bedroom window and lies there thinking about his young wife in her damp grave. The following morning, he goes in search of the grave, but cannot find it. He admits to the director of the cemetery that he and his wife never got on very well and that she had already been living with another man for years when, quite suddenly, death carried her off. Days later, the director phones Basi to tell him that he's found the wife's grave, except that her body isn't there: her lover had applied for a judicial order to have her moved to another niche, where he, too, was buried when he died. So, thinks Basi, his wife can now betray him eternally, lying, as she does, next to another man. But, says the director, the grave is still your property and, remember, you have the grave for future use: it's empty and that space belongs entirely to you.

It seems to me that Sánchez deliberately intended this story to look like a chapter that Walter had, on a whim, added to his memoirs. Having said that, it's also possible that Sánchez included it out of sheer laziness and as a neat way—thanks to a piece of blatant plagiarism—of instantly increasing the page count. Perhaps he added it to this partial autobiography because he was in such a hopeless, drunken state that he didn't realize the gravity of what he was doing. Or else—another hypothesis, mine and, I think, the most plausible—Sánchez simply dashed off the story in order to include, in an almost secret and doubtless very indirect way, an episode from the life of the autobiographer's father. Because I think Basi's unfortunate relationship with his wife recalls Baresi's painful marital relationship as described in "An Old Married Couple." It's therefore worth asking if Basi is a contraction of Baresi. Could it be that Baresi was also the surname of someone who went by the nom de plume of Walter? And what if Baresi of Basel was the father of our Walter? If he was, we would at least be able to clear up one point: we would know who had bequeathed the murder weapon, the sunshade from Java, to Walter the ventriloquist.

As for the epigraph: "What's next isn't the point," it really rang a bell, and, although I didn't know which of Malamud's books it could have come from, it took only five seconds of googling to resolve the matter: it was in a book of interviews and essays by Philip Roth; it was the answer Malamud had given to the risky question Roth had asked him the last time they had met; he'd responded almost at the end of Roth's visit to Malamud's house in Bennington. The previous summer, Malamud had suffered a stroke, and the debilitating after-effects had left him in no condition to travel or to leave his house. Roth had driven up from Connecticut to see his master in Bennington and realized at once how weak Malamud had become, because, up until then, regardless of the weather, he had always managed to be waiting in the driveway to greet visitors or see them off, and that day was no different, except that although Malamud was waiting there in his poplin jacket and nodded Roth a rather grim welcome, he appeared to be listing slightly to one side, while, at the same time, by dint of sheer willpower, keeping himself perfectly still, as if the slightest movement could bring him crashing down: "... he was now a frail and very sick old man, his tenacity about used up."

At the end of the visit, Malamud insisted on reading the beginning of the precarious novel he had begun to work on and which consisted of only a few typewritten sheets. Roth tried unsuccessfully to stop him, but Malamud insisted on reading out loud to him in a tremulous voice. A brutal silence followed. And not knowing what to say, Roth finally asked him what happened next.

"What's next isn't the point," said a furious Malamud.

For Roth, hearing what his master had written on that piece of paper was like discovering that "he hadn't got started, really, however much he wanted to think otherwise. Listening to what he read was like being led into a dark hole to see by torchlight the first Malamud story ever scratched upon a cave wall."

Apart from showing off his own skill with words, I have no idea what the point was of Roth's meticulous description of his much-admired master's decline. There are times when I don't like Roth at all. Malamud, on the other hand, has always aroused my sympathies as a reader. Roth comments that Malamud "looked to someone who'd grown up among such people like nothing so much as an insurance agent—he could have passed for one of my father's colleagues." I'm drawn to the Malamud who stubbornly circles around the human capacity to better ourselves, incredible though that may seem. And I'm drawn to him as well because he creates all kinds of discreet, gray beings, all of whom have a touch of the insurance agent about them, and who, because of that something they carry inside them, try to get at the truth of the matter and, as is the case with the somber, stricken Russian protagonist of *The Fixer*—my favorite Malamud novel—become splendidly obstinate, always engaged in the struggle to go ever deeper into everything.

For a beginner like me, Malamud, so gray and so tenacious, could serve as the perfect model of the writer, never that keen to go anywhere, a writer eager to avoid the fixer's constant battle to evolve. Malamud is a good model for me, because while his heroes always strive to better themselves, the writer never moves from the same landscape of drab rocks and austere oak trees, never strives to test the limits of his own "modest knowledge" of the art of storytelling.

For a beginner like me, the gray, tenacious Malamud could prove a blessing. Choosing grayness might be a way of seeing no urgent need to evolve, when evolution is always seen as so absurdly prestigious. Are animals that don't evolve—like the eagle—not entirely happy with their status? If we hadn't had parents, teachers, and friends insisting that we improve, we should probably have been much happier. That's why it seems to me that here, in this diary, I will continue investigating what I call *modest knowledge*, which implies a knowledge of literary matters, and which allows one to make steady progress *without becoming too successful*, however paradoxical that seems, even to me. And the thing is, that *modest knowledge*— available only to a minority, because it doesn't usually reveal itself— generates its own protection against advancement and contributes to confirming what so many of us have always suspected, namely, that to be too successful can be suicidal.

"I do not evolve: I travel," wrote Pessoa.

In a way, this reminds me sometimes that one can know a man better by what he despises than by what he admires, and it reminds me, too, as I believe Piglia says, that, in literature, what we call progress doesn't exist, just as, for example, we don't get better at dreaming over time: perhaps what we learn most from writing is what we would prefer not to do; we advance, rejection by rejection.

I was thinking about this just a few moments ago, while I was looking out of my window, trying to relive the pleasure I've always felt in the very intense drawings made by certain painters, images that spring impulsively out of the moment. These are pictures that emerge from the beauty of this gray day, serenely advancing along the streets of Coyote, and which emerge, too, from my own debutant artist's world: those mental sketches, always so close to what is actually happening, that are rather charming and, fortunately, rather naive mental engravings; naive, in my case, because the person producing them is still in the initial phase of everything and has no aspirations to go much beyond that, satisfied with the calm state of being *the beginner*, satisfied with the happy state of the beginner, able to travel from his place at the window, never losing sight of the fact that he is content with the comfortable grayness of his *modest knowledge*.

In short: let others advance.

Or, as Malamud would say: perhaps it would be more useful to settle into the stubbornly modest gray classroom and accept it as it is, like an eternal Monday in nursery school. After all, we don't know if things aren't better that way: *deliberately insufficient*. Yet, depending on which way I look at them from my study, things are increasingly brimming with life. This would confirm my suspicion that being successful in unassuming Malamud style is simply a matter of secretly improving my normal vision, as if I were suddenly equipped with special magnifying glasses and everything I studied, saw, and learned were illuminated by a kind of potent light I can't identify, perhaps because it's merely the subtle glow given off by everything that I am starting to learn.

18

This morning, beneath an almost literally scorching sun, I wandered the streets of Coyote, so immersed in my search for something remarkable going on that a keen-eyed observer might well have spotted that I was looking for something, however small, to record in this diary—a coded wink, for example, or a dust particle in which, with a healthy dose of imagination, I might see the whole world. If this keen-eyed observer had existed, he or she might have said:

"Look at that beginner over there, on the hunt in Coyote."

I thought about all the years I've been walking around this neighborhood, a slave to my daily rituals. I have all sorts of set habits and routines, and I couldn't even say now how long I've been living this deliberately provincial life in the heart of the big city. My entire family comes from this neighborhood: from my Germanophile great-grandfather to my six grandchildren, the children of my children, Miguel, Antonio and Ramiro, all staunch supporters of misguided political parties with whom I occasionally sympathize, although only at that time of day when I forget that idiocy isn't a shortcoming specific to a particular age, it's always existed. It's part of the human condition.

I haven't often left this neighborhood over the course of my life, but I've seen my fair share of the world as a keen tourist, and also because I was obliged, when I worked in the construction business, to seek out new markets, sometimes traveling very far afield. For a while now, though, I've been following the same short routes that always lead me to the exact same spots in Coyote, and this helps to prevent my diary from turning into a novel, which I'm still dead set against. But this morning, I foolishly forgot about this, and, on several occasions, unwittingly opened the floodgates, exposing my-self to events that could very easily have turned into scenes from a novel. I was roaming the streets this morning, on the lookout for the first noteworthy episode, when the voice—the voice of that dead man still lodged in my head—reappeared to tell me:

"You don't need to look for anything. Believe me, your life—the one and only great adventure—is enough."

"What a cliché!" I replied.

And not long after, as if it were a consequence of having criticized the voice, I began to get the unpleasant feeling that I was becoming terribly dehydrated. I urgently needed to find a water fountain, or a bar. I felt slightly dizzy, and then my thoughts—one thinks the strangest things at such times—my thoughts turned to the humble status of a man whose highest aspiration at any given moment is simply to get hold of a glass of water. And then a few lines by Borges came to mind, lines which, given my state at the time, I wasn't sure I'd be able to remember in full, although in the end I did: "… a man who has learned to be thankful for the modest everyday gifts of sleep, routine, and the taste of water."

Feeling considerably more worried than I had been even mo-ments before, I came face-to-face with the news vendor, who, at that very instant, happened to be drinking some water. I felt like snatching the bottle from her, but managed to contain myself.

"That's global warming for you," said the ineffable Venus (as local people call her, I assume with a touch of irony, because she's far from being beauty personified), and, at first, I didn't know if she was referring to her own thirst or to me with my ghastly, sweat-drenched look of a man overwhelmed by the heat. When I saw that she was merely referring to her thirst, I felt like venting my anger on that poor Venus and her plastic bottle; then I recalled a friend from earlier days, who was despised by all environmentalists everywhere because, as an industrialist, he was a specialist in contributing to greenhouse gases. And that made me hold my tongue, and instead I simply smiled, as if I were the guardian of some secret.

"Do you think the heat will last into next week?" she asked.

Suppressing the urge to tell her that the temperature, if not my fever, would eventually go down, I found myself saying:

"What's next isn't the point."

I didn't hang around to see Venus's reaction. I left the newsstand without even attempting to buy my usual paper, and entered a bar, where I quenched my thirst, and took a moment to be thankful for life's modest gifts.

Minutes later, I was walking happily back from my outing in the suffocating heat; I was only a few steps from home when, in the distance, I thought I saw Sánchez entering Carson's patisserie, completely oblivious, of course, to the disproportionately large space that he and his ventriloquist's memoirs have occupied in my mind for the last two weeks. And right there and then I realized how accustomed I've become to spending hours each day thinking about either him or that decades-old novel of his, and yet I hardly know the man himself. In fact, he's a complete stranger. He leads a busy alternative life inside my head—or, at least, he has done so for the last two weeks—but if I told him as much, he wouldn't have a clue what I was on about.

Events then seemed to move very quickly. Or perhaps I set them off.

Standing some way away, with my vision impaired by the sweltering fug, I watched, agog, as I saw Carmen go into Carson's after him. Wasn't she at work? I wanted to believe that, as on other occasions, she had managed to get away from the workshop an hour early. The sun was beating down, and it was true that the figures around me were distorted by a kind of shimmering haze, and I told myself that I couldn't be certain that it was Sánchez I'd seen, still less Carmen close behind him, as if she were pursuing him. But the seed of doubt had been sown. And instead of walking over to the spot where I thought I'd seen Carmen, instead of shedding light on that whole business straight away—or perhaps for fear of shedding too much light on it—I went into our lobby, then crossed the lobby itself, got into the elevator, and finally asked myself what to make of what I'd seen.

Was it pure coincidence? Or were Carmen and Sánchez involved in some kind of relationship, and was this the story of a long betrayal (as in the title of that story, the one my neighbor plagiarized from Malamud and which I read just yesterday)? Or was it possible that I'd seen neither Sánchez nor Carmen, and the whole episode was a product of the heat wave, which was distorting everything?

Once inside our apartment, I poured myself a glass of ice-cold water. I then deliberated over whether or not to put this trivial gesture in my diary. The answer wasn't long in coming. I absolutely must write it down if I didn't want to lose the sense that what I'm writing is a diary and not a novel. Even more important, I mustn't forget that, when it comes to writing a diary, anything goes. You can write what you like, even—of course—trivialities; actually, these work especially well in a diary, which is also perfectly suited to reflections, dreams, fictions, short essays, fears, suspicions, confessions, aphorisms, and reading notes.

I sat down in my favorite armchair and told myself to play it cool and, when Carmen arrived home, not launch straight into an interrogation, still less accuse her of something as ambiguous as the vague something of which I wanted to accuse her. I sat down and resumed my reading of *Walter and His Problem*. The title of the seventh story was "Carmen."

19

Perhaps because I found yesterday quite emotion-laden enough, I decided to leave it until today to comment on reading "Carmen." The story opens with a quote from Petronius: "Once again, having to be modest wearies me, as, all my life, has the need to speak slightingly of myself in order to fit in with those who speak slightingly of me, with those who haven't even an inkling of who or what I am."

The words don't sound like Petronius, but I checked yesterday and found nothing to indicate that they might not be his. Anyway, what Petronius—or whoever—says has little bearing on what happens in the story, which suggests that the quotation is there simply in order to mention Petronius and to point out, indirectly, that "Carmen" belongs to the category of *imaginary lives* created by Marcel Schwob.

For Petronius appears in one of the stories told by that French writer's 1896 book *Imaginary Lives*. I've loved Schwob's work for many years now. He was the pioneer of a genre that mingles invention and historical facts and which, in the last century, influenced such authors as Borges, Bolaño, and Pierre Michon.

In the case of "Carmen," there is a certain amount of invention, and, of course, a complete absence of historical facts. And yet the facts drawn from reality—selected solely from the life Carmen led just before I met her—are so skillfully intermingled with fiction that the entire thing could be historical. In other words, the story is well constructed, and even the inevitable "dizzy spell" works, because unlike the others I've so far encountered, this "dizzy spell" lasts only a few seconds and, while it isn't the least bit tedious, it is slightly dizzying. "Poor Carmen kept accumulating little pellets of Kleenex in her jeans pocket because she was always forgetting to remove the ones she'd left in there."

Entering that story was a very strange, not to say incredible, experience for me, but I had to accept it, because there could be no doubt that Sánchez had written about Carmen when she was very young: "So, here we have a young woman with a broad, anemic face, which perhaps highlights the harmonious nature of her features, but who is, nonetheless, very charming. She's tall, with delicate breasts, and always wears a dark sweater, and, around her pale neck, a scarf...."

At first, I felt like killing him. Because, hard though I found it to believe, this was definitely Carmen, my wife, and also because I didn't know what else to do when confronted by Sánchez serenely describing, for example, her "delicate breasts." And how come Sánchez had written about her thirty years ago, and yet I knew nothing about it?

Then, in order to not go entirely crazy and while I waited for Carmen to come home and perhaps explain everything, I amused myself by analyzing the story's place within *Walter and His Problem*. And I told myself that the most likely answer was that "Carmen" was a totally independent text that could function as a hint to attentive readers that the whole of Walter's memoir was one long imaginary life; but it also occurred to me that while the story might seem to bear no relation at all to the ventriloquist's autobiography, it might, in time, become integrated into the whole and could even be seen as a story, for example, about Walter's first girlfriend.

Of course, when I thought about it, I had to acknowledge that the life of the young Carmen could not be said to be exactly imaginary, at least not to me, since I was familiar with many of the things he described, and which were taken directly from her real life before she met me. Reading the story yesterday really shocked me, but now, in the cold light of day, and, I won't deny it, with some effort on my part, I can see that it was a good idea to include the story in the ventriloquist's autobiography, because at least that way there are two women in the book—Francesca and the first girlfriend, or whatever role Carmen appears to play—and it makes the whole thing more flexible somehow—a young woman with a broad, anemic face could well be relevant to Walter's life—and also because it paves the way for the great Petronius to make his entrance.

That was the best thing of all. I've been drawn to Petronius ever since I was a child. For a long time, I thought of this Roman writer merely as the genial character in *Quo Vadis*, the movie which, every year, over the Easter holidays, my school would show at one of their matinees of "religious cinema."

The apparent fixation on *Quo Vadis* on the part of those Jesuit priests must have arisen out of a misunderstanding, because it isn't exactly a serious movie or, indeed, religious: the Emperor Nero, for example, thanks to Peter Ustinov's performance, was a highly comic figure, a Nero who thought he was a poet and would torment poor Petronius with the ghastly poems he wrote. Petronius would sometimes have to express a view on them, until the day when, unable to cope with the stress of being Nero's sole critic, he committed suicide. Petronius also had his comic side in *Quo Vadis*, because, shortly before taking his own life, he wrote a wonderful farewell letter to Nero:

"I can forgive you for murdering your wife and your mother, for burning our beloved Rome, for befouling our fair country with the stench of your crimes. But one thing I cannot forgive is the boredom of having to listen to your verses, your second-rate songs, your mediocre performances. Adhere to your special gifts, Nero—murder and arson, betrayal and terror. Mutilate your subjects if you must; but with my last breath I beg you—do not mutilate the arts. Farewell, but compose no more music. Brutalize the people, but do not bore them, as you have bored to death your friend, the late Gaius Petronius, so much so that I've chosen to kill myself rather than have to continue listening to your ridiculous attempts at poetry."

These words are from the movie based on the Polish writer Henryk Sienkiewicz's novel, but, for many years, I thought they were the actual words Petronius had written to Nero before liberating himself from him in the most effective way possible, by taking his own life. I didn't discover the other Petronius until I came across Schwob's book, in which I encountered a very different character to the one created by Sienkiewicz. Schwob's Petronius had written sixteen adventure stories, all of which had been read by only one person, his servant Syrus, whose enthusiasm for them bordered on the hysterical. So enthusiastic was he, in fact, that his master decided that the two of them should go forth and live the adventures described in those sixteen stories. And thus, one night, knowing that Nero had sentenced him to death, Petronius, accompanied by his faithful slave Syrus, discreetly, silently, fled the Emperor's court. They took turns carrying the small leather satchel containing their clothes and their money. They slept out in the open, tramped country roads, and even, possibly, stole…. In short, they began to experience for real the sixteen adventures that Petronius had written. They went here, there, and everywhere, always with their leather satchel. They were traveling magicians, provincial charlatans, the companions of vagabond soldiers. And finally, in his memorable conclusion to this biography, Schwob says: "While living out the life he had imagined, Petronius completely forgot about the art of writing."

These were the thoughts with which I distracted myself yesterday, pondering the entirely unimaginary part Petronius had played in my life, until—since Carmen still hadn't come home—I again asked myself that unavoidable question: why had Sánchez written a story about her thirty years ago?

The anemic young woman in the story was different from the one I knew, but she was still perfectly recognizable, because what Sánchez described, in however distorted a form, was her life just before we had met—in a strange and genuinely amusing way, perhaps manipulated by invisible forces. She had happened to bump into me on a street corner in Coyote, we had gone for coffee together, and, four months later, crazy about each other in the best sense of the word, we got married.

Everything Sánchez describes in the story took place before that fateful encounter in Coyote, and sometimes it's pure invention, like the marriage of a very youthful Carmen to a gentleman from Olot, who, of course, never existed in real life. He's described in my neighbor's book as a complete and utter bore, and, luckily, he died very young. Carmen had already had enough of this husband—or, rather, character—even before they married, as can be seen from this fragment: "I never met Carmen's husband, an industrialist from Olot, who, according to what I've been told, was a real hick—which was bad enough—and not her type at all. They got married in Barcelona, in the church of Nuestra Señora de Pompeya, and all that remains of the big day are a few faded photos in which Carmen appears wearing the most brazen of smiles. Ah, dear God, how boring, she apparently said as the car set off for their honeymoon, all of which was to be spent in the endless tedium of the Plain of Vic, the long north-south depression constituting the nucleus of the administrative region of Osona, in the province of Barcelona...."

Having got sidetracked along unexpected paths to Osona, I now return to the mystery of how, thirty years ago, Sánchez came to write about the life of the young Carmen, a mystery that was easily re-solved when Carmen returned home thirty minutes after I'd seen her go into Carson's patisserie. In response to my almost tremulously urgent question, she told me, quite calmly, that Sánchez had indeed written that story thirty years ago, taking his inspiration from the life she'd led when she was very young, adding a little "imaginary life" to the mix in the form of the dead, boring industrialist, and other equally minor and doubtless cloyingly sentimental details.

My discovery of the story had, nevertheless, left me feeling lost and half-crazed. What was she doing there in the very book I was thinking of rewriting and improving?

I can see the scene as clearly as if it were happening now, when, as soon as Carmen arrived home, I asked if she'd just come from the patisserie.

"Of course, where do you think I got these cakes from?" she said.

"Did you meet anyone else?"

This question rather disconcerted her, and she paused briefly before answering.

"No. Why?"

That's when I told her that, incredible though it might seem, I had just read a story about her written by Ander Sánchez.

"Really?" she said.

At no point did she seem in the least troubled. She told me that she'd briefly gone out with Sánchez, about a million years ago, one summer lost in the depths of time, and before she met me. Young Sánchez wrote the story afterward, inventing a hideous husband from Olot for her and promptly killing him off, and it was then that she'd decided never to give the matter another thought, for, as I was doubtless aware, she didn't care a bit about "literature and or any other such literordure."

"Wasn't Sánchez in the patisserie today?" I asked.

"Have you installed a secret camera there or something?"

"No, I just happened to see the two of you going in there together, that's all."

She looked at me incredulously, as if she thought I must have lost my mind. And then she shrugged, unconcerned by what I was insinuating.

"You really should find something to fill your time," she said. "You must be very bored. Besides, Mac, all that happened years ago. Three decades ago, I think. And 'decades' really tells you how remote it feels. Decades, yes, decades!"

Her relationship with Sánchez, she explained, had been nothing but a brief youthful fling, one of many she'd had at the time and had never told me about, because it never crossed her mind that there was any need to reignite the dead flame of insignificant passions, to stir the ashes of so many banal affairs. She sometimes saw Sánchez around the neighborhood, and had done so for years. Yes, she saw him in the supermarket, outside the Baltimore and in Bar Tender, and at the patisserie—indeed, a moment ago, she'd watched as, with excruciating slowness, he bought some éclairs—and at Bar Treno and in the Korean restaurant and in Bar Congo and in the watchmaker's owned by the Ferré brothers and in the Caligari cinema and in the cramped changing room at the local tailor's, at the hairdresser's and at Restaurante Viena and at the cash machine in Calle Villarroel, at the florist's and so on. She left our apartment at least three times more than I did, so, obviously, she saw Sánchez more often. She didn't even say hello when she saw him because he was so full of himself and, besides, she was sure he wouldn't recognize her now, all these years after that lost summer.

I eyed her distrustfully, and Carmen held my gaze so fiercely that I froze. We remained silent for a few seconds, and I remember that the only sound was the agonizing tick-tock of a clock which I'd always thought of as fairly discreet. Then, suddenly, Carmen asked why I was reading that book by Sánchez when I'd been told it was dreadful, just like all the others he'd written, at least according to Ana Turner.

"Did Ana Turner tell you that?"

"Don't change the subject," she said.

She asked me how I'd recognized her in the story. Since the question was absurd and the answer glaringly obvious, it seemed to me that she was now the one trying to change the subject. She didn't succeed. You clearly don't remember that, among other details, he lists all your early suitors. That's true, she said. And then, I went on, there's the part where, in a letter, the narrator tries to describe to a girlfriend the color of the sea, when, in fact, he's talking about the color of your eyes.

All that remained was for me to read out the relevant passage: "How can I explain the intense blue of the sea? It was sapphire blue, but a very bright sapphire; the color of her eyes, her transparent but indecipherable eyes, which had a kind of purity, at once limpid and solid, cheerful and bright, and unique beneath this pale blue sky, white with mist."

It's odd, but a moment ago, when I was transcribing that part about the sapphire blue eyes, I experienced a sudden, irrational feeling and I fell hopelessly in love with Carmen all over again, just as I had when we first met.

Are we in control of our destiny or do invisible forces manipulate us? I ask myself this as I hear Carmen going into the kitchen, doubtless to prepare our lunch. I hear her footsteps moving away down the corridor and remember another fragment from the story:

"Rebellious daughter of the Egyptian goddess Isis, lovely and pale as the night, stormy as the Atlantic, Carmen became an expert in causing despair."

I clutch my head in despair, I don't know quite why, perhaps it's merely a sense of doomed love, or despair at feeling so much love and such a terrible fear of losing it.

20

I was aware that certain stories can have quite an overwhelming effect on readers, but I'd never experienced this myself. After the events of yesterday, I now know that they can, for example, make you fall back in love with your wife of many years. And the strangest part of all this is that I've just seen that the next story after "Carmen" in my neighbor's book is called "The Effect of a Story." And faced by this, I no longer know what to think, because this latest coincidence feels like one too many. I refuse to believe that I'll find the story of my renewed love for Carmen, but if that were the case I'd have no choice but to read it as a sign that the real world—and not me, of course—has gone mad.

In any case, the fact that the story after "Carmen" has this title has done me a favor, because it's helped me to imagine something I don't think I've ever thought about before, namely, books in which the reader reads about what's happening in his own real life as it happens.

All of which leads me to suspect that what's going on with me is this: before the time comes for me to set about rewriting my neighbor's novel, my reading of the book is obliging me to actually live out certain scenes first.

Could that be it? At this stage, I wouldn't rule out anything. And since my imagination is on overdrive and my levels of paranoia are running high, I now wonder whether agents from the Adjustment Bureau haven't been secretly plotting my ruin as a businessman in order to lure me more easily into starting a personal diary that would lead to me planning a remake of Sánchez's drunken novel, and, at the same time, that would offer me an irresistible opportunity to fall back in love with my wife, which is precisely what happened to me yesterday.... Although you could also see all of this another way, as one big practical joke played on me by those hypothetical adjustment agents: to leave me bust, with no more options left in the business world, and all so I might come to know the joys of some marginal activity (writing) and the happiness that comes from rediscovering the pleasures of a dull, stable, and decidedly uneventful marriage.

The Adjustment Bureau I'm referring to comes from the movie of the same name, which I saw only recently on TV. It's an adaptation of a very short story by Philip K. Dick involving Kafkaesque clerks or agents of Fate, men from the so-called Adjustment Bureau, functionaries who control and, when necessary, manipulate the fates of human beings.

"Do you think these agents are conspiring to turn your diary into a novel?" the voice asks.

That's precisely what I was thinking, which renders any response redundant.

&

At around midday, I read "The Effect of a Story" and, as was to be expected, the world hadn't gone completely mad, and my dilemma—as to whether we control our own Fate or if invisible forces are manipulating us—was more or less resolved, because the story didn't contain any tales of rekindled love, or anything of the sort; I could rest easy in the knowledge that it bore no relation to my private life.

If there was one obvious detail in that eighth story from *Walter and His Problem*, it was that Sánchez had drawn on "I Used to Live Here Once," a brief, heartrending ghost story written by Jean Rhys. In fact, the epigraph was a line by Rhys: "That was the first time she knew." And the story Walter told had clear echoes of "I Used to Live Here Once," in particular in terms of the plot, which was very similar.

At the beginning of "I Used to Live Here Once," we meet a woman crossing a stream, a precarious route—stepping-stone by stepping-stone—but which she clearly knows by heart. The woman makes her way, convinced that she's returning to her house. Only the sky above gives her a slight sense of unease. It seems to her somehow different, perhaps because of its gray, glassy appearance. Once on the other side of the stream, she stands in front of the worn stone steps up to a house, next to which a car is parked, a detail that surprises her greatly. What—had she never seen a car before? A boy and a little girl are playing under a big mango tree in the garden. "Hello," she says, as if to shore herself up. But the children don't notice her there and carry on playing as if nothing had happened. "I used to live here once," the woman says, and instinctively holds out her arms to them. The boy's gray eyes look directly at her, but he doesn't see her. "Hasn't it gone cold all of a sudden. D'you notice? Let's go in," the boy says to the girl, his playmate. The woman's arms fall to her sides and the reader then reads the line he was so dreading and with which the story ends: "That was the first time she knew."

In "The Effect of a Story," Sánchez/Walter uses Rhys's story as a starting point from which to go on to connect literature and life, describing the sense of alarm provoked in a young boy called Manolín on inadvertently overhearing his father reading the Jean Rhys story out loud to his mother. Young Manolín is deeply affected by what he hears, because the story has revealed to him the fact that all of us, sooner or later, must die, and that, after death, we will revisit our family home and nobody will recognize us. We will be ghosts. Manolín then goes on to ask himself why he had to be born if only to die, and whether his parents conceived him just so that he could experience death.

"It was evening in New Orleans when poor Manolín's hand began to tremble and his glass of milk fell to the floor, and he challenged me to repeat the story. He looked so affected by what he'd overheard that it didn't seem right to repeat a single word of the story which, just moments before, I'd been blithely reading out loud to his mother. And I remember being surprised at the powerful effect the story had on him, given that it was hardly an easy one for a child to understand. But Manolín, visibly upset, kept repeating, like a ghost: 'I used to live here once, I used to live here once ...,' after which he fell silent, thoughtful, uneasy, until he collapsed, exhausted, and finally fell asleep. He didn't leave his bed for three days, although the doctor repeatedly told us that there was nothing wrong with him."

The doctor in the story—and this is hardly an irrelevant detail—

is from Seville, and toward the end of the tale it becomes clear that the action—including the very lengthy "dizzy spell," during which it seems that a mystery narrator, our Jean Rhys impersonator, has the hangover from hell, perhaps from seven thousand shots of neat rum—the action takes place in a New Orleans that bears a remarkable resemblance to Seville. This resemblance is quite a feat, because the two cities have nothing in common, and yet the narrator manages to convince us that they do, and while never actually saying so, the narrator makes it clear that the child from the story is the future barber from Seville at the very moment when he realizes that, sooner or later, he is going to die. Perhaps the only thing young Manolín doesn't know is that he will be murdered by a ventriloquist in a dark alleyway in Portugal. The doctor takes up the story:

"Never in all my life have I seen a sadder face than that of poor Manolín during the three days he spent in bed. 'What time will I die?' he asked us on the afternoon of the third day. His mother didn't know what to say. And I, who am not a member of the family, was equally at a loss to know how to help in such a complex situation. 'I know I'm going to die,' the boy said. 'The story from the other day said so.' And we were so shocked by his remarks that we had to look away, before finally forcing a reassuring smile."

At one point, we're told that near New Orleans, on the seashore, all the young boys and girls wander around with long faces. By now, we're nearing the end of the story:

"That night, Manolín had recovered some of his usually inexhaustible vitality and, as if taking his cue from our earlier smiles, he began to laugh at absolutely everything. The slightest thing would set him off. He wasn't the same boy though. His childhood had come to an abrupt end. He had learned of the indestructible reality that we call death, and all because he happened to overhear that story. This knowledge had made him ill, but also free to respond as he wished. Free to laugh, for example. And God alone could tell how much that boy laughed, because he laughed so much it was impossible to know exactly how much, for he would burst into loud guffaws that left his face contorted into a terrible, anguished grimace."

And so ends "The Effect of a Story," and with it the adventures of a boy who, in time, in a Lisbon alleyway, learned just how much truth there was in the story he chanced to overhear in childhood.

And I'll leave it there for today. I'm sleepy now, and it's probably best just to think that tomorrow's another day, etc. etc. That's how diarists speak, isn't it? Carmen is watching TV in the living room. I double-lock the front door to the apartment, but not without first peering through the spyhole to check the lie of the landing, and I have fun observing the one triangular bit of bannister that's visible. Everything is silent. There appears to be not a single neighbor in the building. Most people, though, will be indoors, and many of them already sound asleep. I imagine Sánchez in the building next door, he, too, safe in his apartment, bedding down for a night of replenishing sleep, but then, quite suddenly, jumping to his feet, as if the slightest of noises, coming from underground, had alerted him to the as-yet-undefined danger that I, his neighbor, represent to him; I, who, unbeknown to him—or anybody—have spent weeks thinking constantly about all the modifications I'll make to Walter's memoirs. And I haven't even finished reading them yet.

[OSCOPE 20]

I've thought about it, and although I am a little the worse for wear and I know I really should take myself off to bed, I've thought about it and I'm keen not to forget it, which is why I think I'd better write it down here, even if I am dog-tired. I don't think it's such a bad thing, or even particularly baffling, that Sánchez should include a story from the barber's childhood in Walter's memoirs. In fact, I'm beginning to think that he's really hit on something by including stories that are only indirectly related to the main body of our ventriloquist's autobiography. After all, a man's life isn't shaped solely by events at which he himself is present. Things that might seem totally unconnected to his world can end up shedding more light on his life than those that involve him directly.

97

This reminds me of the first time I saw something like this going on in an artist's biography. Years ago, I read a book about Baudelaire in which the chronology of his life began with the birth of his grandfather and ended four years after the poet's death with a section in which the biographer examined Baudelaire's mistress Jeanne Duval's aimless wanderings along the boulevards, on crutches and talking to herself. Even then, I found it intriguing that the biographer considered those wanderings to form part of Baudelaire's life.

Sometimes, a few sidelights shining in from the wings can make all the difference center stage.

&

I wake up and waste no time in jotting down the only thing I remember from my nightmare. Someone, with extraordinary persistence, was saying to me:

"The thing is, it's just really weird to be reading a story written by your neighbor donkey's years ago."

21

If you ask me, reality doesn't need anyone to organize it into a plot; it is itself a fascinating, ceaseless creative center. But there are days when reality turns its back on the aimless drifting center that is life and tries to give events a novelish turn. I resist then, because I don't want anything to interrupt my work as a diarist. I resist with the same sense of horror that Jekyll does in the presence of Hyde, when he realizes that he, the good, just man, is totally at odds with the "extraneous evil" he carries within him. This is what happened today when reality insisted on revealing to me, with the best and brightest light at its disposal, its own ruthless novel-writing machine, which, for a long while, made me feel most uncomfortable, until I succumbed and let myself be drawn toward a faltering neon sign at the end of the street where the ancient Bar Treno is located, with its own peculiarly horrible light.

How many years had it been since I last walked down that murky street? Could it be the street I've least frequented of the entire Coyote district? I'd spent years avoiding it and probably for good reasons, and yet, the sight of that neon sign in broad daylight was calling to me, and shortly afterward, I found myself sitting in an inhospitable corner of Bar Treno, the most spacious, but also the most outdated bar in Coyote. I went in for a much-needed double espresso, which is why I didn't bother to look for a more salubrious bar, which, besides, didn't exist, at least not on that street.

I sat down at one of the tables in the least appealing area immediately beyond the old-fashioned bar, that impossibly long ancient bar with shelves above it, resembling an old-style McDonald's. My table was the last one this side of the large smoked-glass screen separating one part of the bar from the next, and which prevents you from seeing the customers on the other side, although you can hear them perfectly well. And there, before I even had time to suspect that I might not emerge unscathed from my choice of table, I was astonished to hear, coming from the other side of the glass screen, the odious, carping, brassy voice of Sanchez's nephew.

Good grief, I thought, it can't be him, but it was. He was ranting on at two young women about the appalling state of the literary world, a world where men in suits were discarding anything they judged to be too weighty, too meaningful.... "We're in the hands of monsters," he suddenly declared. And he began to explain the gulf that existed, according to him, between a novelist who writes bestsellers with all the superficiality of a hack journalist, and a writer of great depth such as ... Mundigiochi.

He said Mundigiochi, that's the name I heard. Perhaps the difference between the *Mundigiochis* and the bestsellers, he said, is the same as that which exists between a writer who knows that any well-crafted description contains both a moral gesture and a desire to say what hasn't yet been expressed, and the writer of bestsellers who uses language simply to achieve an effect and always puts on the same immoral camouflage to deceive the reader. Fortunately, he concluded, there are still a few authors who, in their struggle to create new forms, continue to fight the good fight.

It was like the Sermon on the Mount.

I couldn't believe it: there he was spouting some of the oldest clichés in the book about the publishing industry, and, to judge by the responses of the two young women, they appeared positively dazzled by what the antagonistic nephew was saying. It would seem, I thought, that the people working for the Adjustment Bureau really are doing their best to make things happen to me. However, if that were true and the Bureau really did exist, I have to say they aren't doing a very good job, because the wretched antagonistic nephew's spiel was, to put it mildly, utter drivel. And as if that weren't enough, after a brief pause, I heard him say that the most interesting people were those who have never written anything. What then, I wondered, are we to do with the *Mundigiochis*?

I very nearly asked the question out loud from my side of the glass screen.

Then something curious happened. Seamlessly following on from his declaration in favor of those who write nothing, an ambulance came hurtling down the street with its siren blaring. By the time I could hear the nephew's voice again, it seemed to me that everything had changed.

"People do ask me that," he was saying in a soft, sad voice, "but I'm not afraid of showing my true colors. I really can't stand people who pretend to be reasonable, polite, and all that. When I say something, I'm not worried about the consequences. I don't give a damn how I come across. Although, having said that, I did make the effort to shave today. I'd like that put down on the record, I did shave," and he laughed, or so I thought, a singsong, rather inane titter. "I'm happy as I am and wouldn't want to be any different. Nothing fazes me, you know what I'm saying?"

No one answered, and their silence helped move the conversation on. The nephew finally revealed his real reason for being there and began talking at length about the party he intended to throw in the little hovel where he lived. Then it all became excruciating, because I found myself inadvertently eavesdropping on his cringe-inducing attempts to get those two girls in the sack. At a certain point, I stopped listening, and then, when I reconnected, I heard one of them say:

"Yes, but we'd still like to interview your uncle. You will help us, won't you?"

I preferred not to hear any more. It was clear what was going on: he wanted to get laid, and they wanted something he couldn't provide. And I needed to go home, because there was nothing to keep me there. I headed for the door, paying on my way, and left. Then, as I began walking slowly back up the street, I decided that I'd heard enough from the antagonistic nephew, on two separate occasions, to know that the odious, stupid side of his personality was compensated for by the other side, still unknown to me but occasionally glimpsed in the odd flash of talent. In other words: given that I didn't know what to make of him, the best thing, I told myself, would be to opt for the more favorable impression, because if he had, at some point, displayed signs of genius, it was probably fair to assume that he *was* a genius, or a potential genius. Nevertheless, I had to acknowledge that he had an extremely pathetic, not to say base, side to him, because using his obsessive tirades against his uncle, even as a means of getting laid, really wasn't nice, and that's putting it kindly. But it seemed to me that, despite this, when compared with his uncle, he came out on top, because his uncle was a puffed-up peacock, on top of being a fickle, insufferable urbanite, *and* he had a past life as a former boyfriend of Carmen's, a fact I still hadn't fully digested.

I liked the nephew, mainly because he was perfectly happy to exhibit a kind of genuineness that was, in many respects, prejudicial to him, but which allowed him *to be himself*. Basically, this uninhibited, extremely foulmouthed individual was saying that not writing and refusing to kowtow to the system had at least as much value as scribbling a few pages to produce a cruddy, sellable novel. The nephew didn't know it, but he was simply showing me that I had done well in choosing the writing path furthest from the madding crowd; the path of never publishing; the path of writing for the pleasure of learning to write, of trying to find out what I would write if I wrote.

The nephew aroused conflicting feelings in me, but we had something in common: he seemed to enjoy being a bit of a vagabond, whereas, although I did not, I couldn't deny that a part of me was also attracted to that life, proof of which was my sympathy for Walter's idea of traveling to Arab countries in search of the original story, that is, the very first story. Also the idea of escaping, born of necessity in Walter, was, in me, merely the *idea* of a vagabond life, which I felt I could fulfill in the pages of this diary.

&

"It's completely unimportant. That's why it's so interesting," said Agatha Christie's detective, Poirot. And as I recalled those words—I was by then about five minutes away from Bar Treno—I thought of that poor antagonistic nephew. And suddenly I decided to turn round and go back to the bar. I walked for one long minute alongside some Chinese people who were going at exactly the same speed as I was, which meant that I couldn't overtake or saunter comfortably along behind them. They seemed to be a replica of myself, a sophisticated parody of my way of walking, and that made me remember that yesterday, Carmen, perhaps prompted by her joy at seeing our love renewed, invited me to go on a long trip with her. To China, she said, but then said nothing more about China or about anything else, and nor did I. The word "China" hung there, floating in the air, alone and strange. When I asked her about China a few minutes later, she denied ever mentioning it. It was as if she had suddenly remembered something that would prevent her from going. Anyway, she flatly denied that we'd ever spoken about China.

Before reaching that street, I stopped off at another bar, the Amorós, where I downed a G&T, not, mind you, with any intention of getting all ponderous and heavy, but of arming myself with a drop more Dutch courage than usual. When I reentered grubby Bar Treno, I raced past the long, old-fashioned bar, past the smoked glass screen, and planted myself in front of the nephew at the very moment when he—more repetitively repetitious than ever—was repeating that his uncle had nothing more to say. Earlier on, I hadn't been able to see him, but only hear him from behind the screen. Now, before me, he seemed rather better groomed than the last time I'd seen him, his shoulders even broader, probably the effect of the particularly large shoulder pads in the red jacket he was wearing, which gave him a more boyish, almost healthy look.

"Even assuming that's true and he does have nothing more to say," I broke in, "I would like to have a conversation with your uncle, your illustrious uncle. I need to interview him right away."

He looked at me, terrified. And his two female companions— who were, as I'd imagined, extremely young, and looking quite the intellectuals in their tortoiseshell-framed spectacles—appeared to be equally alarmed, although they both ended up laughing, indeed, they laughed so much that one of them even dropped her glasses, then herself collapsed onto the floor.

Having first been given a fright from my outburst, they'd then got the giggles. I must keep my cool, I told myself. But then I realized what an unnecessary mess I'd gotten myself into. The antagonistic nephew was drunker than I'd thought and seemed about to get to his feet and rip into me, or perhaps even punch me. Then, rather timidly, but lying through my teeth, I told him I was a reporter from *La Vanguardia*. And I pointed vaguely in an easterly direction, where that newspaper had its headquarters, having moved out of the center of Barcelona a few years ago into the Coyote district.

I immediately realized how crazy it was to have suggested wanting to meet Sánchez. What would he think if he found out? I beat a hasty retreat on all fronts and apologized, trying to give the nephew the impression that I was just another passing nutcase. I even quite enjoyed pretending to be crazy. I quoted Horace, as if I were talking to myself: "You have amused yourself, you have eaten and drunk enough; it is time for you to depart. *Tempus abire tibi est.*"

"You're not trying to muscle in on our interview, are you?" asked one of the girls rather cheekily.

In fact, I'd only wanted to take the chip off of that muscleman's shoulder, the chippiness that he uses to his advantage in all situations; I was aware that the less time I stuck around, the less likely he was to remember my face.

"No, I don't want to muscle in on anything, but you watch out for Mundigiochi, he's a real leech," I said.

I didn't hang around to be laughed at, or for the nephew to punch me in the face, and I skedaddled at top speed—like Petronius fleeing at night from Nero's palace, with my little leather satchel—almost flying past the long, old-fashioned bar, where a baldheaded waiter, who hadn't been there earlier, was idly washing dishes. He reminded me of someone. I thought I heard him call out my name, but I didn't stop. No, no, I wasn't going to stay a second longer in that bar. As I went out onto the street, though, I looked back, and saw that he really should have been called Mac, too, because he was the spitting image of the bartender in the John Ford movie, the man who had always been a bartender and never been in love. These things happen, I said to myself, somewhat bemused. These things happen, I said again. But repeating the line did little to help me understand what that other Mac was doing there.

22

Since Carmen insisted that, ultimately, I was really just vegetating—she refused to accept that writing this personal diary, with all the work that entails, amounted to *doing* something—and since she also insisted on telling me that spending all day twiddling my thumbs was so dangerously dull it could even lead to suicide—"We didn't fall back in love only for you to go and die on me," she said, with enough sarcasm to knock me off my perch, and why the snide tone if she really was back in love with me, too?—I decided that the time had come today, over lunch, to explain to her that although I write my diary by hand and always somewhat impulsively, afterward I painstakingly edit what I've written—hence all the hours spent in the study—as if viewing it through a magnifying glass, before transcribing the copy onto the computer, printing it out, reading it through again on paper, making more changes, and so on, until, finally, I copy and paste it into another Word document, which only yesterday I entitled "Diary of a Washed-Up Contractor."

"Why a contractor?" she asked.

"I see, so the word 'contractor' alarms you, but never mind that I consider myself washed up."

"All of it alarms me. To start with, your insistence that writing a diary constitutes actually doing something. Am I in it, by the way?"

"Of course, and I write the most wonderful things about you, but you won't ever get the chance to read them."

I might have worded that better, but her extreme indifference regarding my work as a beginner—notwithstanding her avowed contempt for all literary endeavors—was starting to get on my nerves. Such is her disdain for my diary that she didn't even ask why she wouldn't get to read it, not that this stopped me from explaining it to her anyway.

"It isn't that I've anything to hide," I told her, "I merely want to write in total freedom. And even so, I do occasionally speak to a hypothetical reader. I don't search him out, but I find myself speaking to him anyway."

As I might have expected, she still had a "this isn't squaring with me" look etched on her face. Her aversion to books stems from a childhood trauma, which she's never wanted to discuss with me, but which I know is related in some way to her dyslexia. This trauma is doubtless related to the fact that her parents were also dyslexic, and, as time went by, it even developed into a phobia of the printed page—mild at first, but ultimately uncontrollable.

"Yes, I write wonderful things about you," I told her, "wouldn't you like to hear some of them? You don't have to read them yourself, I know you won't want to do that, but I can read you some right now."

Not even this made her take an interest in my diary.

In the ensuing silence, I thought about how, if, under mysterious circumstances—circumstances related to some heinous crime, for example—I were forced to flee with only the clothes on my back—let's say with a white shirt, a pair of dark pants, and a small leather satchel containing a few bare essentials—and wander God's earth, the big wide world, and if, in my haste, I left my diary at home, perhaps Carmen would have no option but to take charge of those secret pages—at the request of the police, say—in which someone—perhaps even she herself—would discover just how much I loved her, and how infuriating I found her indifference toward my writing exercises, not to mention her strangely sarcastic attitude, which, for the life of me, I can't understand.

What sweet revenge it would be to escape to the Orient and leave her with that diary, forcing her to acknowledge it, even if all that involved was handing it over to the police.

But this is all just hot air, because I do love her. And yet the urge to disappear, to follow in Walter's footsteps and run away never to be seen again—in my case without having to murder anyone—really is quite strong.

What would Carmen do with the pages of my diary in that case? She might just leave them to gather dust for all eternity, or perhaps she'd follow Max Brod's example and give them to someone from a publishing company to read. "After all, even if he did write only for himself, deep down he was looking for a reader," Carmen would say piously, but without dropping her apathetic attitude toward all things literary, or, as she would call it, "all that bookish drivel."

So she might quickly forget all about the diary, but, equally, you never know, she might turn out to be my very own Brod. And wherever I might be—an errant, roaming vagabond—I would silently applaud its publication and approve of my readers doing with me exactly as I intend to do with Sánchez, that is, reading me and, as they read, modifying whatever I'd written.

And where would I be in the meantime? Perpetually on the move? This is all just speculation of course, but I think I'd be hiding out in some spot resembling, as far as possible, what the Romans called Arabia Felix—fortunate or fertile Arabia—doubtless because of all the coffee and incense exported out of Mocha; I'd be holed up somewhere resembling that African territory, where happiness reigned for years and which, today, is a place of pure panic, a land plagued by misfortune.

I'd stay so hidden from view that people would think I was dead. I'd be perfectly untraceable, à la Wakefield, that character from one of Hawthorne's stories, the husband who walks out of the front door one day telling his wife he'll be back on Friday at the latest, but then continually postpones his return home and spends the next twenty years living in a mansion down the road, until one stormy winter's day, he spots a log fire burning in what was once his house, and he decides to go back, and, just like that, raps on his wife's front door, and is home.

What anyone reading my diary would find strange is that, despite having been interrupted by some serious problem—the author's disappearance or death—the diary would have been found to be ready for immediate publication, with no need to touch a single comma.

The manuscript would be divided clearly into two parts: the second of these would modify the diaristic pages of the first part, which would include the story of the crime.

It would turn out that, despite appearances, the manuscript hadn't been interrupted by its author's sudden departure; nor, therefore, would it be unfinished. Quite the contrary: the whole thing would have been planned so that the all-important disappearance of the author—who either went traveling the world, or actually died, whichever suited him best, because the only requisite would be for him to vanish into thin air—brought to a close the game which the text itself had been engineering in such a way that the death or departure of its author was absolutely essential in order for the diaristic artifact to reach its ideal conclusion, and thus end up perfectly complete, while appearing to be incomplete. This, then, would make it a diary that had been carefully planned to appear to be "unfinished," and even conceived in such a way that some would find camouflaged among its pages an "unresolved posthumous novel," always provided, of course, that the author, the Wakefield of our times, removed himself from the picture when the moment came.

Would Carmen become my Brod? Stranger things have happened. Perhaps she herself would end up publishing my deceptively "incomplete" diary.

But all of this, I told myself today, is mere speculation on my part, an attempt to satisfy my thirst for revenge for Carmen's indifference toward my "modest knowledge." Speculation which, ultimately, sprang from the initial confession made in this diary: my weakness for posthumous, unfinished books and my desire to make my own forgery; one that would only appear to have been interrupted.... If one day I managed to pull off that fake book trick, I would really be doing little more than enlisting it in an increasingly popular contemporary literary trend, that of the so-called "posthumous forgery," a fairly overlooked genre in the history of literature.

&

This afternoon, once I'd heard Carmen put down the telephone after a lengthy conversation, I entrusted myself to the protection of the Kafkaesque clerks from the Adjustment Bureau, begging them, above all, not to accidently hook me up with the Department of Maladjustment (a dark subdivision within the main Bureau); I asked them if—provided that they really do exist—they could give me a hand in achieving the impossible and make Carmen pay the slightest attention to what I intended to tell her about my work as a beginner.

Believing myself to be protected, or, rather, preferring to believe that I was now protected by the employees of the Bureau's Kafkaesque Soul (one of the many subdivisions in that place), I marched over to Carmen and, without further ado, told her that nothing I wrote in the diary was made up, apart from my identity as a washed-up building contractor. I waited for a reaction, but it seemed not even this approach was working, and so I then delved back into our recent private abyss and told her that I'd invented that past life as a contractor so that I wouldn't have to give any more thought to "the drama."

At this point, she did react. With a look of panic. The second I mentioned "the drama," her entire expression changed. She even began to pay attention to what I was saying, because, for weeks now, there was nothing that struck more fear into her heart than the appearance of that word "drama" in our conversations. And this is because that word, spoken straight out like that, immediately took her back to my obsessive state during the seemingly endless days following my dismissal from the lawyer's firm where I'd worked my entire life.

In an attempt to hold her attention, to tie it to an imaginary post so that I could say everything I needed her to hear, I told her, as if in passing, that I didn't want this diary to "open the door to the black dog"—a horrible, hackneyed expression, this metaphor for melancholy—at which point she stared at me in sheer terror. The mere mention of that dog still terrifies her, even more so than the word "drama," because it reminds her of the days when I lost my job, went completely to pieces, and moped around referring to my despair as the black dog.

I took advantage of her moment of panic—panic at the possible return of the emotional problems which she believed I'd more or less overcome—to tell her that I began writing the diary in part because I thought it might help haul me out of the deep depression I had sunk into when the firm fired me a couple of months ago. And if I wanted the diary to have a therapeutic effect, I had to think up a profession that was a world away from the Law—building contractor was the ideal solution—one that stopped me constantly going over and over my past as a lawyer, at least until—and that day has now come—I noticed that the wounds inflicted by my ruthless, humiliating removal had begun to heal. Despite not being completely sold on the therapeutic value of writing, I had the vague hope that it might help put at least a modicum of that great humiliation behind me. And I was fairly confident that the journal would help me to do just that. It was a matter of untangling, as far as possible, and by means of this discreet apprenticeship in writing, the knotty core of my shame and mortification, my rage at the disgraceful manner in which they threw me out on the street, the scandal of my paltry severance payment, and the shock of finding myself, quite suddenly, with nothing, not even a stern, phlegmatic goodbye from one of my colleagues.

It was a matter of blocking out everything that had the power to upset me and that might seriously hinder the diary's legitimate function: to make me happy. I was loving these carefree days, where even my strongest-held beliefs were dissolving into easy indifference. And yet, before I could slip into those tantalizing leisurely moments, two things had to happen: I had to spend some of the day working on the diary, and this activity had to bear as little relation as possible to my past as a lawyer, the very thought of which sent me straight back to the drama, the trauma, the black dog, despair, and suicide.

I said all this to Carmen, at which point the strangest thing happened: despite teetering on the edge of that abyss, she allowed herself to make a joke, trying to downplay the whole thing, and declaring in a dulcet, singsong, but nevertheless flippant tone of voice:

"Better an honest but humiliated lawyer than a failed property developer."

I couldn't believe my ears. A failed property developer!

Love is blind. I repeated this to myself two or three times. I had to if I didn't want to slide back into the dark days of my breakdown and go completely to pieces again.

[OSCOPE 22]

It appears we're only just discovering that the gentle, compassionate approach to leadership makes better business sense than that of "command and control." Studies in brain function (carried out by such methods as functional MRI) have detected that being treated disrespectfully raises one's blood pressure and generates stress. "It's the sure path to depression, the second-fastest-growing condition in developed countries, according to the World Health Organization. *Bosses* are by definition disrespectful, even if their lack of respect doesn't always manifest itself in barked-out orders. *Leaders*, on the other hand, do their best to draw out people's talent, and for that there needs to be respect, trust, and motivation," explained the Co-Director of the Executive Education program at Deusto Business School. But I find this hard to believe. The means and methods may have changed, but actually things are even more terrifying than before, perhaps precisely because you trust those around you more and believe that things really are better, and you don't expect to discover, all of a sudden, out of nowhere, just when you least expect it, the real truth: they don't love you because they've never loved you and they're firing you because you're past it and because you're always causing scenes and because you drink too much and because one day you quoted a few lines from Wallace Stevens when tension was at its highest in that emergency meeting.

23

The ninth story, "The Visit to the Master," opens with an epigraph from Edgar Allan Poe's "The Raven":

> *"'Tis some visitor," I muttered, "tapping at my chamber door—*
> *Only this and nothing more."*

Yes, only this and nothing more; the Raven is always there in the background, about to rap on the door, or indeed already rapping, or already inside the house, flapping along the corridors. The Raven is Death for someone like me, who, despite my clear vocation as a modifier, is incapable of reading that fragment from Poe in any other way. It's odd that when confronted by the Raven, I lose all ability to modify. I become a quivering wreck. The Raven always wins. It's like the zero in roulette. The House always wins. And yet, there are ways to manipulate and cheat that zero. A fake *posthumous, unfinished book* is one that can laugh at Death, which is otherwise so brazenly, stubbornly accustomed to getting its own way.

Today, for some reason—if I knew why I would feel much better—I woke thinking about the crocodile-skin purse my mother used to carry, and shortly afterward, I recalled the clear plastic purses that reminded Joe Brainard of lunch boxes with a scarf hanging out of them. I remember, as I have said, the ties that came already knotted with a rubber band to hang them round your neck. And then I remembered a time when I found the Raven in everything I read, sometimes as frighteningly clear as one of those plastic purses, like when Bardamu, in Céline's *Journey to the End of the Night*, said: "You have to listen for the melody without notes that underlies all music, a melody composed just for us, the melody of death."

I seemed to find an echo of Bardamu's words in that ninth story, in the sudden pronouncement of a man who is Walter's master: a man who, when he speaks, seems to be that melody without notes that underlies all music.

I was going to read the story this morning, but, in the end, I left it until tonight, and spent all day waiting for darkness to fall so as to increase the likelihood of the Raven making an appearance; this gave rise to several rather comical situations, with that bird appearing on several occasions ahead of time, in the morning and afternoon, in various places in the house, like in a comedy horror movie…. How many times a day does it brush past? If we could count them, I think we would go mad.

Jünger describes Céline telling him: "I always have death by my side," and pointing to a spot next to his armchair, as if a small dog were sitting there.

Ah, if only I'd been able to domesticate Death today as it seems Céline did, demonstrating his remarkable talent as a tamer of beasts.

Anyway, I spent the day waiting for the midnight hour before reading the story, a day interspersed with brief, but repeated surprise appearances by the Raven, who seemed to possess the gift of ubiquity. Who was this master that Walter was going to visit? Another ventriloquist would be the most logical answer. To find out, I had to start reading the story which, since it was the penultimate in the book, would bring me almost to the end of my (re)reading of my neighbor's novel. As the first shadows began to fall, as dusk came on, I could wait no longer and launched into the story that tells of Walter's visit to Claramunt, who was, he says, "his great master," although, at first, there's no way of knowing just what that mastery consists of, not that there's anything strange about that, because Walter himself doesn't seem to know as he travels toward the remote, out-of-the-way village of Dorm, with no clear idea as to why he has placed Claramunt on a pedestal.

Claramunt had been a ventriloquist for years, but it was not because he was a ventriloquist that he was Walter's master. As Walter himself writes: "I admired him, but not necessarily for his legendary ability to provide different voices for his multiple dummies, but because of something I couldn't quite put my finger on. I adored him, but, strange though it may seem, I had no way of knowing how to pinpoint the root cause of that admiration, although I was quite sure I did admire him greatly, enormously...."

Walter travels to Dorm for precisely that reason, to find out why, for years, he's been having a recurrent dream telling him that he should travel to the Catalan Pyrenees, to the village of Dorm, and there try to ascertain why the once famous Claramunt is his master. Perhaps that insistent, extremely stubborn dream is a mere delusion. But what if it isn't? Walter can't simply do nothing and close the door on a revelation that might perhaps prove vital to him. Intrigued, he travels to Dorm accompanied by María, an old lady brimming with vitality, who, having been both a close friend of his mother and a close friend of Claramunt's sister, has offered to intercede with the reclusive ventriloquist and persuade the monster to receive them. For it seems that Claramunt is a very bad-tempered fellow, who lives as far as possible from the madding crowd, and who, according to all indications, has become a toothless old grouch, a terrible man, who spits on the floor, lives surrounded by dogs, and who makes a habit of being as unpleasant as possible to anyone who dares come anywhere near his farm.

Claramunt is in a particularly foul mood when, after their long journey, Walter and María knock at the door of his rambling house. At first, because we, as readers, need to speculate about something, we suspect that perhaps what Walter admires about the man is the great panache he showed when he bade farewell to the artistic life, because, as Walter describes the long journey with María to Dorm, he frequently comments on the nobility of Claramunt's final gesture, on the majesty of that abrupt, unceremonious farewell. More than that, when he evokes the master's final performance at the Teatro Veranda in Valencia, he recalls Claramunt's parting words on stage, words that have become the stuff of legend among the older inhabitants of Malvarrosa.

"I am someone whom you have come to know very gradually, step by uncertain step. I am someone who has no name and who never will have a name, someone who is many people and, at the same time, only one person. And I am someone who has demanded your patience, too, because, without ever putting this thought into words, I have asked you to bear tranquil witness, over years and years of performances, to the slow, tentative construction of a human figure...."

While I was reading this farewell speech, I couldn't help relating that "slow, tentative construction of a human figure" to another almost identical process, the one Walter is following in his partial memoir, where he is slowly constructing (with diversions along the way, for he does allow various other voices to speak) a tentative human figure with a complex personality; his memoir gradually traces the silhouette of a murderer, even though, for perfectly sensible reasons relating to his own safety, he never says as much.

I was impressed by Walter's faith in going to visit the master, because he remains convinced that he'll find what he's gone looking for at the house of the old grouch. And the reason he seems so confident is because he trusts in his own instinctive ability to decipher riddles.

María suggests that Claramunt's mastery may have its roots in something very simple, possibly in something so obvious that, like the purloined letter in the Edgar Allan Poe story of the same name, it's hard to see at first because it's all too visible.

"You'll have to hone that instinct of yours," says María.

In the midst of a great cacophony of relentless barking, Walter and María knock at the door of the house. And something unexpected happens, because it turns out that the monster has a heart:

"When he recognized María, Claramunt was deeply moved and embraced her warmly and shed a few tears. Shortly afterward, the supposed grouch made a very theatrical gesture indicating that we should enter his tumbledown house. We sat at a small table next to the fire, and the monster brought us tea and cakes and wine from the vineyards of Dorm. He wasn't as fierce as we had been told. But he looked much as we had expected: he wore a dark corduroy suit and was wrapped in various scarves and shawls; he hadn't shaved for several days, and his one good eye was terrifying. Outside, enclosed in a fenced-off area, the dogs kept up their barking. The pack would stop for a few minutes, then immediately recommence their horrendous howling. It was as if a stranger were constantly trying to break into the house only to be repeatedly driven back by the dogs. I asked Claramunt if he kept them there as protection. No, he said roundly, I keep them *for the noise*. He pronounced "noise" as if the very word gave him great pleasure. For a moment, I said nothing, glancing surreptitiously around the room, playing to perfection my role as María's nephew, for that is how she had introduced me, so as to make matters easier."

María tells Claramunt endless stories about mutual friends, all of whom are now dead, and he listens to her, sometimes even with a glimmer of interest. Every now and then, he spits on the floor. At one point—in a voice that, from the narrator's description, I imagined to be like the voice of the dead man lodged in my head—he speaks of the lunar eclipse forecast for that night and begins listing the names of cemeteries in Rome, one after another, like a strange funereal litany, his words punctuated by the barking of the dogs.

Night falls, and María and Walter stay for supper, dining on a cheese omelet freshly cooked by the grouch himself, and the talk turns to Portugal, "where I was due to travel some days later for a long tour of the theaters there, but which, in Claramunt's presence and in keeping with my role as María's irrelevant nephew, I disguised as a holiday."

"I understand that the cafés of Lisbon are abuzz with the random ideas of a great many nobodies," says Claramunt.

And his words sound strange in the night. They seem to have come from some lost piece of prose by Pessoa. What Walter doesn't yet know is that he will soon be going to Lisbon, where he will kill a barber from Seville with his Javan sunshade.

"The random ideas of a great many nobodies," María repeated, as if wanting to underline Claramunt's words.

Shortly afterward, apparently infected by Claramunt's turn of phrase, she tells a rather weird story about a young man and a parrot traveling on an old French train in a carriage packed with murderers. When she finishes the story, she is absolutely exhausted and so sleepy that her head droops and ends up resting gently on a cooking pot on the table where they have dined.

"Let's go for a walk," Claramunt says to Walter.

It's a very starry night, and the lunar eclipse is due to take place in exactly an hour. They head for a small hill from where, according to Claramunt, they will get a clear view of the phenomenon. At first, they walk along gravel paths and then along dirt tracks, until they reach the top of the hill from which they will have a view of the whole of Dorm.

As they walk, Walter casually asks Claramunt if he can think of any reason why he—as the recurrent dream he's been having for years seems to suggest—should be his master. "I don't understand," says Claramunt. "I've admired you for years," Walter says, "but I still don't know why." Claramunt becomes angry and asks if Walter really expects him to explain. With a heavy heart, Walter carries on walking, aware that he has made a blunder asking Claramunt that question, because he alone can find the answer to the puzzle he has come there to solve.

In the distance, they hear music coming from a radio, doubtless from some nearby house. "The neighbors are ghastly," says Claramunt, breaking the silence. "If you say so," responds Walter. When they reach the top of the hill, they sit down on the hard ground to await the spectacle of the moon's disappearance. And there Walter has the impression that, although the opposite may have been true initially, Claramunt is, in fact, prepared to help him find out why he admires him. And so it proves. His master has a sudden flash of inspiration, and, allowing himself to be swept along by it, he begins a litany—almost like a prayer—of his daily activities:

"I wake at eight, and take a ritual dip in a cold bath, where I linger for just a few minutes in winter, but longer in spring. This clears away the cobwebs. I sing while I shave, not very tunefully, because I don't really have a musical ear, but all the same, I sing along happily enough. I go for a walk around the outskirts of the village, in the opposite direction to where we are now. Then I come home, and breakfast on milk and honey and toast. At midday, I look to see if there's any mail, but I never get any letters, not a single wretched sign from the outside world. (At first, I thought it was Durán, the postman, withholding my letters because he hated me, but I soon had to accept that all of humanity hated me, not just Durán.) Then it's lunch, served by Señora Carlina, and a nap. In the afternoon, I imagine there's an ancient lime tree opposite my house and I sometimes listen to the Beatles on vinyl. From time to time, at night, even though I know all the people of Dorm are afraid of me, I go down to the village and tell them anecdotes from my life as a ventriloquist."

A light goes on in Walter's mind, because he suddenly understands where Claramunt's mastery lies. María was quite right when she said that Claramunt's mastery might lie in something very simple and straightforward, something hiding in plain sight.

"I understood then why he had abandoned his art. His finest work was now his daily routine," Walter writes.

Claramunt was a master of the intelligent use of his time. Proof that there was life beyond ventriloquism.

"I remember the moment of illumination that preceded the eclipse. A crow flew past, and it was as if a wall had crumbled, and I had the sense that Claramunt and I could understand each other in a zone that went far beyond our meeting there and beyond this life. He could read my thoughts, and had realized that what had happened to him was happening to me. And even if this wasn't true, everything led me to believe that we were both in agreement that not only were we meeting somewhere outside of Dorm, we were also somewhere far beyond that starry night encompassing the world."

&

In a wing of the mezzanine, in the middle of the night, a woman with long black hair sat bent over some papers. I admired her profile, her dark, dark hair, her air of being a workaholic. Excuse me, I said, does anyone here know Mr. Poe's daily routine?

24

Thankfully, I wasn't so paranoid as to imagine that the neighbor in "The Neighbor," the tenth and final story in the book, would turn out to be Sánchez, or even myself. All the same, I began reading it with some trepidation. Ever since Carmen had appeared in "Carmen," it made sense to be ready for anything, even for the totally unexpected, which I suppose might, for example, be the sudden reappearance of death, even though I have a relatively good handle on that eventuality, because I'm keeping the Raven well under control: he's a poor black dog. He's also the dog of my depression, of my crisis following my dismissal; I keep him down there on a leash.

I won't say any more about that, because I want to lighten the tone a little and explain that "The Neighbor" begins with an epigraph from G. K. Chesterton: "We make our friends; we make our enemies; but God makes our next-door neighbor."

This quote had some influence over my reading of the story's opening lines, where I had a very curious sensation, as if I were reading a fine English short story that had been translated into Spanish with exquisite care. Walter, who shows a real talent for parodying Chesterton, recommends that we dive into his story as if we were "at home, with chestnuts roasting on an open fire." And how could you resist such an invitation, even if you didn't happen to have any chestnuts handy or a fireplace, and even if, outside, the temperature had reached sweltering, record-breaking highs?

The story begins auspiciously, but soon forgets all about this wintry setting, and so we, the readers, can only assume that, due to sheer laziness on the author's part, the narrative thread involving chestnuts has fallen by the wayside. Whatever the truth of the matter, the story's astonishing opening, with its meticulous description—amounting almost to personification—of each and every spark flying up from that blazing fire, finally loses momentum, and we find ourselves trapped inside a strangely soporific, smoldering atmosphere, in a bland, confusing passage—almost like an homage to the book's own "dizzy spells"—which made me stop reading and look up from the page.

An extraordinary beginning can sometimes be prejudicial to the rest of a story, because the rest of the text cannot possibly maintain the same high standard. I looked from the page up at the ceiling—as if nostalgic for the story's now fading brilliance—and my eyes alighted on a tiny spider in one corner of the ceiling, and, in my mind, I began to wander through Chesterton's world and remembered his story "The Head of Caesar," in which Father Brown says: "What we all dread most is a maze with no center. That is why atheism is only a nightmare."

How long had it been since I'd thought about those words? And why had they suddenly come back to me on glimpsing, or perhaps only sensing, the presence of that tiny spider? As I searched for an explanation I was sure existed, I became entangled in a mental spider's web, which eventually led me to *Citizen Kane*, the Orson Welles movie, in which the fragments we're shown of the life of Mr. Charles Foster Kane have always seemed to me the very image of a nightmarish existence, a maze with no center. And I thought, first, about the movie's opening sequence, when we see what remains of Foster Kane's accumulated treasures. Next, I thought about one of the movie's final sequences, in which we see an elegant but wretched-looking woman, Foster Kane's second wife, sitting on the floor in a mansion doing an enormous jigsaw puzzle. This scene provides us with the vital clue: there is no unity to these fragments, and the vile Charles Foster Kane, the business magnate whose strange biopic we thought we were watching, is a mere simulacrum, a jumble of illusory appearances…. There are great gaps in Kane's life story, important events are left out, and the movie focuses instead on the tiniest of details, as well as on minor characters who have only a tangential relationship with the tycoon.

With my own thoughts still lost in this maze of illusions, it occurred to me that *Citizen Kane* had certain points in common with Walter's memoir, which is also made up of brief snapshots of life, of fragments that lack any unity, but which, at all times, seek to relate, however obliquely, the twists and turns, however insignificant, of an artist's life; a trajectory composed of pieces that gradually form a grim jigsaw puzzle that might have been called *A Ventriloquist's Life*; a life that is, simultaneously, a maze in the form of a spider's web with no center, and also a nightmare, although in this case, in the final chapter, the narrator not only finds the center of the maze, he also discovers within it an unforeseen and decidedly anomalous clearing in the undergrowth, which leads him to think that any escape follows its own entirely separate path….

As soon as I set off along said path, I felt my spirits lift. It seemed to me that "The Neighbor" had picked up again, and it began to dawn on me that, despite the usual anxieties, I couldn't go on ignoring the fact that my life had entered a phase not unlike a mirror that reflects, however vaguely, only the most sublime things. As a reader, the sky was my limit. Or, to paraphrase Gombrowicz, as a reader I was nothing, and so could get away with anything. Such feelings of joy don't come around very often, which made me suspect that my sense of well-being must emanate from my tireless work as a literary novice.

From then on, I flew through "The Neighbor" as if there were a perfect confluence between the story and my reading of it, which meant I was soon captivated by a scene in which I seemed to identify completely with the vagabond Walter, who, "walking in the light of the star of my destiny," as he puts it, finally came to a small Portuguese town near Évora. There, in a dimly lit local bar, he chanced to overhear a story told almost in a whisper by a fellow customer; a story that was as much about a young man from the town—a Jew called David, known for his stern, unforgiving nature—as about his next-door neighbors, a family of black Angolans—a husband and wife and their three children—who, according to the locals in the bar, were recent arrivals.

The João family had been berated by everyone for trying to pass themselves off as genuine country folk, when, in fact, they knew nothing at all about farming. That evening's story in the local bar, the one Walter overheard, had actually begun the moment the Jewish neighbor told the João family, or rather bellowed at them, that when it came to matters agricultural they were downright useless; that is, it all started the moment he repeated to them what the rest of the town had already been saying—sometimes in rather vicious terms.

That story of the young Jew and the João family, told in the dim light of that local bar in a small Portuguese town, continued with a chilling scene that took place only days later: on finding a chicken from his Angolan neighbors' farm running loose on his lawn for the umpteenth time, the stern, unforgiving young David fired eight shots at the unsuspecting chicken, reducing it to a ball of blood and feathers. From that moment on, and with good reason, the Angolan family were terrified of their neighbor.

"But that was all just a preamble to the story I really wanted to tell you, and which happened only yesterday," said the customer recounting the tale, and there was a slight change in the inflection of his voice.

And what he told them was this: in the absence of their parents, who had gone off on a flying visit to Évora, the three children had spent the whole of the previous afternoon trotting about on the family horse, an ancient, world-weary mare bought at a knockdown price by their kindly parents. They rode the poor animal for so long that, finally, utterly exhausted, she strayed from the path and collapsed on the lawn of the stern, unforgiving young Jew. And right there, on that very spot, probably the worst place she could possibly have chosen, she promptly died. The three children froze in terror and then, as if they were chickens at risk of being turned into a ball of blood and feathers, they ran home and hid in the barn, where they decided to stay put until their parents returned from Évora. Every now and then, the children peered out of the barn window to see what the neighbor was doing. The young Jew stood staring in disbelief at the dead horse lying on his lawn, and then he looked over at the barn, where the children quickly ducked away from the window. When night fell, the neighbor again went out into his backyard and, sitting on the lawn very close to the mare, he, too, waited for the parents to return. When they did, at around midnight, they were dumbstruck, horrified to discover what had happened. They knelt down beside the poor beast and wept; they wept as if they were weeping for themselves and for the whole world. By the light of the small fire the young Jew had lit in his backyard and which cast ever deeper shadows over the dead body, the mare seemed to take on monstrous proportions. The couple feared the even more monstrous words that the young Jew would say, and the measures he would take, but, instead, most unexpectedly, he went gently over to them and began to console them. He fondly patted them on the head, and, still by the light of the fire, he very slowly and softly told them in more detail about the poor animal's sudden demise before going on to recount—taking his time and speaking with extraordinary gentleness—a story that was, in fact, an ancient Hasidic legend, although he didn't reveal its Hasidic origins to the Angolans, because having to explain the meaning of the word "Hasidic" seemed unnecessarily complicated.

The story went as follows: once upon a time, on the outskirts of a village, a group of Jews were observing the end of the Sabbath together, seated on the floor of a wretched little hovel. They were all from those parts, with the exception of one man, who nobody knew: an extremely poor, raggedly dressed man crouched in a dark corner of that cheerless house.... The conversation, which had touched upon all sorts of topics, finally threw up one particular question, which seemed to please all of the men there: if they could be granted one wish, what would it be? One said he would ask for money; the other, a son-in-law; the third, a new woodworking bench, and on they went in turn around the circle. After they'd all had their say, the only one who hadn't spoken was the ragged man crouched in the dark corner. Reluctantly and hesitantly, and seeing that they wouldn't take no for an answer, he responded thus: "I would wish to be a powerful king and to reign over a vast kingdom, and find myself sleeping one night in my palace as the enemy breached our borders, and for those horsemen to appear, before sunrise, at the walls of my castle, and for nobody to offer any resistance, at which point I, having woken in sheer terror and with no time to get dressed, would make my escape in nothing but my nightshirt, and, after being pursued over hill and dale, through woods and valleys, with no sleep or rest, I would arrive unharmed at this very corner in this very room. That would be my wish." The men looked at each other, confused, and asked him what he would gain from such a wish. To which he replied: "My nightshirt." And there ended the Hasidic tale, and the Angolans, after a few seconds of bemusement, smiled in gratitude for their neighbor's strange words of solace.

There is a subtle time shift in the next paragraph, and, after a kind of cinematic dissolve, we move from the expressions of bemused joy on the faces of the Angolans and travel far, far away from that backyard and the dead mare. Thanks to a series of short vignettes,

we begin to learn about the various places visited by the ventriloquist on his pilgrimage from the small Portuguese town to the devastated hills of Sana'a, a pilgrimage "in search of the origins of the
oral tradition."

Having first traveled to several locations, always heading east, we
follow the narrator as he boards an airplane, which is slow to take
off, but eventually leaves the sun-scorched runway and, in almost
no time, has risen above the extraordinarily white clouds, beneath
which, out of sight, lie the endless sands extending beyond the lovely
hills of the ancient kingdom of Saba.... The ventriloquist then describes how, as he flies over Arabia Felix—where he expects to land
that very night—he realizes that he isn't, hasn't been, and never
will be an angel. He isn't, nor will he ever be, because, among other
reasons—and here you have to read between the lines, I think—he
killed that barber back in Lisbon; but his words also seem to be a
kind of veiled reference to something Saul Bellow once said: that
from a certain point in the last century, air travel afforded modern
writers a possibility that no other writer before them had ever had:
that of seeing for themselves that there is no trace of any angels up
in the sky, among the clouds, where it has always been said that the
angels keep their cloudy quarters.

&

I'm surprised that, a few days ago, I seemed to recall that, toward the
end of "The Neighbor," Walter threw himself into a canal *in which
there was a kind of whirlpool that went deep down into the Earth's core*, and
I recalled how *just when it seemed that our man was completely lost in that
endless darkness, the whirlpool whisked him back up to the surface again and
deposited him in a strange, remote region of the world....* I must have read
that somewhere else, though, because there is no sign of it at the end
of the story, which also happens to be the end of the novel.

Where did this memory spring from? It's possible that I was mix-
ing it up with something I read in another book. In fact, there is an

airplane at the end of Walter's memoirs, but there's nothing about a whirlpool whisking him upward, nor any mention of angels. What there is, as I have just remembered, is a scene set on an airplane with a fellow passenger—a man, and something of a know-it-all—who amuses himself telling the story of the family he has just left for good—and he keeps insisting that it is "for good"—in Toronto. At one point, just as an in-flight announcement tells them that they'll soon be touching down in the land where the oral tradition began, in that long-forgotten land of Arabia,* the man sitting next to Walter tells him that his father, on his death bed in the town of Rutherford, New Jersey, told him he'd believed in many things over the course of his life, all of which he'd gradually lost faith in, until he was left with just one absolute conviction: he believed in a fiction that admits to being a fiction, in the knowledge that nothing else exists and that the exquisite truth lies in knowing that it's a fiction, and yet believing in it all the same.

25

Walking along Calle Londres, I was so immersed in my obsessive thoughts, and finding it hard to breathe in the asphyxiating heat, that I was sure there was no one else on that street, or anywhere else

---

* There, in that once fortunate land of Arabia where it might just be possible to trace the origins of the story, the ventriloquist—as my neighbor recounts in the final lines of *Walter and His Problem*—practices as a storyteller, fulfilling his dream of traveling toward the world's first story, the original story, the very first story: "I live near Saba four leagues from the city of Sana'a, where each night I go to tell stories to people who are unswervingly respectful and loyal—the ideal audience. The Europeans no longer listen to stories told aloud. They become restless, or they fall asleep. But here, close to Saba, everyone who comes and listens stays to hear me out. I tell story after story to people who, armed with the janbiya—the dagger symbolizing their fighting spirit—gather around me each day in warm, welcoming semicircles and give me their undivided attention. There are days when, as I tell my stories, I feel as if I were creating the world."

in the city. That's why it came as a brutal surprise when, out of the blue, another human being addressed me. And "brutal" is the right word, because it was the kind of surprise you get as a child at the age when you haven't yet come to terms with the existence of other beings who resemble you, but are not you: beings who appear one day, by surprise, when you least expect them and when you're most convinced of your own individuality.

Underlying what I say is something I've never told anyone before, but which I consider to be undeniable: I've always had trouble being confronted by the sight of a person similar to me but not me—that is, the same idea contained in another body, someone identical to me and yet different. I've always found that very hard, because on those occasions—it still happens to me now—I feel what Gombrowicz described as "a painful splitting in two." Painful because it transforms me into an unbounded being, whom even I can't predict; all my possibilities multiplied by that strange new and yet identical force suddenly approaching me, as if I were approaching myself from the outside.

Today I was walking along Calle Londres, and such was my extreme state of introversion, it was almost like having a veil over my eyes, which is why I had to open them very wide and rub them to see who was blocking my path and addressing me so cheerfully. He was a man of about fifty, with very bright eyes, curly fair hair à la Harpo Marx, and very shabby clothes. He was dragging along—as if in a dream—a supermarket cart, laden with all kinds of street detritus, with objects piled one on top of the other to form a tower of junk crowned by a very tall mop, which resembled the flagpole of a newly created union of local beggars.

Pessoa said that some men rule the world and others are the world. The vagabond, who I'll call Harpo, obviously belonged to the latter group.

"I woke up late with a splitting headache," he said, as if he'd known me all his life. "Which means I've got a lot of catching up to do."

I was so surprised by the familiarity with which Harpo spoke to me that I even wondered if I knew him from somewhere, perhaps we'd been fellow partygoers in our youth.

Surprising as his manner was, I was even more amazed that, whereas I found it perfectly normal to be addressed by the voice of the dead person lodged in my head, having this vagabond speak to me in such friendly terms made me feel distinctly on edge. In fact, the truth is, I felt terrified. Because there was no one else on the street, and, since there wasn't another person for half a mile around to bear witness to whatever might happen there, I couldn't quite see how to deal with that request for alms, which is what I took it to be, a hand held out asking for charity, although it was also the hand of someone with a hangover and possible ulterior motives.

"Bad night's sleep, was it?" I asked, trying to pretend I wasn't afraid.

"Yes, and when I woke up, I looked like I'd been dragged through a hedge backward!"

He clearly had a sense of humor, but I thought it best just to get on and give him some money. I felt in my pocket and found a two-euro coin, which I immediately handed to him. Harpo took it at once. Rummaging around in my pocket again, I found five smaller coins and handed him the whole lot. However, he rejected this second gift outright, reacting as if I were a vampire dangling a string of garlic in front of him.

"No, please," he said, almost imploringly.

I even began to doubt that he had actually asked for any money. I made a fresh attempt to give him the coins, and he looked even more horrified. I couldn't understand what was going on, but, just in case, I thought it best to leave him. In the desert, I recalled, one shouldn't stop to speak to strangers. But first I took a closer look at him, as if this would provide me with the necessary moment of reflection to help consolidate my precarious grip on what I was seeing. Then, without wasting any more time, I set off again, and when I'd already left him behind, I heard him repeating those same words:

"No, please."

Two hours later, there was more of a breeze on the streets and more pedestrians out and about, so there would be plenty of witnesses to anything that might happen. I felt tired after all my meanderings, stopping off in various bars, walking aimlessly but always in circles, never leaving the more monotonous parts of the neighborhood and always reemerging onto yet another stretch of Calle Londres. In a way, this process reminded me of something a friend used to say, that any road, even the road to Entepfuhl, would lead you to the end of world, but the road to Entepfuhl, if followed right to the end, would lead straight back to Entepfuhl.

I felt there was no escape, that I was stranded in the circular geography of Coyote, and, at the same time, at the end of the world, knowing that, even if I traveled to the ends of the earth, I would always return to Calle Londres. The truth is that noting down all these incidents or simple details was doing me good, perhaps because I was immersed in the kind of banal activities described in all my favorite diaries. That's why, for some time, while I walked, I devoted myself to seeking out the irrelevant. I even had a sense that in doing so, I was rebelling in some way against the clerks of the Adjustment Bureau, who might well be imaginary beings, but might also actually exist, in which case I'd be foolish to try and erase them from my mind. And what if those clerks weren't as brilliant, fierce, and determined as I had imagined, but instead toiled ceaselessly away in a decidedly gray environment? Of course, that didn't mean they weren't capable of changing our lives with a single line.

I had just reemerged, for the nth time, onto Calle Londres—feeling slightly tipsy now—and I was just wondering why they didn't think to rename that street to which I always returned as Ithaca, when suddenly I caught sight of Sánchez's nephew or, rather, the back of his flamboyantly shaven neck. No, I couldn't believe it! There he was again, the hateful hater. It was only what I deserved really, having walked for hours in circles round and round the neighborhood. The ghastly nephew was swaggering along just ahead of me, nonchalant, and, at the same time—for he'd definitely had a few drinks too many—slightly unsteady on his feet. I decided to follow him so as to find out where he lived or who he was going to see and what he had got up to and what he did for a living, always supposing he was capable of holding down a job. I was still wondering whether or not to approach him when he came to an abrupt halt and remained glued to the spot outside the window of a small store. In an attempt to creep nimbly into the shelter of a nearby doorway, I performed a strange kind of pirouette, spun round, then took two very short steps that nearly achieved precisely the opposite of my desired effect, namely, landing me slap-bang in his field of vision.

When he finally managed to drag himself away from the window and set off again, I followed suit, pausing to see what it was that had so captured his attention. A pair of sneakers. What an anticlimax! I mean, sneakers! I was so overwhelmed by this disappointment that, when I finally recovered from my state of disillusionment, I assumed that the nephew would be out of sight. But as I prepared myself to scan the horizon, I found him right there, staring at me, in the grip of some stubborn thought, until he finally spoke and demanded to know where he had seen me before.

I managed to blurt out that I was the journalist from La Vanguardia who had wanted to interview his uncle. The nephew leaned ominously toward me and seemed even more of a giant. I was, however, saved by the bell, an imaginary bell. Just when things were looking really bleak, I had a brilliant idea and promptly invited him to have a drink with me in Bar Tender, barely two steps away. He accepted at once with unusual enthusiasm, because it seemed—as I would soon find out—he didn't have a penny to his name and needed a drink, several, he said.

Not that I was rolling in money myself, because, having given away most of my change, all I had left was a twenty-euro note. But this was, in any case, more than he had, for, as I saw quite clearly, he was one of those creatures who drift through life doing nothing; although, of course, he may have been one of the tragically unemployed, and I was perhaps unfairly dismissing him as a mere idler. Besides, setting aside certain insurmountable differences, he did have something in common with me, because I, too, was unemployed, although I'm very active in my unemployment, and this diary is my apprenticeship, an apprenticeship in becoming a writer.

"Good God, this just gets funnier and funnier," he said.

"What do you mean?"

"I mean people are falling over themselves to pay me for information about my uncle."

Ah, now I understood. He was an out-and-out rogue. Not that I minded. On the contrary, a few doors opened to me when I saw him so ready to talk. But talk about what? I didn't need him to tell me any more about his uncle—he was far too hostile to Sánchez and would be totally biased; but the first story in *Walter and His Problem* was entitled "I Had an Enemy," and, unless I was very much mistaken, the plot of that story—with the presence of Pedro, the ventriloquist's gratuitous antagonist who disappears off to the South Seas—did, in some respects, resemble what the nephew was up to in the neighborhood, although he would doubtless be unaware of his resemblance to the ventriloquist's gratuitous enemy from the first story of that book published all those years ago. I could perhaps ask if he'd read it?

I thought so many things in that moment that, when I glanced up again, I found the nephew staring at me even more fixedly than before. I was about to ask him what he was looking at when he took the initiative himself and asked me what I was looking at. Then, I decided to make an instant enemy of the nephew and told him I was taking in, very carefully, very closely, his indescribable loathing.

He smiled, but I could see I'd ruffled his feathers, and he eyed me with great hostility.

"Why 'indescribable'? What do you mean 'loathing'?" He had ordered a drink and they hadn't brought it, he said, and he complained to the bar staff. I asked him his name. Julio, he said. Julio what? Julio, he said. It seemed to me that this wasn't his name at all, but that of the month we happened to be in. I had to accept it, though, what else could I do?

As if I'd suddenly turned private detective, I surreptitiously slipped him my twenty-euro note. I was preparing my interview with his uncle, I said, and wanted to know if he'd read a story by

Sánchez called "I Had an Enemy." Julio asked me to repeat this more slowly, and so I did. I was left none the wiser as to whether he'd read it or not, but I did, on the other hand, learn that Sánchez's real enemy was none other than Sánchez himself.

"Because Sánchez," he said, "is a complete neurotic, totally egocentric. He's spectacularly egotistical, the very epitome of egocentricity. Everything has to revolve around him, he can't bear it otherwise. That's why he's such a disaster in company, because he can't always surround himself with enough flatterers to make him the center of attention. Yes, he's a bona fide egocentric. He can't see beyond the end of his nose. He's a fucking neurotic. And the mistake we humans often make is to think that neurotics are interesting, when they never are, because neurotics are perpetually unhappy, self-absorbed, malicious, ungrateful—people incapable of making any constructive criticism, who only ever see doom and gloom."

It seemed to me that Julio was painting a pretty good picture of himself here, but I said nothing. And then, while I was thinking all this, something ridiculous happened. Julio, without even asking my permission, took a sip of my G&T. I felt quite disgusted and was about to demand, at the very least, some explanation, when he began telling me to give up on the idea of interviewing his uncle, although he wouldn't explain why. It seemed more like a subterfuge so that I wouldn't catch on that he was in no position to act as go-between.

Well into his second drink, he suddenly announced that, although he wasn't one to boast, he was the best writer in the world, and he was about to give me a perfectly abridged version of what was going on with Sánchez. His uncle's life, he said, could be summarized easily enough by giving a detailed account of how idleness, fear, and anxiety were gradually dulling a great intellect, and by describing how that intellect was very slowly disappearing, just as all that remains of an object you drop into the ocean are a few ephemeral bubbles.

He went on to say that, in recent months, things had gotten worse, and Sánchez's sole ambition was to emulate a certain Norwegian writer whom some misguided critics were comparing with Proust. What saved his uncle was a certain sense of dignity when he put on his public persona at speaking engagements, but little more. On one occasion, back when they were still on speaking terms, he'd heard his uncle say that he intended to adopt a pseudonym and devote himself to criticism, to being implacably honest, especially about his own work; he'd heard him say that he was prepared to analyze his own books in those implacably honest reviews, which he would publish under that pseudonym. These, his uncle said, would be the only really intelligent reviews he would get, because no one knew better than he did where his faults lay…. That's what his uncle had said on that one occasion, and then Julio had put a damper on this rush of self-critical enthusiasm, telling him that, as a good nephew, he was equally aware of his literary faults and could, if he liked, list them right there and then, although perhaps he'd best keep them to himself, in case he wounded his uncle's feelings. And that was the last time we spoke, Julio concluded.

Well, I said, I'm not exactly surprised you don't see each other anymore. But that's all I said, because I was reluctant to tell him that I'd given him my twenty euros and that I couldn't, therefore, pay for our drinks. I then pretended that I'd just received a text message (I said this in English just to see if I could manage to impress him at least once) and that I had to shoot off.

I had interrupted him almost in midsentence. I went over to the bar, where they know me quite well, and said that I'd pay them to-morrow for any drinks we'd had.

"And what if that gentleman over there orders something else? Should we give it to him?" asked one of the two idle barmen.

"I wouldn't if I were you, stranger."

I answered like a character out of a Western, as befitted someone called Mac, who'd picked up his name in the saloon of a Wild West town.

I left with a spring in my step. Armed with the knowledge that Sánchez was his own worst enemy, I could begin planning my re-make of *Walter and His Problem*.

I left so quickly that anyone seeing me might have thought I was skipping out. At a pedestrian crossing, I came across a beggar, who, if I'm not mistaken, usually sits on the corner of Calle París and Calle Muntaner. I surprised myself at how easily I recognized him. He seemed about to leave and looked just like any other man going home after work. Then I realized that exactly the opposite was true: he was, in fact, heading for his place of work. Under one arm he was carrying a notice saying something to the tune of that he was hungry and had three children to support. He glared at me, and I thought he was about to ask for money. If he did, I had my answer ready: my last twenty euros had gone to another beggar. He said nothing, but merely looked me up and down. That look made me squirm, but I defended myself in a most peculiar way, invisible not only to him, but to anyone else as well. I silently invoked a favorite saying of a friend of mine—a great expert on clochards and on very friendly terms with a fair few of them in Paris—which I repeated as a kind of private prayer: "Born to us will come the man who, having nothing, will want nothing more than to be left with that nothing he has."

I thought then of the Jew and his wish to escape dressed only in his nightshirt, and, at the next traffic light, as I left behind the man whose sign said he was hungry, I wondered if the various beggars who appeared to be accompanying, almost punctuating, my walk today weren't perhaps different versions of my own image reflected in a mirror in continual movement. If so, I told myself, I should kill them off, one by one, at each set of traffic lights; that would be one way of bringing about my own death—or disappearance.

On the corner of Calle París and Calle Casanova, I saw—and, in the circumstances, I barely felt a glimmer of surprise—the same group of gray, forty-something bohemians I'd seen months before, on the day I'd first spotted Julio. They seemed to be handing around bottles of wine and looked more like clochards than bohemians. They seemed in far worse shape than the last time. Had they gone entirely to the dogs in those few months? I considered telling them that they would find the slanderous nephew in Bar Tender, but then

I began to wonder if the economic crisis was driving more beggars into the Coyote neighborhood. Or was this, rather, an invasion of misunderstood geniuses?

&

I wake up and get out of bed to note down all I can remember of the end of a dream I would very much have liked to continue. Through the open windows of the saxophone school in Coyote came the languid sound of the music classes, a monstrous buzzing in the midst of the pervading summer heat, which mingled with the din of the street performer belting out his carefree song to the rhythm of *bamba, la bamba, bamba,* his voice reaching every corner of the neighborhood. Everyone was dancing. And I had to agree that Coyote was much improved when transplanted to New York.

26

If I rewrote "I Had an Enemy," the new plot would revolve around the problem of Walter the ventriloquist's extreme egocentrism, which was doubtless what lay behind his lack of other voices. It would also mention a rehab center for egomaniacs, newly opened right next door, and which, while he would certainly know all about it, he would never consider to be an appropriate place for himself.

My "I Had an Enemy" wouldn't begin with the Cheever quote, but with the line from William Faulkner that Roberto Bolaño used as an epigraph in his novella *Distant Star*: "What star is there falls, with none to watch it?"

As far as I know, no one has yet been able to locate this line in Faulkner's work, which suggests that the quote could be made-up, although everything else points to it being Faulkner's handiwork, and Bolaño experts all agree that he wasn't in the habit of inventing quotes, and certainly not if he was going to use them as epigraphs.

Just as we might ask ourselves which star we mean when we speak of a star that has fallen with none to watch it, we might well ask what kind of diary we're talking about when we speak of a diary with none to read it. Both the falling star's need for a spectator and the paradoxical need for a reader shared by some personal, private diaries have led me to imagine a diary in which someone writes down his daily thoughts and activities with no intention of ever being read, only for that diary to take on a life of its own and to rebel against the intentional absence of a reader and slowly insist on being seen, on escaping its fate as a fallen star with none to watch it.

I'm suddenly reminded of how, four days ago, I had an idea for that fake posthumous book (posthumous *and* falsely interrupted by death), a book I haven't really lost sight of for a moment since I began this diary.

After writing this last line, I took a break from the page as a way of simulating a genuine break in the diary, which meant, in reality, that I cracked open another bottle of Vega Sicilia, the last in the pantry, and drank a toast to a return to the idea of creating an entirely artificial and counterfeit work, consistent with the genre of "incomplete and posthumous works."

Wasn't this the very first thing I thought when I began my diary, and also what ultimately led me to remember the character of Wakefield and to feel a growing need for Carmen, or indeed anyone, to, at some point, acknowledge the existence of this diary? Sometimes, even if it involves us temporarily absenting ourselves, we must fight to achieve something as essential and, at the same time, as simple as having someone acknowledge our existence.

After that break, I returned to the study, to these pages which I began almost a month ago with no idea where they would lead or what I would talk about, always assuming I would have something to say, but in which a theme soon emerged and so promptly that I felt it must be the theme meant for me. It had come to me sooner than expected, one sunny morning as I was listening to Antonio Lauro's "Vals Venezolano No. 3, Natalia," a song I never tire of hearing. The theme was repetition, and I soon became immersed in it, especially in its importance in music, where sounds and sequences tend to be repeated, and where everyone agrees that repetition is fundamental if it works in harmony with a composition's opening themes and variations.

I was soon utterly gripped by this theme of repetition, the proof being that I'm now planning the modified and improved rewrite of my neighbor's novel, a misguided, insignificant book, full of now forgotten sound and fury, but nonetheless one that I've chosen to study with a care compatible with my plan eventually to change it. If one day I do rewrite "I Had an Enemy," the first thing I think I'll do is replace the Cheever quote with a Faulknerian epigraph, a modification that would not only make Sánchez's novel perform a triple somersault of thirty years, it would also prevent the narrator telling the story as if he hadn't read the literary masterpieces produced by Bolaño.

At the same time, I'm adamant that this Faulknerian epigraph will bear no relation to the plot of "I Had an Enemy"; I mustn't forget that I've always longed to demystify the assumed significance of epigraphs, and to follow in the footsteps of Alberto Savinio, for instance, who began his book *Maupassant e "l'altro"* with a line by Nietzsche: "Maupassant, a true Roman."

"Maupassant, a true Roman." I repeat it to myself now for the sheer pleasure of saying it. The number of times I've returned to that line, and yet I have always read it in the same way, however often I repeat it. I see Nietzsche's definition as illuminating the figure of Maupassant, but, as Savinio himself said in a footnote, he does so by bathing him in the light of the absurd; he illuminates him so much more clearly because we can't be sure what Nietzsche meant by calling Maupassant a Roman, and perhaps, as is often the case with Nietzsche, he didn't mean anything at all.

And so, if one day I decided to rewrite "I Had an Enemy," Faulkner's epigraph would bear no relation to the story itself, but instead would make its own way, would travel on alone, unconnected to anything, basking in a great unconnectedness, like a ghost plane in the skies over Chile.

As to how much I would preserve of Sánchez's "I Had an Enemy," one thing I know I would keep is the skeleton of the subplot in which the gratuitous antagonist heaps odium on the object of his hatred, that story so strangely comparable to Julio's hatred of his uncle. I would also hold on to the part about how the owner of that voice— who in Sánchez's story does a fairly good job of imitating John Cheever—is desperate to stop drinking. This would simultaneously preserve and modify Walter's character, who would then have an additional enemy in himself and his boundless egoism. Indeed, his egoism was the main criticism leveled at him by his primary enemy—I'd call him Pedro, as he is in the original—that egoism which led him to talk constantly about himself and is the real reason behind his lack of different voices for his dummies. However, for this primary enemy, Pedro, I would take my inspiration from the tremendous egoism and vanity that I've observed in Julio, who, despite showing the occasional glimmer of genuine talent, is actually the classic raving lunatic who goes around accusing others of having what are, in fact, his own flaws.

If, some day, I were to rewrite "I Had an Enemy," I would describe a night when the ventriloquist finally came up with an effective way of solving the problem of having only one voice: the realization that what constrained him were his antagonist's constant attacks on him, thus forcing him to rely on his one voice, to cling steadfastly to what he did on stage and in his private life, and to dig in his heels still harder in that ongoing battle.

One night, all of this would come to a head. There would be a backstreet encounter, and, after some illegal shenanigans, Pedro would win a trip to the South Seas in an unofficial lottery run by the local church. And once Pedro had left, Walter would ease up on his tactic of defensive egocentrism. There would be less need to defend himself, and he would begin to relax, shake off his old self, his infuriatingly singular voice, "the voice that writers so yearn to find," becoming, from that moment on, the various voices in which he would go on to tell the remaining nine stories.

And so I would give Walter what I imagined to be Sánchez's

personality, while Pedro the enemy would take on the difficult and ultimately mean-spirited character of Julio.

In the final lines of "I Had an Enemy," Walter would feel very satisfied with his role as a full-time ventriloquist, and very happy at last to be so many other people, and not himself. Walter would be a mixture of Sánchez and Julio, with a touch of my own discreet, humble nature, plus he would have a few of the inflexible, tiresome characteristics of some of his dummies. Walter would wear jackets with padded shoulders, white shirts (for a quick getaway when the time came), and a bamboo cane concealing a Javan sunshade.

But the reader would only learn all this at the end of that first story, because at the beginning of the second one, "The Duel of Grimaces," there would be no trace in Walter of the different traits that made up his identity.

I'm imagining the following style for the opening of "I Had an Enemy" that I might one day rewrite:

"Picture a ventriloquist. His voice seems to come from someone else. But if we weren't sitting in a theater, we would take no pleasure in his art. His appeal, therefore, consists in being both present and absent; in fact, he is far more himself when he is being, simultaneously, another. And, in fact, as soon the curtain comes down, he is neither. Let's follow him now that he's alone, walking along in the pitch-black night, now that he's neither of those other two men he has left behind, and is, therefore, a third man we know nothing about, and yet we'd still like to know where he's heading. But what with the beard, the Irish cap, the sunglasses, and the dim lighting, it's hard to get a good look at the face of that broken creature...."

[OSCOPE 26]

By pure coincidence—and we tend to say "pure coincidence" whenever we can't fathom how something happened, but we suspect there might be an Adjustment Bureau lurking in the shadows, either that or some other, perfectly reasonable explanation that we'll never find out about—while reading Antonio Di Benedetto's *Zama* this evening, I came across a line that Roberto Bolaño might well have read and which perhaps accompanied him for some time and over long distances; it's surprisingly similar to Faulkner's line:

"It was the sky's own secret hour, when it shines brightest because all mankind is sleeping and no one is watching."

27

This morning, making the most of the overcast sky, I took a pleasant stroll around the neighborhood. I bought the daily papers, had a laugh with the woman at the newsstand (who was in a more cheerful mood than usual), waved to the tobacconist and the owner of the patisserie, purchased five apples at the organic store, and chatted to the group of retirees who congregate in Bar Tender. The triumph of the trivial, which suits this diary to perfection. That's what I need, trivialities; at least the occasional one, because seemingly banal matters help keep at bay the novel lurking stubbornly in the dark forest I sometimes imagine lies right outside my apartment.

The sky, pale gray, the bottom of each cloud edged with blue. A bicycle with a slightly bent front wheel. The triumph of the trivial. Roland Barthes once said that the only possible success a personal diary can hope for is to have survived the battle, even if that means distancing oneself from the world. Alan Pauls said: "Any diary is, then, the literary incarnation of a zombie, the living dead, the person who has seen everything and lived to tell the tale."

Most of the retired gentlemen at Bar Tender—there are usually between five and seven of them, depending on the day—are chain-smokers, which makes me think that this is probably their chosen route to death. Normally, the most talkative member of the group is Darío, a naval engineer, long since retired, who always has a cheap cigar clamped between his lips, but there's not one there today. I've had more to do with him than with the others, and that relationship—plus a rather banal excuse—qualified me to join them this morning. Darío was complaining about his summer cold and saying that, even though it was nothing serious, it was nonetheless depressing, first, because people don't get colds in July, and second, because the persistent slight fever and, in particular, the dreadful phlegm were affecting his mental balance. It occurred to me that perhaps he was craving his cigar, and I was about to say so, but decided not to risk making such an overly familiar remark. Nevertheless, in the ensuing silence, I took an even greater risk—I somehow couldn't stop myself—and asked them all what they would wish for if they knew their wish would be granted. No one said a word, some pretended not to have heard me, and the others genuinely didn't hear me—a combination of slight deafness and complete indifference to any comment made by an interloper. Only Darío answered, and after saying a few words which, this time, I had difficulty hearing, he said that if he could do anything he wanted, he would journey to the center of the Earth and look for rubies and gold, then he would set off on an adventure in search of perfect monsters.

He spoke a little like the mysterious vagabond in that Hasidic tale, but also like a child, and it made me laugh to hear him say "perfect monsters," because there was really no need to go looking for them in the center of the Earth. *We* were the monsters.

Ana Turner came racing past. She was walking a little dog or, rather, it was walking her, for it was dragging her along so violently that she seemed to be in permanent danger of stumbling and falling flat on her face. With a mischievous smile, she announced that she'd just been on a secret mission. I wasn't expecting to see her there, and would have given anything at that moment to vanish, because I didn't want her to think I belonged to that gang of boorish retirees.

Shortly afterward, as I was about to say goodbye to the gentlemen and was gazing distractedly over at the sunny horizon of Calle Londres, I experienced what can only be called an hallucination, when, for a few seconds, I thought I saw Sánchez and Carmen walking along together on the opposite sidewalk. They weren't holding hands, but it looked as if they were. The sight so upset me, I instinctively looked away, but when I looked back two seconds later, there wasn't a soul to be seen.

Does one consult a doctor after having just one hallucination? I felt distinctly worried. Were Carmen and Sánchez simply midday ghosts? Perhaps it was merely a projection of my own fears, and I had imagined seeing them because of all the many emotions that have been boiling away in my head for days now, what with my suspicions about Carmen and being so immersed in the amorous intrigues described in the ventriloquist's memoirs.

Seeing my look of distress, Darío asked if anything was wrong. No, it's nothing, I said, I happened to see something over there which isn't there anymore. I stood up and, despite my disquiet about what I thought I'd seen, I was amused to see how getting up to leave unleashed a minor duel of grimaces among the retirees. Was I considering including this battle in "The Duel of Grimaces," the story I was thinking of rewriting one day? I immediately saw that this was a bad idea. One learns some lessons very quickly when it comes to concocting and planning writing projects, and this message came across to me loud and clear: the fact that the plot of "I Had an Enemy" resembled one I was experiencing in the real world—Sánchez being criticized by a nephew who loathed him utterly—didn't mean that, from then on, one by one, the plots of the nine chapters—which I still hadn't worked out quite how to rewrite—should bear any resemblance to what might happen to me in the next few days in the real world.

Thinking about this and that, and still unable to conceal my unease, I said goodbye to the old boors, crossed over to the other side of the street, then walked around the corner and, just in case I had really seen them, went looking for Carmen and her companion in Calle Urgell; but there was no one there, only an imposing sun blazing down on the asphalt. I continued on my way and, on the final corner, was approached by a very smartly dressed beggar—well, smartly dressed from the ankles up, for the total effect was ruined by his feet, which were shod in a pair of enormous, battered boots, like something straight out of a Charlie Chaplin movie; they were the only thing that indicated to me that he was, very politely, begging. He was clearly one of the new wave of beggars, of whom there were already quite a few in Barcelona. They wear expensive clothes and don't care in the least if this proves off-putting. They tend to do their begging in a very studied, professional manner, and their style is certainly very different from that historically associated with people asking for help. The man in the monstrous boots began by saying that, to him, health means a certain capacity—one that had been beyond his reach for years—to live a full life. I gave him some change, even though he was wearing a floral shirt and didn't seem in the least bit sad. And I didn't for one moment regret having allowed myself to be taken in by his gestures, always assuming he was an impostor. Indeed, as I watched him walk away, I found myself admiring the way he walked, making sure no one could possibly fail to notice his boots: they were like a kind of theatrical prop and—along with his little spiel about health—were doubtless an essential part of his unique method for getting his hands on money intelligently and, equally important, with great aplomb and dignity.

Back home, with the air-conditioning on at an almost subzero temperature, I tried to forget that ghostly vision of Carmen and Sánchez on the opposite sidewalk, and, after racking my brains, I finally found a way—not very long-lasting but interesting nonetheless—of passing the time and blocking out my problems. I began to rummage around in my memories for the best of all the many periods of doubt into which I've slumped over the years.

My thoughts led me to Cyril Connolly's book *The Unquiet Grave*, in which he very intelligently reflects upon states of uncertainty. I read it for the first time when I was working as a law clerk in the office of Señor Gavaldá, my first employer. Grim days spent opening the door to his colorful bunch of clients and years of traipsing up and down corridors taking coffee and sugar to my ghastly bosses. Fortunately, I always carried in my right pocket a copy of Connolly's book of doubts, which I would secretly stroke, and which gave me the necessary strength to go on opening doors in my role as a poor young lawyer-cum-tea-boy. Never more so than during that period—I'd still never been in love, I was just a bartender—was the name "Mac" so appropriate.

Ah, the great Cyril Connolly: "We think we recognize someone we pass in the street. It turns out to be a complete stranger and yet, a moment later, we meet that very person. This pre-vision indicates the moment we entered into his wavelength, his magnetic orbit."

Despite my best efforts, I can't forget that, at midday, shortly after leaving the old boors and rounding the corner in pursuit of Carmen's ghost, I bumped into the woman herself carrying her shopping along Calle Buenos Aires. It all happened in a few tenths of a second.

"Are you alone?" I asked her.

She stared at me in amazement.

"Are you stupid or what?"

28

Carmen went off to the movies, while I chose to stay at home, and almost instantly Sunday filled me with such anxiety that, quite soon, I was imagining myself in a white coat, transformed into the on-duty doctor of a provincial hospital. I emerged from that fit of anxiety feeling even more anxious, remembering a few verses written one Sunday by Luís Pimentel, the doctor and poet from Lugo, Galicia: "Here I sit, / alone and still, / in my white coat. / The afternoon stretches blandly before me, / outside, the cold kiss of concrete / and, lying on the grass, a dead angel. / A doctor passes. / A nun passes. / The operating room rises up, lit by cotton-wool lights."

In that Sunday solitude, the operating room in the poem began to rise up in my imagination, and I had no choice but to go for a walk around Coyote, which was deserted at that hour.

The stillness and peace of the street was a blessing. Not a sound. Sunday, and everyone in their homes, snoozing, playing, fucking, dreaming, and, in truth, most of them feeling slightly nauseous, because Sundays create an unfailing sense of emptiness and ruin.

But I was thankful for those tranquil streets. I thought I would go to the cinema and wait for Carmen to come out. And I was on my way there when, suddenly, in a split second, everything was turned on its head. A Buick screeched to a halt just inches in front of me, and from the passenger side there emerged a young man, a prominently nosed fellow dressed in matching white shirt and pants. I say "emerged," but, in fact, he literally leapt out of the car. He seemed very on edge, and then he asked why I was so on edge too, a question I didn't answer, precisely because I was so on edge. What struck me most was how pale he was, and, for a fraction of a second, he looked like an unexpected replica of the white-coat-clad doctor from the poem. So much so, that I even asked myself why I'd bothered to come out for a stroll if, in some way, what I was seeing was there back at home, in that Pimentel poem I'd been thinking about moments before leaving the apartment. But I soon saw that the man was nothing like the doctor in the poem; rather, he was a young guy walking in a strange way and moving his feet very oddly. A kind of black wallet was poking out next to the buckle of his showy but not inelegant belt, and he patted it, as if it were a holster, as if he wanted me to think he was carrying a gun. Then, suddenly, as clear as day, I saw that he was.

A fleeting metaphysical doubt crossed my mind. If that whole situation was merely the crazy consequence of a poem I'd remembered and that had suddenly taken on a most unpleasant life of its own, I had no reason to be afraid. If not, though, it was clear that this prominently nosed stranger had mistaken me for someone else, and that the best thing for me to do would be to get the hell out of there, perhaps taking refuge in one of the pool halls—which were always open on Sundays—the closest being next to Piera's barbershop. Or, better still, I thought: I could run round the corner and race up the stairs to the second floor of the Chinese restaurant, where they'd surely be glad to take me in.

It's very strange, but in a situation like this I'm quite capable of completely zoning out from the action and asking myself if, in my time as a lawyer, I'd made any enemies who might now be seeking revenge, and even asking myself what the hell had made me think of that poem about a white coat. But I'm also coolheaded enough to stop and ask myself why I left my apartment when everyone knows that calm and silence often turn into the exact opposite, into something noisy and terrible…. In any case, this moment of distraction lasted only a moment, because events were heating up and I saw that the youth in the white shirt was striding toward me. In my mind's eye, I was already a dead man, when, at the very last minute, the killer changed course and ran straight past me. In fact, he ignored me completely, he couldn't have cared less about me, and, deep down, I found this rather disappointing. Instead he chased after a very tall Colombian guy well known in the Coyote neighborhood because he sells Cuban cigars "fresh from Havana," sometimes by means—in terms of his approach—of an almost intimidating sales method.

Anyway, like many others on the street, I was curious to see how that pursuit would end and I joined forces with a chorus of circumspect bystanders, and the whole thing ended in the worst way possible, for it was no longer merely unliterary in tone, it was also utterly uncivilized. A short, sharp karate chop brought the Colombian to the ground, where he lay motionless, having hit his head on the edge of the curb. Was he dead? His aggressor, who showed no interest in stealing his Havana cigars, turned to see what was going on behind him and, pausing for the briefest of moments, he scowled menacingly at us onlookers. That set my mind off again, although only for a second, allowing me to notice that, despite his youth, he could equally well have passed for an old man, because his nose ended in a bulbous white tip, as if it were making a foolish attempt to match his white outfit.

As tends to happen in real life—and as I see all too clearly in this diary as well—events come and go, usually with no great dramatic twist, however cataclysmic they might seem at the time. And thank goodness, because this stops me having to behave, in my diary, like certain novelists who insult the reader's intelligence by filling their stories with spectacular events, inventing great fires, for example, or getting their characters to go around killing each other, or having the nice guy win the jackpot, or someone drown in the sea on the happiest day of his life, or having a twelve-story building come crashing down, or for seven shots to ring out on a blissfully peaceful Sunday....

Some novels even overdramatize events, which, in real life, happen in a far more unassuming and inconsequential way; they happen, then they're over, they run into one another, floating like clouds scattered by the wind between the odd deceptive pause that turns out to be impossible, because time—which no one understands—stops for nothing. This "flaw" in certain novels is another reason why I tend to prefer short stories. Of course, I do sometimes come across excellent novels, but that doesn't change my overall opinion, because the novels I like always resemble Chinese boxes, containing tales within tales.

Short story collections—which can seem very similar to personal diaries, made up as they are of days that resemble chapters, chapters that, in turn, resemble fragments—are perfect machines when, thanks to the brevity and concision demanded by the form itself, they manage to appear in every way more closely linked to reality, as opposed to novels, which so often dance around it.

Not unusually for me, in the midst of that crazy incident involving the man with the flashy belt and the possibly deceased Colombian, my mind wandered off and I ended up pondering the tension between the genres of the short story and the novel, the friction that existed in my own diary. Nor was it unusual for me, despite the apparent importance of that sudden fracas on the street, to see the whole thing as utterly insignificant, and by the time the ambulance arrived, I'd almost forgotten all about it, the proof of this being that I calmly turned on my heel and went home as if nothing had happened. Carmen was back by then, having returned from the movies, where I was sure she'd seen less "action" than I had on my stroll around Coyote. Idiotically, I somehow failed to notice the surly look on her face. Had I noticed, I wouldn't have asked if she'd found

146

the heat unbearable; I wouldn't have asked her anything, because I know how badly she reacts when she's in a bad mood and is asked a question, any kind of question.

She replied furiously, demanding to know why my shirt was drenched in sweat. I just narrowly escaped death, I said. And I told her about the chase and the karate chop and the possible corpse in the midst of it all....

"You can't go on like this," she cut in authoritatively.

She then started saying how I do less and less each day—as if, once again, she were making a concerted effort to ignore the existence of my diary, and as if my having witnessed a possible murder were proof of my idleness—and she asked what I'd done that morning, wanting to know—as she put it—if I'd spent it sitting on my hands. I considered how fickle a thing falling in love can be and how it can flare up or die down in a moment. My hands were kept pretty busy, I told her. And if plates didn't fly, that's only because they happened to be out of Carmen's reach.

Later on, when things had calmed down, Carmen asked, apropos of nothing, when I planned to give her my shirt so she could sew on its missing button. I asked if she meant the sweaty shirt I'd been wearing. And in the middle of our absurd and increasingly heated argument—in which I repeated several times that none of my shirts had a button missing—she called me Ander.

"Ander!" she said. Sánchez's name. I heard it as clear as a bell. Everything in the house froze, even time itself seemed to stop. There, right in front of me, was the unexpected evidence that Carmen was in the habit of arguing with Sánchez and calling him by his given name, which meant not only was she lying when she said that she never had any contact with him, she also seemed accustomed to arguing with him in the same familiar tones as she did with me.

But the strangest part of all this is that Carmen denied the whole thing. She repeated over and over that, at no point, had she called me Ander. She even swore on her mother's life, and then—quite unnecessarily—on His Holiness the Pope (this one *and* the Pole, she said). In the face of her adamant denial, there wasn't much I could do apart from begin to doubt myself and accept that perhaps I had misheard, even though I knew I'd heard perfectly well.

And now, at this very moment, along with a sense that today has been a less than felicitous Sunday, I realize again that she *did*, without a shadow of a doubt, say what I heard her say. I can't change things, because it is what it is; I can't rewrite in my mind the fateful moment when "Ander!" escaped from her lips.

I remember it perfectly, including the particular way in which she shouted it out, then stopped short when she realized her blunder. But I just told her, yes, perhaps I had misheard and maybe she had actually said "And another thing!" or even just "And er …!" And then came the strangest part of my Sunday. She looked at me, incensed, and said: "For crying out loud, Mac, I didn't say either of those things either." And I said: "Oh, really?" "No," she assured me with such a beatific look that I was stunned. And I replied: "No, it turns out you didn't say anything …" "Exactly, I didn't say anything," she said, and if her composure was merely a front —it had to be, it simply had to—it was a masterpiece of pretense.

29

In the late afternoon, still shaken by what happened yesterday, I tottered wearily round to see the local tailor and ask if he could let out the pants I bought last year and which I can now barely do up.

On the way, despite the extra nine pounds I'm carrying around, I felt so frail that I was sure the slightest breeze would knock me down.

The tailor could not have been nicer, but he only has one changing room in his very cramped shop and he's chosen to furnish it with not one, but two full-length mirrors and a tiny stool. It's terribly confined, like a tomb. Feeling flustered behind the curtain, I almost lost my balance and risked falling and breaking one of the two mirrors. Then I felt an overwhelming fear that I might die in the very moment I slipped my foot into the narrow pant leg. And shortly afterward, having overcome my fear of losing my balance just as I breathed my last, everything grew still bleaker: I felt very alone and, for a few seconds, couldn't even see myself in the mirror.

I broke out in a cold sweat and realized I was alive. Lucky me. When I went home, I recalled the story I'd heard some time ago, about a wife who left her husband for another man. The husband placed a naked statue of her in the garden of a friend. Was this a kind of "Renaissance revenge," or did he simply give it to his friend because it was no longer of any value to him?

30

I spent the whole morning telling myself that there wasn't a moment to waste.

By the afternoon, nothing much had changed. Once again, I obsessed over not wasting a minute while wasting them all.

"Just get up and leave the house," the voice said.

(The voice of death.)

But I didn't want to leave my apartment. I was paralyzed by a sudden insight into the most contradictory aspect of the artist's condition, however much of a beginner he might be, namely, that when going out onto the streets, he must observe whatever he sees there as if he were oblivious to it all, but then he must do something with it, make a carbon copy of it at home, as if he had understood absolutely everything.

Paralyzed. And on top of this, the day seemed determined to be the shortest I've known in all my days on this planet, probably a decision made by that devious bunch from the Adjustment Bureau.

I watched the clouds racing by, but still couldn't make up my mind to do anything. I spent the entire day eager to get myself into gear before the day ended. Carmen came into the study to let me know it was getting late. I looked out of the window, and, lo and behold, night was falling, and there I was, having done nothing all day, knocked senseless by jealousy, by my suspicions about Carmen, by my wretched state of mind.

Now, as I think about heading to bed, I can see that the only thing I should have written today is the following: "Death speaks to us in a deep voice only to say nothing, nothing, nothing...." I should have read this and then written it out a hundred times and in that way gone to bed believing that I had at least written something today. And then this, another hundred times (as an homage to the dark parasite of repetition that lies at the heart of all literary creation): "We know far less than we think we know, but we can always know more, there's always room to learn."

"Mac, what are you doing?" Carmen calls, or almost bellows, from the living room.

In response, I cover my mouth with one hand, while with the other I remove my pajama pants, put them away in the closet, and, standing there stark naked, I reply:

"Nothing, darling, still just repeating the neighbor's novel."

And I imagine Sánchez, also naked, forty years, or who knows, perhaps only a couple of hours ago, standing ready before Carmen as I am now, ready for anything.

31

If it came to it, the first thing I'd change in "The Duel of Grimaces" would be the epigraph by Djuna Barnes. I'd replace it with a piece of dialogue taken from *Fever Dream* by Samanta Schweblin:

"'Carla, a child is for life.'

'No, dear,' she says. She has long nails and points one finger at me, level with my eyes."

The epigraph would then chime fully with the contents of the story.

Schweblin is an Argentinian writer who doesn't necessarily see madness as a disorder, perhaps because she feels that the strange and anomalous make most sense. She particularly admires the short stories of Cortázar, Bioy Casares, and Antonio Di Benedetto, and that, I think, gives a really good clue as to where she's going with her writing, because those authors are three of the finest practitioners of the kind of Argentinian literature that inhabits gray, disquieting, everyday worlds and which someone has named "the literature of disappointment." I'll never forget Di Benedetto reaching the old wharf and saying: "There we were, all set to go and not going."

In her stories, Schweblin usually tries to make some of the things she describes *happen inside the reader*. If, one day, I do rewrite "The Duel of Grimaces," I'd like to achieve the same effect, or at least try. I could choose other writers who place the reader in a similar position, but I would take Schweblin as a reference point for "The Duel of Grimaces," because I've read her only recently and still feel very much under the spell of *Fever Dream*, with its atmosphere of rural drought mingled with herbicides and the poison some mothers exude. I still haven't gotten over the shock. When I finished reading the book, I felt as if I'd been transformed into a mother who harbored murderous feelings for her children, and that Schweblin really had succeeded in making that story *happen inside me*.

That's why, if, one day, I do rewrite "The Duel of Grimaces," I would make a point of imitating her way of writing, although I'm sure that in order to do that, I'd have to spend years steeped in the sadness and the difficult art of those Argentinian writers.

In my story, the egotism of the ventriloquist would be the determining factor, especially as regards his relationship with his only son. Walter would be a jealous man—as I have been these last two days, terribly jealous, despite having no evidence that Carmen is deceiving me, and convinced, too, that I'm making a complete fool of myself; it's as if I wanted her to betray me, so that I would then have a reason for running away—yes, Walter would be neurotic, self-absorbed, egotistical, with a very real feeling of physical disgust for his only son, a disgust that would, in a way, already have been announced in that quote from Schweblin and would lie at the center of everything.

My rewrite of "The Duel of Grimaces" would be totally different from Sánchez's original: the father would, quite simply, want to do away with his son, to kill him. We wouldn't, then, be faced with just the horror of someone who discovers that his son and heir is as vile an individual as he is, but of someone with the entirely unnatural desire to murder his thirty-year-old son, whom he judges to be unacceptable and monstrous. Needless to say, I don't identify in the least with Walter's criminal desire, among other things because I don't desire the death of anyone, and mainly because I adore my three lovely sons. In fact, only yesterday, Miguel and Antonio, the two oldest, phoned from Sardinia, where they're having an amazing time on vacation near the ruins of Pula, which is where Carmen and I spent our honeymoon thirty years ago. Love you, I said. And then, wanting to let them know that their mother and I were currently basking in the glow of a second honeymoon, I added: "We both do."

It's the sort of thing I only ever dare say over the phone, and never to their faces. And yesterday, I didn't hold back.

"We love you, too!" cried Miguel, the most affectionate of my three sons, and possibly the most intelligent, although that doesn't really come into it if you love your three children equally.

"But I love you more!" I said.

And Carmen told me off for joshing with them like that. To which I replied: They're grown men, they can take a bit of joshing.

"Love you!" we could hear Antonio saying, so as not to be left out.

They have their own lives to lead. Far from us. If we'd had a girl, she would probably have stayed closer to home. I think sons tend to do their own thing—they like to be free, and ours are no exception. Our third son is an aeronautical engineer; he has found a very well-paid job in Abu Dhabi, and we speak to him now and then on Skype. I couldn't be prouder of all three of them. If, one day, I were to commit suicide or disappear, I'd like them to know that they have my unreserved admiration. I haven't seen any of them for a while now and haven't had a chance to tell them that I'm working hard every day on this diary, but I don't think I really need to tell them what I'm up to, however much it bothers me that they might think me stupid and idle, not to mention an old fool, an idle retiree or still worse: a lawyer who was dismissed because he wasn't up to the job and hit the bottle too hard. Let them think what they like. It's enough for me to love them and feel proud of them, and also to know—this is rather more prosaic, but I have to include it—that they could help me out financially if I were to split with their mother and needed their help. When they were little—when their tender ages required it—I spoiled them rotten, and Carmen was a perfect mother, affectionate, impeccable. I keep thinking about fatherhood now, and I can't deny that when we give life to another being, we should be conscious of the fact that we're also giving them death.

Do we give them death? If I were to rewrite "The Duel of Grimaces," that would be the son's gripe with his ventriloquist father. I'm already practicing putting myself in Walter's shoes in order to be better equipped to write that story. Not that I actually believe we do give our children death; I believe we give them life. And that's an idea, a conviction if you like, over which almost nothing can cast a shadow, apart from once—a while ago—when, as I strolled down to the port of Barcelona, I thought I saw—my imagination doubtless playing tricks on me—a shape floating in the water that came and went and that appeared to be—how can I put this clearly?—a dead monkey.

While I was imagining seeing this, I stood for quite a long time, asking myself if it really was a monkey and, if so, was it a whole monkey.

I just want you to explain one thing, the son would say in "The Duel of Grimaces," why did you tell me so early on, when I was only fifteen, that everything would end in death and that after death there was nothing? As I explained at the time, his father would say in reply, I couldn't bear to see that—just like a dog—you had no concept of death.

"But that was a terrible thing to do. Are you sure it wasn't because you were already wanting to see me dead and buried? And wasn't it true that you hated having a son and wanted to live your own life and have no paternal commitments?"

When he heard this, Walter would start to believe, there and then, that his son was a complete and utter monster, and begin to feel an urge to kill him. Strange though it may seem, his own son would have given him that idea, which is pretty much what Walter would say, although not in so many words:

"What's wrong? Are you so very delicate? You just have to put up with it. You are a being made for death."

And then his son would completely lose it.

"You're really getting on my nerves, you know. I'm a poet, and you, on the other hand, are a second-rate, out-of-work ventriloquist, a failure with a foul temper, full of resentment for all the ventriloquists who you sense are better than you. Because everything has to be centered on you, isn't that right? You're a complete egocentrist."

"You mean egocentric. No one would think you were a son of mine, you haven't even learned to speak properly. I'm beginning to suspect that you rather dislike the idea that you're mortal."

Shortly afterward, the insolent son and the "egocentrist" father would fall silent, at which point I would begin to feed in elements that would doubtless become central to the slender plotline of the ventriloquist's memoirs; one of those elements—which only appears to be an insignificant detail—would be the Javan sunshade, which, just as in Sánchez's novel, would turn out to be important because of its suggestion of criminality, but also perhaps because it would be useful, at various points in Walter's indirect autobiography, to have him simply wave it around and thus frighten away the ghosts roaming about in his mind.

I can see it now, the misanthrope Walter shooing away flies during his argument with his son and, tragically, blindly hitting out with the sunshade, thus signaling his real intention: to murder his chief enemy—himself.

What I see with utter clarity is the absolute need—if, one day, I do end up rewriting the story—to preserve intact the scene in which Sánchez describes the duel of grimaces between father and son. With that same clarity, I think I can also see the need to add to that scene a series of footnotes—one per grimace—in pure David Foster Wallace style: footnotes that would create a huge creative contrast between two powerful and totally contrasting styles (Schweblin and David Foster Wallace); footnotes capable of unleashing a perfect storm.

There's no point in denying that I adore the enormous, mad, limitless extravagance of Foster Wallace's obsessive footnotes. I see in them a kind of troubling, irrepressible impulse to keep on writing, to write until you've written everything, and to transform the world into one great perpetual commentary, with no final page.

That's why I'd love to parody or pay homage to the recalcitrant tone of those notes, and I'd do so by writing several long footnotes that would establish a direct link between Walter's duel with his son and an actual episode from the history of Polish literature: the face-duels held, in the winter of 1942, in Nazi-occupied Warsaw, in the houses, respectively, of Stanisław Witkiewicz and Bruno Schulz.

According to Jan Kott, it was common in both households, in the bedroom or the corridor, to see two people in face-to-face combat, each seeking the complete destruction of their opponent by coming up with a grimace so horrifying that no better counter-grimace was possible.

Kott explains that their faces were the best game of ping-pong at their disposal. He writes: "Strange sounds reached me from the next room. I opened the door a crack and found two geniuses of Polish literature kneeling opposite each other. They were banging their heads on the floor, and then, on the count of three, they raised their heads and mimicked each other, grimacing in the most sinister way. It was a duel of grimaces until the opponent had been completely wiped out, until a face was made against which there could be no counter-face."

My long footnotes—a duel of grimaces between Schweblin's Argentinian style and David Foster Wallace's more expansive style— would expound on whatever needed expounding upon, although, inevitably, my neighbor's novel would not emerge unscathed from such an intervention, which would be, at once, strange and amusing or perhaps tireless and tiring, or else just plain tiresome.

I said "strange and amusing," but perhaps it wouldn't be so very strange. You just have to remember what Foster Wallace once said, when he shed both light and enigma on the probable meaning of his inexhaustible glosses, explaining that they were almost like "a second voice in his head" (something in which I believe myself to be an expert).

I just know that I would have such fun writing those apparently endless footnotes; I would use impossibly long sentences, which, for all their exquisite style, would demand a huge effort on the part of the reader. I would so enjoy the infinite joke of those footnotes that I'd like to believe I wouldn't shy away from including more digressions than were strictly necessary, each apparently more unnecessary than the last, and almost all included out of sheer malice, because I would try to find the most convoluted way possible of fitting them in, that is, I'd try to be even more "ponderous" than usual in my attempt to experience the pleasurably scandalous impunity achieved by David Foster Wallace each time he lingers over his "very Germanic" footnotes; after all, Schopenhauer did say that the true national characteristic of the Germans was ponderousness.

I've always been fascinated by that German quality. More than that, I'd like to spend one day of my life, or at least part of a day, just being a German writer of deeply tedious prose, the most incredibly boring German writer ever, a German who would take real delight in the pleasure it would give him to write those boring, knotty sentences, in which one's memory, without any help at all, would, for five whole minutes, follow the lesson being taught, until, finally, at the end of that protracted Teutonic sentence, the meaning behind what is being said would appear like a lightning flash and the puzzle would be solved.

The motto of many German writers was always this: may heaven grant the reader patience. And now that I think about it, the same motto could also suit me, because I love the very idea of being able to live for just one day as a truly sleep-inducing German author. I also love the possibility that in my version of "The Duel of Grimaces," just when it seems that those footnotes would never end, they could come to an abrupt halt and leave the field open for the end of the story, a dénouement in which we would find the defeated son wandering aimlessly through dark, cheerless landscapes. The son, a dead man walking. Having lost the duel with his father. Grave fodder. A corpse already snug in his coffin. A corpse preparing for the cold of the long winter nights to come, for the terrible German nights that surely weigh heavier than lead: the endless nights now free from all excess and in which no one would lay chrysanthemums on his grave, and where, no longer able to hear, he wouldn't hear a single goddamned prayer.

32

Tidying up back issues of magazines this morning, I came across a Sunday supplement whose cover I recognized at once—Scarlett Johansson at a Zebda concert—but which I'd forgotten contained an interview with Sánchez. Banal questions and correspondingly banal answers. I felt a flicker of joy when the female interviewer asked if he had any intention of ever giving up writing. Sánchez said he found the question amusing, "because just an hour or so ago, in my local bookstore, I was told my work was going through a particularly good phase, and I found myself replying, speaking from the heart, that I was going to retire. My reaction reminded me of a time, back when I was twenty, and, standing in the last bar of the night, just before heading home, I told the old gang that I wasn't going to write anymore. But you don't write now, they reminded me. You see? I hadn't even begun to write and already I wanted to quit."

He must have enjoyed himself describing Walter's retirement from the stage in "The Whole Theater Laughs." Because Sánchez seemed to love parting gestures, farewells of all kinds. In the final story, where there is also a goodbye of sorts, we read about the ventriloquist's departure for distant Arabia: a journey both slow and beautiful, in search of the origin of oral storytelling, although in reality Walter is hiding the true motive behind his escape. He tries to cover it up, but the reader knows he's hiding something, because it's hard to believe that he's traveling to the Orient purely in the hope of finding there *the first voice*, the source from which all stories spring....

Every ventriloquist knows that if there's one thing that characterizes a voice, any voice—including *the first voice*—it's the knowledge that the voice will not last; it emerges, shines brightly only to fade again, consumed by its own brilliance. A voice has something in common with a falling star with none to see it. There is no voice that doesn't eventually burn out. You can recapture it, but you never truly find it again; to think otherwise is as naive as thinking that a time machine could carry us back to *the beginning of everything*.

You can imitate a voice, or repeat what a voice has said, and in that way prevent it from disappearing altogether, but it will no longer be *the* voice, nor will it say exactly what that voice said. Repetitions, versions, perversions, interpretations of what the extinguished voice said will inevitably produce distortions. Voices are the building blocks of literature, which, for me, is a way of keeping alive the flame of tales told around the fire since the dawn of time: a way of turning around the impossibility of accessing something that is lost by at least reconstructing it, even when we know that it doesn't exist and that the best we can hope for is an imitation.

In the afternoon, I went out for a while and, right outside Bar Tender, I literally bumped into Julio, who seemed half-asleep, as if he had just returned from some shameful escapade. He was so drunk that I came straight out and boldly asked him if Sánchez had a lover. He knew at once what I was getting at.

"What matters is the passionate energy behind the thought," he shot back.

"Oh, quit fooling around. Does Sánchez have a lover or not?"

"You mean you don't know? You know Ana Turner, don't you? Well, the old goat is crazy about her. Everybody knows they're an item. They don't hide it. You must be the only person left who hasn't caught on."

I froze—for want of a better word—in that stifling heat. On the one hand, I felt relieved, because my jealousy over Carmen was driving me to distraction. But on the other hand, I was deeply upset. Upset with Ana. Disappointed in her, for her extraordinary bad taste. Why is it that when a woman falls for someone else, we always think she's chosen a complete numbskull? What does that ass, that jerk, have that we don't? we ask ourselves.

Julio and I took a table outside Bar Tender, and he proceeded to prattle on about matters so utterly moronic that, for a few minutes, I didn't even listen to what he was saying. After a while, though, I began to pay attention to his murmurings—he was speaking in an ever quieter and more inflammatory whisper—and I did catch one comment in midsentence which I can't reproduce word for word, but a version of which I include here (duly blushing): "She, admired by so many, languishes in the evenings, a prisoner of her own mind, bound to a place, to a spuriously pleasant Mediterranean city, to an unremarkable bookstore, and to her single's apartment and the awful tedium of her years, bound to a tiny place, waiting for her lover to visit...."

It was his tone, above all, that irritated me, and also his frustrated-writer pretensions, his clumsy attempt—if I'd understood him correctly—to tell me cruelly and almost certainly mistakenly that the splendid Ana Turner lived a wretched life as a languishing prisoner of her own mind and of her lover.... Or perhaps he meant something else. It hardly mattered either way, because the really unbearable part was his pose as poète maudit. That and his outrageously bad literature, because all that stuff about Ana being "a languishing prisoner of her own mind" was enough to make me cringe.

That's why I was even more shocked when, suddenly, in almost insufferably hushed tones, he told me that he was the best writer in the world.

I decided it was high time I left Julio to his own devices. But beforehand, bursting with curiosity, I asked him if he had a job of some description.

"I don't want to fall in love with you," was his reply.

I chose to believe that he was merely trying to get to me; perhaps by now he really had had one too many. Given that reply of his, it seemed to me that the best thing to do—or even the proper thing—would be to start making my exit. But even then I held back, because I wanted to know what he had worked as before. He'd been a high school teacher for many years, he babbled, poking around in the pockets of his shabby old jacket, as if looking for a dog-end. They'd fired him, for some serious failure to comply with the authorities. Which authorities? I asked. He carried on talking as if he hadn't heard me. His sons had reproached him bitterly for getting fired, and his wife had left him. Now all of them—the losers, Julio stressed—lived in Binissalem, in Mallorca. They left him alone. He had no one in the world—he said this so loudly that the whole of Bar Tender turned to look at us, all that we needed was for them to burst out laughing—but he wasn't about to change, he said, he felt "lucid as hell," and he survived on tea and alcohol, which helped him to see that the future was his for the taking; one day he'd be a truly incredible poet and the whole world would then bow down to him; and I would be the first, he said, because I was—how could I deny it—far beneath him, a poor wretch whose curiosity had left him covered in oil stains. I couldn't be bothered to tell him I didn't understand that last comment. By the way, he said, you'd better give me some more. More what? Oil, he said, almost dribbling. And he asked me for money. I rebuked him for this, but, in response, he laid his head on my shoulder. I realized that, if I let him rest it there any longer, matters could get rather complicated, and soon we'd be the object of all kinds of nasty neighborhood gossip. I didn't want that, and still less did I want the echoes of such gossip to reach Ana Turner. But don't worry, he told me, you're not so very far beneath me, a couple of feet or so.

I thanked him for having had the delicacy to whisper as much, and managed to extricate myself from him and his greasy head, the whole weight of which had, for a few seconds, ended up slumped on my shoulder. In order to distance myself from the rest of his body, I pushed him gently to one side, but to no avail, because he didn't budge an inch, and we looked like two twins attached to the same umbilical cord. Or, worse still, if someone seeing us had paid us any serious attention, he or she might have thought that, in our unwitting reenactment of Sánchez's story, we had, momentarily, become a father fighting with his crazy son, or—which amounts to the same thing—two loners on a sad, bland, afternoon, poised to do battle in a duel of grimaces, sorehead versus nuthead.

33

In the popular imagination, the profession of ventriloquism is often linked with terror, which is why, when Sánchez turned Walter into a criminal, the book's few readers must have found the plotline perfectly normal, involving, as it did, a ventriloquist's dummy and a murder. Ventriloquists—or their dummies—are always frightening.

The first ventriloquist I ever saw, however, was a woman, not a man, and she wasn't scary at all, nor did she aim to be. Her name was Herta Frankel, and she was Austrian. Fleeing from Nazi barbarism and destruction, she had ended up in Barcelona in 1942 as part of a company called The Viennese, whose cast also included Artur Kaps, Franz Johan and Gustavo Re, all of whom remained in Barcelona for the rest of their lives and became very famous here.

In the early years of Televisión Española, Frankel—better known as "Señorita Herta"—was well-known as a ventriloquist on children's shows, working hand and string puppets. Her most famous puppet was an insolent poodle called Marilín, who made a point, whenever she appeared, of announcing to her mistress: "Señorita Herta, I don't like television." What Frankel intended to say with these words—or so it always seemed to me—was that Fate had played a nasty trick by having her work on something as crass and modern as television; she doubtless felt she belonged elsewhere, in some Central European cabaret or a variety theater back in her hometown.

The other ventriloquists I recall from my childhood were all horribly sinister. Among the most memorable was the one who appeared in "The Glass Eye," the best episode in Hitchcock's television series *Alfred Hitchcock Presents*. In "The Glass Eye," a dwarf reverses the usual roles by pretending to be the dummy, when he is, in fact, the ventriloquist manipulating a large and extremely handsome model. The dummy is so convincing that the dwarf manages to make an innocent young woman fall in love with it. According to legend, the actress and the dwarf and seven other actors in that episode all died in mysterious circumstances.

However, the most unforgettable of all those sinister ventriloquists was perhaps the one who appears in *The Great Gabbo*, Erich von Stroheim's deeply troubling movie. Gabbo is someone who works perfectly happily with his dummy Otto until he falls in love with a dancer who doesn't love him, and Otto has to give him advice—sometimes even on stage—on how to go about capturing the young woman's affections. The plot becomes increasingly sordid and unsettling, and is clearly going to end badly, in a crude, harsh underworld. It's highly likely—and I must try to confirm this one day—that Sánchez drew his inspiration from this movie when he came to write *Walter and His Problem*.

Among other stories connected to this universe of dummies and terror is one my father used to tell me about an Argentinian ventriloquist, a man who went by the rather odd name of Firulaiz. When his son was born, Firulaiz saw how his favorite dummy became hopelessly jealous, dejected, and dumb. One day, Firulaiz left the bedroom for a moment, and, while he was gone, the baby put the puppet's hand in his mouth as if it were a pacifier. Noticing that things had gone strangely quiet, Firulaiz burst into the room and saw that his son had turned completely purple, having been strangled by the dummy's hand, which had closed too tightly about the child's throat. In his despair, Firulaiz threw the papier-mâché puppet onto the fire, and, overwhelmed by what had happened, crouched over his son's dead body, weeping bitterly. It seems, though, that, at one point, he glanced over at the fire and saw, staring back at him from among the flames, the ceramic eyes of his dummy, still supported on its fragile wire frame. This final image appears to have driven Firulaiz permanently insane.

The most famous ventriloquist ever—at least according to the multivolume encyclopedia I inherited twenty years ago from my father and which, at the time, despite Carmen's fierce opposition, was a fine addition to my study—was probably Edgar Bergen, a Swede, but born in Chicago. When he was still only an adolescent, he began to go about accompanied by a puppet made for him by a carpenter friend: this puppet represented an Irish news vendor called Charlie McCarthy, who became his regular companion on stage. Bergen always wore a smart tailcoat, while his puppet wore an elegant monocle, a top hat, and a dress suit. Charlie was a mouthy creature and would lash out at all kinds of people, aiming his mordant comments at the powerful and the proletarian alike. In the mid-1940s, when Bergen was at the height of his success and popularity, he married Frances Westerman and they had a daughter, Candice, who went on to become a famous actress.

As soon as the child was born, Charlie McCarthy turned into an absolute monster. Years later, Candice Bergen told the whole traumatic story in a television interview, explaining how awful she felt when she became aware that her "wooden brother" was always insulting her and coming between her and her father. Charlie McCarthy had a bed in the same room as Candice—or perhaps it was the other way around, and Candice was put in spiteful little Charlie McCarthy's room—and she recalled how, as a girl, she'd had to get used to falling asleep at night with the puppet's inert body lying in the next bed—a pure corpse—staring up at the ceiling with grim fixity.

This morning, while I, too, was staring up at the ceiling—in this case in my study—I couldn't help wondering how I would go about rewriting "The Whole Theater Laughs" (if I ever do make up my mind to rewrite it). Why would I want to change the one story in the book that I really enjoyed? What's more, it contained a very attractive "exit stage left," a fascinatingly dramatic interruption to the life of the artist. I realized then that I only needed to change the Borges epigraph—which was completely inappropriate anyway, since in the story Borges's easily detectable style is nowhere to be found—and to replace it with one by Pierre Menard, that creative repeater par excellence: "There are as many Don Quixotes as there are readers of Don Quixote." Everything else could remain the same, without changing so much as a single comma.

And so I decided that, in Pierre Menard style, I would simply repeat the whole story, for it seemed to me that, as a reader, I, in some way, identified with the ventriloquist and his crime. I fancied acting the story out, even if only in the privacy of my study. I fancied creating an imaginary audience and repeating the touching moment when Walter sang, almost sobbing: "Don't marry her, she's already been kissed. Kissed by her lover, back when he loved her."

To sing that song well would, paradoxically, mean singing it as badly as Walter did, revealing the full tragedy of that poor humiliated man, who, in front of his Lisbon audience, desperately sang a song of jealousy and love, only, at the last moment, for his voice to crack, thus ending the song on a shrill wrong note, as tragic as it was ridiculous. To achieve this, I would have to think myself into the role of the ventriloquist, which I could probably do in the solitude of my study, imagining my nonexistent audience breaking into a loud, unanimous guffaw.

Since this very special performance would take place only in my head, and given that I'm free to do whatever I like in my own head, it would hardly come as a surprise if I nominated Ander Sánchez as the ideal candidate to share the murdered barber's fate.

I laughed when I thought of this, for it was what one might call the symbolic murder of the author. But he did, on balance, deserve it. It may have all happened in the dim and distant past, but there was no denying that the great writer had once been Carmen's boyfriend and had, as such, placed his grubby paws on her. And I certainly hadn't forgotten how, as I'd heard only a few days ago, he had captivated Ana Turner, and I found that even more unforgivable.

"Death to Sánchez, death to the author!" I cried out to myself in the solitude of my invented theater.

And I did, then, perform that third chapter before an imaginary audience. I acted in what you might call Petronius style, because all I did was bring to life what had previously been written—in this case, thirty years before—and, in a sense, what was written for me alone.

I began to identify so closely with Walter that I even found myself wondering whom I might one day hire as a hitman to murder the author and, with a single bullet, lay him low on some local street corner. The antagonistic nephew, I decided, would make the perfect hitman.

How easy it is sometimes to persuade someone else to commit a murder, I told myself, especially being safe in the knowledge that you would never feel guilty.

I said as much this morning, out loud, standing in the middle of my study:

"No one would ever think I was the culprit."

And the whole theater laughed, and asked me to repeat it.

No problem, I said, repetition is my strong point.

I felt so good that I even looked out of the window to see if, by chance, I might see the murdered Sánchez strolling by, alive and kicking. If I did, I would probably have shouted down to him:

"Hey, what do you think you're doing down there when I paid good money for someone to kill you? Can't you see you've been bumped off?"

To my surprise, Sánchez wasn't in the street at all, but in my study, eyeing me indignantly, reproachfully.

"Look, it isn't what it seems," I said to him, frightened. "It wasn't me. It's all a mistake. How can I possibly be guilty if all that is happening is fiction?"

"Good question," said Sánchez, "but that, as you know, is precisely what guilty men say."

[OSCOPE 33]

If I were to disappear and my diary were found by someone who didn't know me from Adam, but who, for whatever reason, had access to my computer, that person, should he take the trouble to read these pages, might get the idea that—given my fascination with falsification, and given that, for days, I concealed my true identity as a lawyer and pretended instead to be the owner of a construction company—I might also have been lying when I said I was a beginner at writing. However, that reader, that person, who would be quite within his rights to think I'm not a beginner, would not only be making a big mistake, he would also be grossly underestimating the long, hard hours I put in every day editing this text, a task made meaningful by the reward of seeing the progress I'm making in this diary, where I try out different paths each day, always eager to know more, always hoping to find out what I would write if I wrote: each day stitching together my imaginary world, weaving a structure that I may or may not finish; each day building a repertoire that I sense will be as finite and perpetual as any family lexicon: a diary on which I could work for a long time, making tiny changes to every passage, every sentence, repeating the whole thing in so many thousands of different ways that I would eventually exhaust my repertoire and find myself gazing out at the limits of the never-before-said or, rather, at the gates of the unsayable.

34

When, the day before yesterday, Julio repeated, again, that he was the best writer in the world, I was reminded of an unfinished tale by Dostoyevsky, which I'd read in an old anthology I lost years ago. In this story, a young Russian violinist from the provinces, who considers himself to be the greatest musician in the world, travels to Moscow because, he thinks, he has outgrown the town where he was born. In the capital he finds work in an orchestra, but is soon dismissed. He is hired by another, but again he gets fired, either because of his excessive vanity or sheer musical ineptitude—or perhaps several things at once. We never learn the exact reason why he keeps being rejected by the working world. No one appreciates his gift, apart from a poor, ailing maidservant who is so besotted with him that she doesn't dare to contradict him when he says that he's the greatest violinist in the world. The girl, unbeknown to her masters, lets him stay in her attic room, gives him money, what little money she has, so that he can continue his quest for recognition. When the poor maid can no longer finance his aimless drifting (and boasting), we see the "greatest violinist in the world" roaming Moscow's harsh winter streets, pausing before all the posters publicizing the city's musical program, posters that never feature the name of the best violinist in the world, the unsurpassable genius whom no one notices. This, thinks the violinist, is rank injustice. And there the story ends abruptly, or, rather, Dostoyevsky stops writing. Perhaps there was no need to go on. Perhaps everything had been said.

[OSCOPE 34]

I opened my inbox and found it filled with spam and mortifying messages from the bank: notifications about loan interest rates and commissions, and my expenditure over the course of this year. And in among all that digital mulch, I found a message from Damián, a close childhood friend who was in the middle of an intentionally solitary "journey of introspection"—that's what he called it—on the near-deserted island of Corvo, in the western Azores: a kind of experiment, living in a cabin Robinson Crusoe–style, fully immersing himself in the experience of being alone in deserted places. Corvo Island boasts fewer than four hundred inhabitants in winter. Damián's previous email had reached me from there: in it, he described his "primitive" lodgings and the complete absence of any social life, apart—he told me—from his contact with some adventurous botanists who had come to Damián's rescue when, shortly after he arrived, he broke a finger on his left hand.

In today's email he told me that he was on the island of Pico, in the central Azores, and that although the island had more inhabitants—some fourteen thousand—he was feeling far more alone than he had on Corvo. He described the volcano with its snowy peak, which took up the best part of Pico and was the tallest mountain in Portugal, and he also explained how the island had once been very economically robust, thanks to its magnificent vineyards. The next island on his list, and to which he was thinking of moving in a couple of days, was São Miguel, the largest in the archipelago, with more than a hundred thousand inhabitants.

His email set me thinking about desert islands and, after searching on Google for some witty, amusing comment on the subject to include in my response to my friend, I stumbled upon Gilles Deleuze's short text "Desert Islands," written in the fifties but not published in his lifetime, although he did include it in the bibliography of his book *Difference and Repetition*.

It had never occurred to me that while every island is unique, and different from all others, at the same time it is never alone, because it has to be framed in something like a series, in something which, paradoxically, is repeated in each island.

The reappearance of the theme of repetition led me to think more deeply about Deleuze's book and, in full research mode, I came across an observation by Marcelo Alé, which really hit the mark: "It is because there is no original that there is no copy, and, as a result, no repetition of the same."

A very good point, and yet, it didn't help me with my reply to Damián, who had no idea that I'd spent longer than a month mulling over the theme of repetition. Coming from me, Alé's comment would have unsettled him, so I opted, instead, to reply that if he felt more alone on Pico, with its larger population, than he did on Corvo, he had better prepare himself to feel even more alone on São Miguel. It's quite likely, I told him, that on São Miguel he'd find that he craved an island even more deserted than Corvo, Crusoe's island, for example, in order to finally stop feeling so alone.

Brilliant, came his almost instant reply.

That, I thought, is direct communication with desert islands.

35

In the fourth story, "Something in Mind," I would respect Sán-chez's decision to impose a Hemingwayesque stamp on it, indeed, Hemingway's Iceberg Theory is vital to the story, because the plot of "Something in Mind" is nothing without a hidden second narrative, the untold part of the story.

In the story, the two young party-animal protagonists are very much the worse for wear and both in love with the young woman they never mention, but with whom we deduce they are both obsessed—rivals in love. If they have *something in mind* throughout the whole story, it is that girl, hence the title.

In the three previous stories, the narrator was the ventriloquist, but the narrator of this fourth chapter is anonymous. If I were to rewrite "Something in Mind," that narrator would be a double of me—but it would never be me myself, because I consider that impossible: as far as I know, the person speaking (in a story) is not the person writing (in real life), and the person writing is not the person he is—he would be a duplicate Mac who would restrict himself to being faithful to the idea of telling a banal story like the one Sánchez gives us in "Something in Mind," but I would replace the plot of the two pathetic partygoers with the trivial conversation I had this morning with Julio, when I was unfortunate enough to meet him sitting outside Bar Tender. Everything we talked about then bordered either on the utterly futile or the absolutely inane, but it did reveal an unexpected characteristic in him. One that was unexpected and very dangerous.

This is what happened: I found Julio stationed outside Bar Tender, smoking a cigarette and apparently gazing off into the distance; my first reaction was to hope he hadn't seen me so that I could slip past unnoticed. But not only had he seen me, he even asked the time, as if time could be of any importance to a despicable bum like him. Was he hoping to pass himself off as a man of action? Some people dread others finding out that they not only have nothing to do, but they also exist in a state of utter vacuity.

Instead of telling him the time, I allowed myself to be carried away by a kind of instinctive meanness of spirit and I suggested that he kill his uncle. To justify this alarming proposition, I immediately invented an excuse and told him I was in need of inspiration for a story that I was thinking of writing, and had hoped to glimpse on his face, just for a moment, the look of an implacable murderer.

"You see," I said, backpedaling slightly, "for the novel I'm planning I need to imagine you as a hired assassin, but you mustn't go thinking I'm actually suggesting that you murder anyone. If you'd be so kind as to look at me as if you *were* an actual lone hitman, that would be quite enough, that would be really helpful."

"Basically," he said, "you're saying you need to believe in what you're about to write."

"I wanted to base the character of the hired killer on you, that's all."

"Do I look that hard? A contract killer? Shouldn't I at least earn something out of our contract?"

He then became hostile and smug, and I disliked him even more. To think that the first time I saw him, I'd been deluded enough to see in him a reincarnation of Rameau's nephew! He began by saying that he understood me perfectly—when he didn't understand a thing—and spoke to me rather pedantically about the "effect of verisimilitude," which, according to him, must first convince the author if it is to convince the reader. Yes, yes, he understood what I meant, and he repeated this several times. But, if I didn't mind, he'd very much like me to invite him to lunch and make him into a real hired assassin, or, even better, just pay him the fee. Otherwise, he said, he'd inform the police. Then he remembered that I'd wanted to interview his uncle for *La Vanguardia*, and, ever the wise guy, he wanted to know if he should kill him before or after the interview.

Then, out of nowhere, Julio shot me a look of profound contempt—I'd never seen him look at anyone like that before—after which he appeared to become even more self-absorbed than usual, with the unbearable demeanor of a man sunk in perpetual gloom. How relieved his wife and children must be in far away Binissalem, I thought. The two-faced creep. But why was he like that?

"What was *that* all about?" I asked bluntly.

"What do you mean?"

"I mean: what was that about? Are you even aware of the death-stare you just gave me? Because that really isn't normal behavior...."

When he realized, as he did, I think, that I was basically asking why he was such a total asshole, he tried to change tack and talk about the weather, mentioning the heat and then global warming. We really should be asking ourselves, he concluded, what's behind the extreme summer we're having.

"Why waste time thinking about what's behind it?" I asked, in an attempt to shut down this pointless conversation. "We just have to accept that it's a mystery, and one we're unlikely to solve. Besides, isn't that what our friend reality is like: inscrutable and chaotic? It's hot and it's no one's fault. Or do you think there's an Adjustment Bureau manipulating the weather too?"

"A what?"

At last, new avenues were opening up in this suffocating exchange about the heat, but just when I thought I was finally going to be able to tell him about the agents of Fate, he again brought up the tired old topic of the weather and spoke to me about the terrible heat wave in Paris in the summer of 2003 and about the afternoons he wasted at the bookstalls on Quai Voltaire, and about a nearby hothouse of a pet store, where even today, he said, you could still see cartloads of crazy capuchin monkeys wrangling over a piece of rotten banana....

Capuchins? I realized that I hadn't heard that word for fifty years. As a child, my mother once told me about the capuchins she'd seen in Brazil: monkeys who were far more sociable than chimpanzees and took turns speaking when they talked among themselves.

As the heat appeared to rise several degrees, Julio himself, with his wild gesticulations and his banal, unstoppable chatter, reminded me momentarily of a rather whiny capuchin monkey. All he lacked was a rotten banana in place of the chair he was sitting on.

He must have sensed that I'd already gotten his number and thoroughly disapproved, because he again changed the subject and fell back on his old hobbyhorse, his uncle's sterility as a writer, perhaps because he thought he'd be on safer ground. And there we were, trapped in what I thought was a scene of the utmost banality, when something happened that changed everything once and for all, because, almost out of nowhere, came the thing that had remained invisible up until then, like a silent background presence, the reality underlying all that apparently trivial chitchat.

The revelation arose as a consequence of a chance movement of Julio's mouth, which lasted, at most, a few fractions of a second, but long enough for me to capture the very essence of his being, or, rather—because that might sound rather pretentious—to capture exactly *the something in his mind* at that moment.

It was the merest twitch: his fleshy mouth opened and then closed, as if he were about to articulate a vowel or else say something that would require a great effort on his part. And for a few brief seconds, I could read precisely what was on his mind: he had focused all of his loathing for humanity on me; he wanted to see me crushed. This was, of course, irrational and capricious on his part, but his failed attempt to utter a single sound made me realize how much he hated me, perhaps because it bothered him that I was going to write a novel, or simply because he belonged to the tribe of those who think: since I'm never going to be happy, I don't want anyone else to be happy either, because that would really grate on my nerves.

It reminded me of a shitty trick played by a young poète maudit, who lived in Barcelona in the 1960s and spent his time discouraging his friends from writing. If he didn't have enough talent to create anything himself, he didn't want others to either. Now he lives saddled with debts and with women who once admired his bad-boy ways.

And I thought: what I imagined to be Sánchez's haughtiness, eccentricity, perversity, and craziness was infinitely preferable to what we might call "petty, sordid malice," which, I believe, is pretty much the driving force behind Julio's poisonous moral ugliness.

Sometimes, strange though it may seem, all it takes for us to discover the unknown is the faintest curl of the lip, a tiny random gesture, the briefest flash of insight, and we discover it—as Rimbaud said—"not in some far-off terra incognita, but in the very heart of the present moment."

[OSCOPE 35]

It would have been so easy for the antagonistic nephew, in the face of his uncle's brilliance, simply to have remained patient, and—like the husband in Ray Bradbury's "The Picasso Summer"—waited for the tide to come in. In that story, an American couple go on holiday to a seaside resort, somewhere between France and Spain. It's the husband's idea, because he knows Picasso lives there and sometimes visits the beach. He doesn't actually think he'll see the artist, but he wants to at least breathe the same air as him. After lunch, while his wife chooses to stay in and rest, he decides to go for a walk. He strolls down to the beach and along the shore. He spots another man walking ahead of him. He can see him from behind: he's an old man, very tanned, almost naked, and completely bald. In one hand he carries a stick, and every now and then he bends down and draws something in the sand. The husband follows him and his drawings, which are all of fish and flora from the sea. Then Picasso walks off into the distance, getting smaller and smaller until he disappears. The husband crouches beside the drawings and waits. He waits until the tide has erased everything and the sand is smooth once again.

36

Books that leave their mark forever. 53 Days, for example, George Perec's unfinished novel. Indeed, I think it has been surreptitiously influencing this apprentice's diary. Well, I don't so much think it has, I'm now certain of its influence, although that thought only just occurred to me today. I particularly love the title of Perec's book, a direct reference to the number of days Stendhal took to dictate his masterpiece, *The Charterhouse of Parma*.

Perec didn't get the chance to finish his book. He died in the middle of writing it. But perhaps that needs some qualification. Ever since I read *53 Days* a year ago, I've been trying to make sense of the strange fact that the manuscript, which ended up in the hands of his fellow Oulipians, Harry Mathews and Jacques Roubaud, was found practically ready to go to the printers. How do we explain that? The manuscript comprised two separate sections, the second of which explored alternative solutions to the detective story narrated in the first, even modifying the story itself. These two sections are followed by a series of curious "Notes on the Text," which, as well as offering a new twist on the modifications already made to the first part, seem to reveal the following: Perec's novel was *not* prematurely interrupted by the author's death, thus rendering it unfinished; instead, Perec had finished the novel some time prior to his death, but in order to be considered truly complete, it required a problem as momentous as death—which Perec had already incorporated into the text itself—even if, on the face of it, the book appeared interrupted and incomplete.

A "finished" and perfectly thought-out novel, therefore, which Perec planned down to the very last detail, including the final interruption.

Every time I go back to *53 Days*, I want to believe that Perec really wrote it in order to have a laugh at Death's expense. For isn't he mocking arrogant Death by concealing the fact that he's been playing with him all along and allowing the poor vain creature to believe that it was him and his ridiculous scythe that brought *53 Days* to an untimely end?

37

If I were to rewrite "An Old Married Couple," a story whose style is reminiscent of almost anyone else in the history of world literature *except* Raymond Carver, I would very likely replace the epigraph with a quote from another American writer, Ben Hecht, whose style is more suited to the story of Baresi and Pirelli. Unless, of course, I decide—in homage to Nietzsche's ridiculous "Maupassant, a true Roman"—to keep the Carver epigraph, leaving the story with two epigraphs, neither of which bears any relation to the plot.

If I did decide to change the epigraph, I would take one from Hecht's story "The Rival Dummy," the basis for Erich von Stroheim's *The Great Gabbo*.

Ben Hecht was a brilliant short-story writer and an extraordinary screenwriter, whose style, as legend would have it, emerged out of what he had learned from his fruitful early reading of Mallarmé—yes, that most difficult of French poets—although this was an influence that gradually waned and is barely noticeable in Hecht's best-known book, *I Hate Actors!*

The epigraph by Hecht would be the rather shocking line I remember from the von Stroheim movie.

"Little Otto is the only human thing about you."

These words were spoken by Mary, the Great Gabbo's assistant, who was very much in love with him, even though she couldn't understand why the ventriloquist had to say everything through his dummy Otto.

This is why she ends up speaking those terrible words to the Great Gabbo—who is anything but great.

When I saw the movie, I was so struck by those words that they stayed with me, perhaps because I would hate anyone ever to say the same about me. And who knows, maybe they were the indirect cause of last night's nightmare that featured Otto, or, rather, the one particular scene from the movie in which Mary speaks those words. The rarefied atmosphere of my nightmare was the same as in the movie, but instead of Mary it was Carmen standing in the middle of the amorphous space separating dressing room from stage and saying:

"The thing is, it's just really weird you writing Ander's novel."

"What's even weirder," I retorted, "is you talking to me as if you were talking to yourself. Are you a ventriloquist now?"

Still dazzled by a spotlight, I looked at her more closely and saw that she had indeed become a ventriloquist, complete with impeccable black tuxedo, and I was her dummy, her servant and puppet, and I was also—let it be said—the only human thing about her.

&

If I were to rewrite "An Old Married Couple," I would keep the bare bones of the story, but not the conversation between Baresi and Pirelli at the bar of a hotel in Basel. Because I wouldn't make those two gentlemen the embodiment of the tense relationship between reality and fiction, but between the simple and the complex in literature. The simple, in this case, would be the conventional, which takes no narrative risks. The complex would be the experimental, which presents difficulties for the average reader and can become extremely convoluted, as was the case, years ago, with the *nouveau roman*, and as is still the case with the so-called School of Difficult Writing, a trend that suggests we should see all significant developments in our cosmic history as leaps upward to ever higher levels of complexity.

Among the representatives of the *nouveau roman*—whom I read at the time with interest and a serene belief that I understood it all—were Nathalie Sarraute and Alain Robbe-Grillet. The writers of the School of Difficult Writing whom I found most interesting were David Markson and William Gaddis. This latter movement is still alive and well, full of authors who, without actively seeking consensus, share the idea that the narrative is a process with no end point, no destination. And I couldn't agree more. On the other hand, its departure point is clearly the deliberate abandonment of the traditional ideas on which the concept of the novel is built. The aim is to create a whole program of renewal for the genre of the novel, a transformation in line with the need to give the novel a form that fits with our current historical circumstances. Throughout my life,

I have felt a great deal of empathy— sometimes more intensely than others—with that now old-fashioned American school that never denied that it was still possible to write great novels, but always acknowledged that the problem for novelists—not only now, but a century ago—is how to avoid simply continuing with the genre as it emerged in the nineteenth century and, instead, find new possibilities.

I remember Mathieu Zero saying that the novel is a medium that needs to adapt itself to the essential ambiguity of reality. In order to place "An Old Married Couple" within that tendency, I would keep in mind what one of the theoreticians of the School of Difficult Writing once said, someone whose name I've forgotten, but who I referred to as Zero at the beginning of this paragraph. Yes, I think it was Zero himself who called for the modern novel to achieve the same level of complexity as modern music and contemporary art. And he took as an example the Beatles, who, when they released *Sgt. Pepper's Lonely Hearts Club Band*, were criticized for suddenly introducing so much complexity into their songs. According to Zero, if the Beatles had stuck to their initially simple style, they probably wouldn't be the cultural icon they are now. And given that even their older fans applauded this evolution, he wondered why literary authors don't allow themselves to do the same as pop musicians.

Of course, were I ever to place "An Old Married Couple" within that now outdated literary fad for difficulty, I would need to gain a lot more experience as a writer, something that would take time, always assuming I ever do acquire the necessary experience.

If, one day, one distant day, I felt capable of rewriting "An Old Married Couple," I would keep the bare bones, but I would transform it into a comic piece of "written theater." The simple (Baresi) would converse with the complex (Pirelli). While Baresi would tend to a simplicity that was as astonishing as it was, occasionally, touching, Pirelli, for his part, would provide nothing but healthy doses of complexity. Baresi would be all too comprehensible, while Pirelli would try to make everything as infernally complicated as he could and find himself permanently conspiring against the poor simpler-than-simple gentleman sitting beside him at the bar.

The play would be profoundly comic and grotesque, because it would be clear that the author was as ignorant of experimental literature as he was incapable of parodying, in the most tedious, meaningless way, what he, in dull, pedestrian fashion, believed to be a story from the School of Difficult Writing transposed to the stage, when, in fact, it barely constituted a feeble example of the theater of the absurd.

Some readers would be in stitches from the very first scene, because, bathed in a light reminiscent of a Hopper interior and on a stage bereft of all human movement, two static figures, Baresi and Pirelli, would be visible leaning on the bar of a hotel in Basel, near a window through whose half-drawn curtains a neon sign could be seen changing from red to violet and illuminating a few sheets of dull white paper lying on the bar. Now you might imagine those sheets to contain the dialogue about to take place between those two motionless gentlemen, each with a very different role to play: one of them rooted in the world of the simple in terms of narrative, and the other in the world of the complex. But that is only how things appear, because there's nothing as yet written on those sheets of paper—hence their dull white appearance—and the two unmoving characters are simply preparing themselves to move as soon as they receive instructions from the prompter.

However, the prompter—someone who has traditionally been there to help or direct the actors when they forget their lines or make a wrong move—would not be a person at all. It would become clear at once that the text of the dialogue—basically an exchange of Baresi and Pirelli's respective experiences of love cut short—would be dictated from offstage and would reach them via the constant drip-drip of water falling onto a piece of oilcloth placed beneath a leaky but otherwise inconspicuous radiator in one corner of the bar. That dripping would replace the usual figure of the prompter. This would not only provoke gales of laughter, it would be the drop that made the cup of the absurd run over. And things would only become more ridiculous when it was revealed that the leaky radiator was in reality a backstage computer making the drops of water appear to be dictating the whole dialogue between the simple (Baresi) and the complex (Pirelli); the computer would be playing a hugely important role in the play, because its hard drive contained a complete ethnographic document capable of summing up our entire age with all sorts of signs and details.

Everything would spring from that initial frozen snapshot—Baresi and Pirelli both motionless and preparing themselves to perform that erroneous, grotesque parody of Difficult Literature—and there would be no hint of the hidden aggression that would erupt later on, toward the end.

There would have been violence inflicted by Pirelli, with entirely base intentions, in his eagerness to rape Baresi, who would end up simply and meekly accepting the gift of the Java sunshade, going up to Pirelli's room, and allowing himself to be penetrated with undisguised glee by a completely off-his-head Pirelli, who, after the act, still had enough breath left to inform his poor, shafted friend—in the purest, discursive, most casual fashion—of the complexity of existence and of the many and various uses of a sunshade, as well as the many and various types of marital relationships, which—as Pirelli would say in a voice that was at once weary and euphoric— "have existed, do exist, and, believe me, Baresi, trust me when I say this, will exist, you just wait and see."

> *Editor's note:* I feel I must intervene here, because that notorious old married couple—fiction and reality—was waiting for me this afternoon on the porch when, after pausing in my revision of Mac's diary, I drank two espressos one after the other and, under their caffeinated influence, began reading Paul Klee's notebook about his journey to Tunisia. He went to North Africa in 1914, in order to both paint and discover new places, in the company of

another great painter, his friend and rival, August Macke. They spent their days there eating and drinking. What I gleaned from my reading was that Klee's favorite color was orange. And I particularly remember this sentence: "Here, too, the vulgar reigns supreme, although that can probably be put down to European influence."

Only when I reached the end of Klee's notebook did I discover that it also contains the travel diary of August Macke, although this must have been apocryphal, given that Macke died in the Great War, shortly after returning from Tunisia, and he left no African diary.

In Macke's notebook—which, as I found out later, had, in fact, been written by Barry Gifford, who supplanted him—certain episodes described by Klee are modified or corrected. And a curious thing happens, a phenomenon I was thinking about just last week. If Mac ever carried out his "remake" of Walter's memoirs, would it end up seeming more authentic than Sánchez's original? Something similar happens in the book I read today. Macke's diary seems more credible and truer to life than Klee's, perhaps because the latter only tells us what he would like to have happened, whereas in Macke's diary everything seems very real, as if it had actually been *lived*. I found Macke's diary far more amusing too. "My irrational dislike of Klee begins with his pipe," he writes. And elsewhere: "At supper, Louis and Paul ate like pigs, but I outdid them both."

38

At noon, having, hours before, returned in my mind to the distant past, I wound up feeling utterly exhausted and writing out—thirty times, with spaces in between them—the nine letters of the word

"Wakefield," writing them in a meticulous hand on a sheet of graph paper, and then copying out, also thirty times and on the same page, immediately on top of what I'd just written, the nineteen letters—four of them capitals—of the title "He Who Absents Himself."

The apotheosis of repetition. Words written on words written on top of more words. It's begun to look like the work of performance artist Tim Youd, who types up classic novels on a typewriter, but without ever changing the sheet of paper, so the transcription of the novel ends up as "a sheet of paper saturated with ink."

I was engrossed in this very task of saturating a sheet of paper with ink when Carmen arrived home from work. Believing that I couldn't see her, she chuckled to herself. I couldn't resist asking her why she was so chipper.

"Because I see that I've come home in time to give you a hand," she replied. "I've always wanted to help, but you don't let me. You're making a fine mess of that piece of paper. I mean it, Mac Vives Vehins. I'm pleased for you and your blottings, your paintings, but, don't you think it's time you did something else?"

When she calls me by my full name, it never fails: Carmen thinks I'm a lost soul. And there's nothing to be done about it. I don't know how many times I've told her about my happy role as an apprentice writer, as novice diarist, and yet today I saw that she still thinks my cruel dismissal from the law practice has me locked in the grip of depression. And that's simply not the case, or at least it hasn't been for some time now. But she's stubborn and won't believe me. Thank goodness she doesn't know about my occasional flirtation with the fascinating topic of suicide, although I have no intention of going down that route myself. And how fortunate that she doesn't know about those times I entertain myself by weighing up the pros and cons of the two possibilities Kafka spoke of: either making myself or simply being infinitesimally small. And what a stroke of luck, too, that she's oblivious to those nights when I think dangerous thoughts, although I doubt mine are any different from those of other mortals familiar with the anxiety that comes from knowing oneself to be simultaneously both dead and alive.

39

> *What's next isn't the point.*
> —Bernard Malamud

In his final days, in early 1961, Hemingway—whose heroes had always remained so rough and tough and elegant in the face of heartbreak—traveled from the sanatorium to his house in Ketchum, Idaho. In an attempt to lift his spirits, his friends reminded him that he'd been asked to contribute a note to a book intended as a gift for the recently inaugurated president, John F. Kennedy. After laboring for hours, he had produced nothing, not a word, and all he could write was: "No, I can't. I'm done with that." He'd suspected as much for some time and now his suspicions were confirmed. He was finished.

As for elegance in the face of heartbreak, it can't be said that he showed much sign of it in his final days. Fragrant with the alcohol and the deadly nicotine of his life, he decided one morning to wake everyone up with the sound of the gunshot signaling his divorce from life and literature.

"Last week he tried to commit suicide," says an old waiter of a customer in what is arguably Hemingway's best story, "A Clean, Well-Lighted Place."

And when Mac, the younger waiter, asks his older colleague why, he receives this reply:

"He was in despair."

A heartbroken Hemingway had left Cuba for a house in Ketchum, which was clearly a house made for killing yourself in. You only have to see a photo of the place. One Sunday morning, he got up very early. While his wife was still sleeping, he found the key to the storage room where the guns were kept, loaded a twelve-gauge shotgun that he'd used to shoot pigeons, put the barrel to his head, and fired. Paradoxically, the work he left behind—inhabited by all kinds of heroes who prove stoic in the face of adversity—has had an influence beyond literature; because even the worst Hemingway story is a reminder that in order to commit yourself to literature, you first have to commit yourself to life.

40

What would I modify in "A Long Betrayal," that short story in which a certain Mr. Basi—although everything seems to indicate that Basi is Baresi, Walter's father—has a monumental mix-up with a grave? First of all, I would leave Malamud's epigraph as it is, a heartfelt tribute to his "What's next isn't the point"; but I'd describe the episode in a Kafkaesque way, setting out the story's hidden narrative plainly and clearly while, conversely, obfuscating the main narrative until it became the most enigmatic story in the world.

When the time comes, writing in the clearest possible way, I will describe the lush, green grass that grows inside the grave where Basi buried his wife, and also the parched turf growing on the outside, around the grave. And I will then relate, in the most convoluted way, the interminable bureaucratic red tape that Basi's wife's lover had to cut through in order to obtain a judicial order to transfer the deceased's remains to another grave.

I wouldn't change a thing about sad old Basi. I'd leave him exactly as he appears in the original story: as the likely father of Walter and, as such, as the man from whom our ventriloquist inherited the Java sunshade. When his turn comes to do the paperwork for his wife's exhumation, I will meticulously document every last process and procedure. And I will devote an inordinate amount of time to describing the tedious pacing of the bureaucrats along the galleries and pavilions of the vast, sordid Palace of Justice.

Life, seen through the lens of the most cumbersome administrative procedures, will be—as, indeed, it already is—brutally depressing, a hostile labyrinth of interminable galleries and pavilions, red-taped up to the eyeballs; endless rows of offices and millions of corridors linking together seemingly countless galleries, each with its own sinister distinguishing feature, except perhaps the

183

remote "Chamber of Writing for the Unemployed," where a group of clerks, in their most elegant hand, will copy out addresses and redirect undelivered mail. Duplicating texts, transcribing texts ... these men and women will appear to belong to another time and will prevent that knot of galleries and pavilions from being even more depressing.

But few people, despite their constant toing and froing along those cold corridors, will know how to find that final bastion of life as it once was, that bastion that gathers together all the lost and forgotten things, all those things that are still apt—precariously so, but nonetheless apt—to remind us that there was once a time, a bygone age, in which writing moved within parameters quite different from those in which it moves today.

As I tell myself all of this, I think I glimpse one of the clerks—tucked away in the most hidden corner of the remotest gallery and having finished his work—write down some words on one of the pages of a stack of one hundred and three loose sheets, which, it seems, no one has been able to bind together due to a lack of resources:

"No, I can't. I'm done with that."

41

This morning, in the middle of a trivial conversation with my friend Ligia in the watchmaker's store owned by the Ferré brothers, I happened to find out that, the other day, Julio—flirtatiously and apropos of nothing—said to Ligia, with a confidence she found surprising in such a shabby individual: "When you learn of my death, that will be my moment of triumph! You will never have loved me so much, and I will never have occupied so much space in your life."

Ligia mentioned this to Delia, Sánchez's wife, who was utterly astonished. Her husband, she said, has no nephews.

"Are you sure, Delia?"

"Positive."

Early this afternoon, I tried rewriting "Carmen," but managed only a fragment that I will probably insert toward the end of the story. I pretended to myself that I wasn't in the least surprised to have written it, but, actually, I could have burst with happiness:

"She was still as beautiful as ever, but had spent far too much time—a whole decade—traipsing off to pointless parties, dancing to rock music with idiotic fury, sometimes swaying back and forth on her powerful legs, keeping hold of her spent cigarette until she found an ashtray, and then, without missing a beat, stubbing it out. She was still as beautiful as ever, but she'd wasted the best years of her life. Nevertheless, most of her charms were still intact, especially her nonchalant gait. There was something odd, though, about her black suit, perhaps because she'd been wearing the same one for four years, not to mention the tattered silk stockings. In the holes in those stockings—which apparently had the same power to read the future as coffee grounds—one could see that, in the future, some sad hick would fall in love with poor Carmen and she would marry him, and, two years after the wedding, he would die, his body bloated with the rat poison he'd swallowed."

I didn't get beyond this fragment, but I was aware of the leap I'd made, because, for the first time, I wasn't writing in order to rewrite, but I was going a stage further. Well, I thought, still astonished at my own prowess, you have to start somewhere. But the real surprise came when I realized that actually writing something meant finding out what it felt like to write a fictional fragment rather than a diary fragment. And it almost makes me laugh to say this, but I am, of course, going to say it anyway: it feels exactly the same in both cases. Really? Yes, the same. This only confirms that, as Nathalie Sarraute said, writing is trying to find out what we would write if we wrote. Because writing, real writing, is something we will never do. That's why I felt exactly the same as if I'd merely been speculating and writing about how I would write about something if I did write about it.

We didn't write to fill a sheet of paper with symbols, but to know, or rather *to try to know*. It's a matter of simply creating. And, contrary to what some frustrated haters of creativity think, in order to take on these imaginative challenges, you don't have to renounce humility. Creativity is one's intellect having fun.

In my own case, *trying to know* has accustomed me—during the writing of this diary—to the charm of the obscure, and, day by day, I've become a contented reader, who sometimes enjoys the invisible, the veiled, the clouded, the secret, and who sometimes even likes to powder his face with gray talc in order to seem even grayer in the eyes of other people, were that possible.

&

I wake up feeling confused and retreat here to note down the one thing I can remember from the end of the nightmare, in which someone kept repeating over and over:

"Look, in the original first edition, *Moby Dick* had twenty-five pages of epigrams."

I decide to find out if this extraordinary fact can be true, and when I discover that it is, I stand frozen to the spot, as if I'd been parachuted into Greenland. I probably did know it once and had forgotten. And then I laugh just to think how worried I was that I'd overdone the epigraphs.

42

I took a long stroll around the neighborhood, trying to find out if anything was going on between Carmen and Sánchez, despite finally feeling sure that there wasn't.

And yet, I set myself this task because, notwithstanding the absurdity of carrying out such an unnecessary investigation, and notwithstanding the implicit danger—being seen as a cuckold or a madman—I reckoned it would be time well spent if I could come away with a good tale to replace Sánchez's stupid story, "Carmen."

After all, I told myself, you have to be prepared to take risks if you want to find a good story. Every writer knows this, just as he or she knows that every story runs the risk of turning out to be completely meaningless; and yet without that risk, it would be nothing at all.

I'll pause there a moment to include a detail I know will please the diary itself: when I speak of a "writer," I tend, for reasons unknown to me, to imagine a man removing his scarf and gloves, remarking on the snow to his pet bird, rubbing his hands together, smoothing his hair, hanging up his overcoat, and then settling down to dare all.

If he doesn't dare all, he will never be a writer.

Over the years, that is the most enduring image I have of "the writer," probably a result of my seeing, in the late 1960s, Jean-Pierre Melville's movie *Le Samouraï*, in which a hitman lives in the most complete and utter solitude. The image has stuck. A lone man and a bird, possibly some kind of parrot, I can't quite remember. The whole scene is imbued with the bitterest of solitudes, but—for reasons that escape me, perhaps it's the gloves and the man's arrival home—it has always seemed rather cozy.

The writer as hitman. That could explain why, the other day, when I saw the bogus nephew—in his role as undiscovered talent and as-yet-unrecognized-best-in-the-world—I offered him the chance to become a contract killer.

I set off on a long walk around the neighborhood in search of a story that would fit well with the fragment of "Carmen" I'd already written and of which I secretly felt so proud: "She was still as beautiful as ever, but had spent far too much time …"

I set off convinced that it wouldn't prove very difficult to find things to blend in with that brief passage. Whatever happened, it would be enough to paint a portrait of the present-day Carmen, as seen by the locals.

I set off, fully aware that I was taking a gamble, but aware too that this was the best thing to do, daring to take a risk and becoming a provocateur of stories, seeking them out on my patrols of Coyote, during which I could remove my imaginary scarf and gloves and observe the lay of the land down there on the street, all the while asking my bizarre question.

First, I went to interrogate the clerk in Carson's patisserie, but on my way, as I passed the ATM in Villaroel, I came across the beggar with the fair, curly hair, whom I'd met the other day dragging along a supermarket cart and who had rejected my offer of more money. The door to the ATM place stood open, and there he was, lying on some sheets of cardboard, draped in blankets (at the height of summer too!). As soon as he saw me, he asked with exquisite politeness if I could possibly spare any change. I again had the feeling that we'd known each other in the past, possibly because of the familiar way in which he always addressed me. Do I perhaps see in him a kind of amiable version of the antagonistic Julio, the obverse of the bogus nephew, and is that the reason I like him better with each encounter? I gave him three euros, and he advised me to give him less next time.

"Don't be so extravagant," he said.

He seems more concerned about my welfare than anyone else at the moment, I thought. And I thought, too, that this ghostly beggar could easily have come straight out of that Ana María Matute piece in which the short story is described as having an old vagabond heart and how, after wandering into town and telling its tale, it withdraws, but always leaves its mark in the form of unforgettable memories.

"Don't be so extravagant," I repeated to myself, uncertain as to whether what I'd heard was laughable or rather touching, the gesture of someone worried about my finances, which, contrary to appearances, were in a very precarious state.

As I turned the corner, on my way to the patisserie, I met a very old tramp whom I'd never seen before and who was clearly mad. He was singing, which rather took me by surprise and made me think that you never hear anyone singing these days, not even in the inner courtyards of apartment blocks around the neighborhood. When I was a child, singing was a deep-seated tradition in Barcelona, and whether that made the city a happier, more spontaneous place, I don't know, but people definitely sang. Tramps form part of another very special tradition, since the modern hero of Barcelona is a tramp—the architect Gaudí—who was rather despised in his day, his clothes the object of all kinds of mocking comments. The city's great genius was run down and killed by a tram and, because of his ragged appearance, he was mistaken for a tramp, so much so that the tram driver merely got out, removed the body from the track, and continued on his way, and not a single passerby went to help the man who is now the city's great hero. Needless to say, the secret, unconscious reason why Barcelona remains such a fascinating place to all its visitors is the spirit of that tramp, the most brilliant tramp the city has ever produced.

I finally arrived at the patisserie, where I carried out my first interrogation. After that, I kept on asking questions and digging around, although, in most cases, I avoided doing so too directly. Indeed, I sometimes asked in such a circuitous way that I didn't even seem to be asking a question. Rather than the whole neighborhood thinking me crazy, I'm sure they simply presumed I was letting it all hang out for a day, throwing some kind of private party to mark my forty years in Coyote.

The point is that, in the end, I managed to question—or perhaps merely bamboozle—Carmen's baker friend, the crazy flower seller (a real character), the couple who run the tobacconist's, Piera the barber, Ligia, Julián (of Bar Tender), the Ferré brothers, the news vendor's dimwitted stand-in (for one day only), the lawyer with whom I've been friends since we studied Law together, three local pharmacists, the taxi drivers at the stand in Calle Buenos Aires, the box office clerk at the Caligari....

No one knew anything about Carmen and Sánchez, no one had ever seen them together. I realized that this conspiracy of silence—these sealed lips—was of no use to me, because it didn't provide enough material for that possible story entitled "Carmen." And yet this was all there was, this suspiciously silent neighborhood. Clearly no one knew anything, and it would, of course, have been very odd if they had. Worse, almost everyone I questioned assumed I was joking, apart from the stand-in at the newspaper kiosk, who refused to speak to me because, he said, he didn't give information to the police.

The heat was unbearable, and I was annoyed that someone should have addressed me as "the police." In the end, I sat down outside Bar Congo and had a drink with my lawyer friend, whom I trust and often confide in, perhaps because I've known him since we were young. With his habitual good humor, he asked if I was trying to find out if it had all been a case of "imaginary giants," sleights of hand, fleeting moments of madness on my part, like the other day when I thought I might die in the tailor's tomb-like changing room.

"What has my wife got to do with the tailor?" I asked.

"Oh, don't tell me you suspect the tailor, too? You're terrible, Mac."

&
THE EFFECT OF A STORY

Shortly afterward, I arrived at Bar Tender, still feeling quite shaken up, because what I'd taken to be my friend's jokey remark in Bar Congo has turned out to be true. Carmen must be cheating on me with the tailor. The affair surely started months, possibly more than a year ago. Who would have thought I would ever write such a thing? I suddenly learned that, for some time now, I've been living *a long betrayal*.

This would explain various things; for example, why, the other day, I came so close to dying in that lousy tailor's changing room.

"Still out of work?" asked Julián from the other side of the bar.

I'd told him about my situation last month, and he'd clearly remembered.

"No, Julián, I'm working as a modifier now."

"A modifier of what?"

Julián was confused and so was I; then, at that precise moment, a nasty-looking fellow with a huge beard came in, a middle-aged man who said his name was Tarahumara, and who went from table to table begging in an unusually bullish manner. He appeared to be demanding what he considered his due. As soon as Julián heard the visitor's insolent tones, he shot out from behind the bar and hustled the man back out into the street. I didn't really follow what happened very closely, because I was still too troubled by what I'd just learned about Carmen. I had no idea what to do, although it seemed likely that I would have to follow in Walter's footsteps and head off to Arabia Felix, or somewhere similar. One thing is certain, I have never felt so lost, even though, to be honest, I've spent months unconsciously hoping Carmen was deceiving me so that I would then have a genuine reason to leave, to escape Wakefield-style.

Meanwhile, Julián was yelling at Tarahumara and trying to man-handle him out of the bar. Good grief, I thought, the lengths he's willing to go to just to protect his customers' peace and quiet.

The financial crisis is worsening by the day, and yet the television—which is controlled by the corrupt party currently in power—tells us that, economically speaking, everything's just fine again. And while they cynically feed us this load of crap, there's still no sign of an actual revolution. Nevertheless, revolution is stealthily creeping its way along Coyote's streets, where the crisis sticks to everything, impregnates everything, ensuring that nothing is as it was before, and urging the Tarahumaras of this world to hold out their hands and demand what's theirs.

43

THE VISIT TO THE MASTER

I was visiting the master, the fearsome Claramunt, and it felt like being in one of those bad dreams where you're strolling through a munitions dump carrying a lighted candle. It was clear, just from the way I was walking the streets of Dorm, that I'd embarked on the initial stage of a long journey of escape: as if I'd killed our local tailor and suddenly been transformed into a freshly blood-spattered Walter, and had no choice but to run away.

I knocked three times on the door of the rambling house, and it was opened by the man whose daily routine was his finest work. He cut a very sinister figure: he wore a dark corduroy suit and was wrapped in various scarves and shawls; he hadn't shaved for several days, and his one good eye was terrifying. Outside the house, enclosed in a fenced-off area, his furious dogs were jumping up and barking.

"I keep them for the noise," Claramunt said again, referring to the dogs.

But on that visit, as so often happens in dreams, I knew more than I could be expected to know. I knew, for example, that, despite appearances, this man was not as frightening as people said, and that his finest work was his daily routine. Was that detail so very important? Yes, it was, because in order to make a successful escape after committing my crime, I needed a routine as open and flexible as that of my admired master. Given that I'd killed the tailor, it was absolutely crucial that I leave myself plenty of time to make my getaway.

I sat down with Claramunt and spoke to him about his dogs, about the extraordinary noise they were making and what a useful job they did guarding the house. Claramunt fidgeted in his chair and said he was utterly opposed to any noise that might be deemed aggressive. This was clearly a contradiction, but I wasn't particularly shocked. It was followed by another contradiction, for Claramunt told me that he greatly admired the sudden sound, which, in Antiquity, must have broken the silence of the original chaos of the universe; and he added rather emphatically that he also admired the grandeur and portentousness of humanity's first sages, who invented—wherever it was they did invent it—the most extraordinary of all works of art: grammar. They must have been real marvels, he said, those gentlemen who created the different *parts of the sentence*, those who separated out and established the genders and cases of nouns, adjectives and pronouns, as well as the tenses and moods of verbs....

"When you write," said this grouchy and deadly boring Claramunt, "you should never tell yourself that you know what you're doing. You have to write from the place inside you that harbors your own personal chaos, for the first sentence must be born out of that place, as happened when the first meaning appeared: the Song of Solomon."

"Meaning? Solomon?"

I soon realized that the "Song of Solomon" could mean many things at once, but here it referred to the story that he imagined had sparked all subsequent oral narratives, that is, the world's first story. What you need to do, he said, is to continue writing your memoirs. I am, I said, albeit in an indirect way. And escape, Claramunt added, you must run, flee. I am, I said.

"Mac, Mac, Mac."

I didn't know what the voice of the dead man was telling me, but it was obviously warning me about something.

"Why have you got your head hunched down inside your collar?" Claramunt asked.

His voice sounded strange.

"Why are you doing that?" he asked again.

I had been aware for a while that there was something strange about his voice, but it had become far more obvious: his voice was identical to that of the dead man inside my brain.

Run as far as you can, Claramunt was telling me, leave the city behind you before they can accuse you. I asked him what he thought they could accuse me of. Run, he said, and become more people, speak to all the other people inside you. Escape, let no one persuade you that you won't one day be all the voices in the world and, at last, become yourself by merging with the voices of everyone else.

Then I realized that my master didn't have the same voice as the dead man, he *was* the dead man.

"Mac, Mac, Mac."

44

To leave with just the clothes on my back, or to leave with the clothes on my back and a small leather satchel, Petronius-style, setting off to live out—for real—what I have written or read. The idea of simply leaving everything you own reminded me of the story my father used to tell about the occupation of a large estate during the Spanish Civil War. The owners had been hiding in the cellars of the house for a long time, until, finally, they managed to escape. One morning, after my father and the other soldiers had taken control of the estate, a soldier from his own army turned up. He said he was the brother of the estate owner and asked if he could have the small portrait in oils of his sister, which was hanging in the main bedroom. That soldier's request made my father ponder the meaning of property and how, when everything falls apart, we return to our home, and all we want to salvage is one small painting; nothing else matters.

Leaving with just the clothes on my back, and saving only a small volume by Charles Lamb containing his essay "On the Melancholy of Tailors," in which he speaks of a melancholy common among tailors, a fact that "few will venture to dispute," not even Piera, who, an hour ago, was cutting my hair while I was thinking about all this, about leaving home with only the clothes on my back, but including the "elaborately worked" death I always carry with me, the death stitched to my very self, as if it were—*as it is*—"my personal problem," my most personal problem.

Wasn't it Rilke who talked about each person having "his own personal death"—the supreme problem?

Even as I was thinking this, about leaving with just the clothes on my back, I got drawn into an article about last night's Sevilla-Barça match in Tbilisi. While I was thinking about "escaping in my nightshirt" and, at the same time, engrossed in that article, I became mesmerized by the small bottle of Floid hair tonic that Piera had suddenly produced as a finishing touch. The smell of that tonic has always reminded me of my grandfather, who was addicted to the stuff, and so I quickly turned the pages, simply to avoid that thought, and found myself in the Culture section, where I was surprised to find an article by Joan Leyva, which began by saying that Ander Sánchez, of course, needed no introduction, or perhaps he did: "... or no more than any other real person whose books we can read, whose every move we can follow online, and whose voice we can even hear. And yet it still seems necessary to describe him, because he is also an unreal person, constantly appearing and disappearing in the books he invents. His typical protagonist is someone who is there in order not to be there, rather like an exhalation that hangs in the air."

I laughed when I read "an exhalation that hangs in the air," because that really sums him up. An example: for years now, Sánchez has been going on about leaving Barcelona, but he always gives the impression that he's trying to disappear using the paradoxical method of staying put. Julio, on the other hand, never teased anyone with the idea of disappearing, and yet, for some days now, no one has seen hide nor hair of him. He's vanished from the neighborhood, his very shadow has melted away since his cover was blown. Who is he, then? Now that he's evaporated, we can't ask him. Perhaps our only hope of learning something about him is to read the unforgettable words of Daniele Del Giudice in *Wimbledon Stadium*: "Maybe he had noticed that he'd failed, but then he had always been a failure."

About an hour ago, I began hearing the sound of suitcases being trundled around in the apartment above the barber's shop: presumably the tenants moving out. It lasted a few seconds, and then I wondered if I was just imagining those noises in the attic of my brain, if it was me trundling around the suitcases of my own being.

"Mac, Mac, Mac."

The voice of the dead man was quick to put me right. The only thing you're trundling around, it said, is your indecision about whether or not to kill the tailor, but it really doesn't matter if you don't commit the perfect crime or if you don't commit a crime at all; if I were you, I'd get out all the same.

While I was listening to these words, I had the impression that, on the other side of the far wall in the barber's shop, there was a man sitting on the floor: he had long legs, was wearing a plain pair of boots, and his face oozed vile envy.

Had there been a small hole in the wall, I would have been able to see that poisonous man, who was always pretending he didn't mind not being one of life's creators, but who contaminated everything around him precisely because he wasn't a creator, and he did so by intervening directly in other people's lives with a kind of terrorism of negativity disguised as the critical spirit.

But perhaps it would be best if I just forgot about the man sitting on the floor. I was telling myself this on my way home, when I turned the corner at the Baltimore and saw a group of classic not-so-very-young-men, the kind who have as yet failed to find their place in society, all three sitting on the ground, legs outstretched. It seemed to me that, given their passive faces and their supine indolence, they clearly didn't belong to the stealthy revolution. They may have been unacknowledged geniuses, but they didn't appear to have the kind of energy which, if put to good use, could have formed the basis for a new movement in that area. They weren't, however, the same ones who had been with the antagonistic nephew the first time I saw him. They were so similar, though, that I almost asked if they'd any news of that terrorist of negativity, the vanished Julio. It only confirmed me in my belief, however, that the economic crisis seems to be filling up the neighborhood with great misunderstood geniuses.

"Run, Mac."

45

Why all this interest in Mars? It certainly doesn't interest me. But Carmen has always been crazy about such things. Not that she's alone in that, of course. Mars intrigues many a lost soul, because it has gravity, an atmosphere, and a water cycle. It's also older than the Earth, and might contain clues to the origin of life.

The origin of life! That should be of interest to me, too, given my fascination with the origin of stories. And that perhaps explains why, last night, I agreed to watch an old B movie about Martians with Carmen. First, naturally enough, I was tempted to ask her why she didn't watch it with that scumbag of a tailor and leave me to my own devices. In the end, though, I bit my tongue and decided to continue pretending that I knew nothing, thus gaining more time to ponder what decision to take, a decision I didn't want to ruin with some precipitate, hysterical reaction.

Filmed in 1954, *Killers from Space* is about a scientist whose work involves testing atomic bombs and who dies in an air accident only to be resuscitated by extraterrestrials who want him to work for them as a spy. We watched it while eating supper. I was feeling dreadful because I could see the tailor everywhere, even in my soup, which, appropriately enough, was cold. I tried my best to control myself, because there seemed no point in confronting her with her infidelity, still less unleashing a litany of devastating put-downs about the tailor.

We ate our supper in peace, and when the movie ended, we went into the kitchen to do the dishes. Carmen washed, and I dried. Everything seemed absolutely fine, as it always does when I decide to help with the housework. Yes, everything was going swimmingly, with no unpleasant surprises, until Carmen mentioned that volunteers could sign up for the Mars One Foundation, an organization that is planning to send humans to Mars by 2032 and to set up the first permanent settlement outside of Earth. They reckon, said Carmen, that it would take seven months to reach Mars, and once there, they would live in 540-square-foot tents and grow their own food. The peculiar thing about the journey was that it was one-way only, there would be no coming back: you signed up to go, knowing that you wouldn't return.

I didn't know whether to laugh or cry, the latter because Carmen was suggesting that she would happily sign up for that one-way trip. Just to check that I'd heard her correctly, I commented that surely no one in their right mind would ever volunteer to travel to another planet, knowing that he or she would never return to Earth.

"What do you mean 'in their right mind'?" she asked.

I saw that I was about to get into very deep water, potentially far more perilous than a three-hundred-foot-high tsunami on Mars.

"Escape, Mac," I heard the voice say.

I began drying the plates more quickly, not even looking at Carmen. She wasn't looking at me either, but then she suddenly broke the silence to say that she actually intended signing up for the Mars One Foundation. And she went on to explain that, while it might seem absurd to think they would accept someone her age as an aspiring astronaut, she'd discovered that it wasn't. It had, after all, been her lifelong dream, and she hoped I wouldn't stand in her way. Her eyes were bright with tears. No, I wouldn't stand in her way, I said, meanwhile quietly cursing her absurd determination to reassert herself as a woman of science and not of literature, as if, in order to reaffirm her personality, she had to be the polar opposite of me.

"You really wouldn't stand in my way?"

"No, I wouldn't."

And so as not to get madder still, I thought: I'm Walter, or perhaps I'm just trying to feel that I'm Walter, but there's really no reason why I should get so upset about my wife's spine-chilling idea. I even offered to finish the washing up on my own, an offer Carmen accepted with such alacrity that, only seconds later, I was alone in the kitchen, absolute master of my destiny. I wiped down the table and while I was in cleaning mode, I washed the kitchen floor too. I took the trash out onto the landing and, after hesitating for a moment, carried it down to the street. It was a very humid night and wondrously starry.

The apartment was in darkness when I came back. Carmen was in the bathroom. I stood outside the shower and told her that I wouldn't want her to think I was taking my revenge on her for her interplanetary plans, but I, too, had been considering setting off on a journey of no return. I wouldn't go to Mars, but somewhere nearer, to a village next to an oasis on the outskirts of a desert I'd recently discovered and which didn't appear to be on any map.

Carmen asked me what on earth I was talking about.

"I was just saying that I'm going to an as yet unknown desert, with no return ticket."

She didn't react at all, but asked why my voice sounded so different.

"Why are you talking in that funny voice, Mac?"

It was my voice, but it was gradually mutating to sound more and more like the personality I attributed to Walter; however, trying to explain that to Carmen would only have been asking for trouble.

"Well?" she said.

I could feel an argument brewing and did nothing to avoid it. Indeed, I said that if we were about to have an argument, would she mind if I took notes, so that I could write it up later and ponder what had happened?

"You want to take notes of us arguing?" she asked shrilly.

There followed a Martian tsunami.

46

35 is 53 backward, which made me think of *The Charterhouse of Parma* and the tiny number of days it took Stendhal to write his mighty novel. Thirty-five was also the age reached by Albert, the baker on the corner of Torroella, who died today. He didn't die because of the heat wave in the middle of the hottest summer recorded in Barcelona in more than a hundred years. What killed him was a night out on the town, one of those wild nights out that some people still indulge in: a stupid accident in the early hours, when he was on his way home; one G&T too many as he left the Imperatriz, the most dismal bar in Coyote.

I thought about the fragility of the strange and ultimately improbable air surrounding us and which we never think of as being made for us, and also about our intuitive sense of exile, of rootlessness, all those things that make us long to go home, as if that were still possible. Wallace Stevens, lawyer and poet, put it much better: "From this the poem springs: that we live in a place/That is not our own and, much more, not ourselves/And hard it is in spite of blazoned days."

Familiar faces from the neighborhood that, suddenly, I don't see anymore, nor do I even notice their absence, until, one day, months later, they resurface in my mind and I wonder what could have become of them, and feel sad to realize that the unavoidable has happened. They weren't even friends or even acquaintances, and yet, without my being aware of it, they were perhaps the very symbol of life.

Constant daily disappearances. The whole neighborhood is full of people who are here one day and gone the next. "What has become of those people who, just because I saw them day after day, became part of my life? Tomorrow I, too, will disappear from Rua da Prata, Rua dos Douradores, Rua dos Fanqueiros. Tomorrow I, too, will be someone who no longer walks these streets...." (Fernando Pessoa).

I realize that in the height of this Barcelona summer—which is now officially the hottest on record, and which some are erroneously calling an Indian summer—all my thoughts are cold.

47

THE NEIGHBOR

This morning: an intense writing session in my study. I set about describing a fleeting visit, incognito, to the city of Lisbon. A pause or stop en route to that small town near Évora, where, in some bar or other, I would probably overhear a group of customers engaged in a whispered conversation, a semisecret confab that I imagined would be about a young Jew and a dead horse. The description of that first phase of the journey, the Lisbon phase, took me ages, only to conclude that it had been a complete waste of time and that what I'd written was utter garbage and I would have to repeat the whole thing, which is why I decided to go for a walk and take a good long breather.

My head was pounding like a drum, as they say, and inside that drum were all kinds of shadows and labyrinths, as befitted my guise as Walter fleeing in his nightshirt. Indeed, so deeply immersed was

I in that escape, that I realized all it would take for me to become Walter would be for someone to treat me as if I really were him, which is exactly how I felt when I bumped into Sánchez in La Súbita, and he treated me just as if I were one of his pathetic characters.

I again had the impression that my neighbor was extremely vain. But why? Because of a certain popularity gained from his appearances on television? Because he had flirted with the idea of erasing himself from the map like Robert Walser when, in fact, Walser fell quiet because he followed certain complicated Swiss paths, and, above all, because he vanished into the interstices of his "micrograms," whereas Sánchez chose to do so by ostentatiously receiving prizes and other such vulgarities?

I realize that I'm talking as if I were his worst enemy. I obviously feel deeply humiliated by his treatment of me.

There came a point when I could stand it no longer, and I asked him about his character, Walter, about whether he'd named him after Robert Walser or after Walter Benjamin. Even though I assumed the name was probably a reference to some ventriloquist he'd known in the distant past, he didn't have to think very long before answering.

"No," he said with a broad smile, "I named him after Walter Marciano de Queirós, a Brazilian forward who played for Valencia and died very young in a car accident. When I was a boy, his face was the only one missing from my album of cigarette cards."

I would have laughed along with him if I hadn't felt that even the way he looked at me was somehow scornful, as if I were a slightly inferior being, perhaps because I never presume to be "someone" and I take pleasure in being restrained and humble, keeping strictly to what I've been learning about *modest knowledge*. This may have confused him and made him think I'm just a poor schmuck who used to be a lawyer and who is now a complete nobody.

"By the way," he said, "I've been told that some guy is passing himself off as my nephew and that you know him. How come?"

"How come what? How come I know him?"

"No, how come someone is claiming to be my nephew."

I realized then that, while I might have thought I knew Sánchez really well, he was, in fact, a complete stranger, and that my mistaken impression was due perhaps to having spent all those days steeped in the world of that early novel of his. He was looking at me with such a superior air that my natural reaction was to tell him that the bogus nephew had told me he'd spent weeks now rewriting *Walter and His Problem*.

The look he gave me was unforgettable, a mixture of shock and horror.

"Did I hear you right?" he said.

"Yes, apparently he's brought the whole plot right up to date, and there's one story in particular that he's really improved, the one called 'Carmen.' At least that's what he told me the last time I saw him. According to him, his version of the novel will be a vast improvement on Walter's memoirs."

"Not so fast," he said. "Could you repeat what you just said?"

"Oh, it was nothing, just that the relationship between repetition and literature is the central theme of your nephew's work."

"Hardly surprising given that he's writing a repeat of my book."

And he laughed. He almost split his sides, as people used to say.

He seemed so blithe and pleased with himself that I decided to rain on his parade.

"Your nephew is determined to show that no novel is ever complete, that no text can ever be considered to be finished."

"But he isn't my nephew. And that's just for starters," he said, looking me up and down, doubtless thinking exactly what I was thinking about him: you never really know your neighbor.

I explained that his bogus nephew believed that the history of literature was a kind of succession of works, a sequence of short-story collections, for example, that never stop in one place, which means that they're all susceptible to being given another turn of the screw.

Sánchez again roared with laughter, apparently having the time of his life. "I had no idea," he said, "that you spoke in such a weird way." I felt offended, but pretended not to care. I could have asked him if it was my discretion and humility that made him take me for a fool, but preferred to pretend that I hadn't even noticed his barely concealed contempt, although I did try to get a dig in somewhere.

"Your nephew wants revenge for something or other," I said. "The first time I saw him, I thought he was a clochard, then it seemed to me he was an intelligent clochard; eventually, though, I worked out that he was just a shady individual consumed with envy, that his real name is Pedro, and he works for another Pedro, the local tailor. Do you know him?"

"Who?"

"The tailor."

"Is there a local tailor?"

I told him that this chirpy little needleworker was paying the false nephew a lot of money on the pretext of having him create a free version of Walter's memoirs, his real aim being to get him to make radical changes to the story entitled "Carmen," which was the only story the tailor really cared about.

"And what has that got to do with me?" asked Sánchez, again smiling broadly.

"It seems he wants to avenge himself, through your nephew, for the affair you once had with the real Carmen."

Even that didn't wipe the smile off his face. On the contrary, he laughed even louder.

"So the tailor is her lover?" he concluded.

Whether intentionally or not, this question made me see myself as I really was: a duped husband. What's more, I'd brought it on myself. There I was thinking I was being so clever, when really I'd landed myself in another fine mess.

The most unbearable part was that Sánchez was still greatly tickled, as if some detail that completely escaped me were provoking his endless, uncontrollable laughter.

I was, though, obliged to answer his question. If I told him the tailor wasn't Carmen's lover, then I would be what I am: a cuckold. And if I told him he was, the result would be the same.

"Oh, and another thing your bogus nephew said," I told him bluntly, "he said that whenever he rereads one of the chapters about your Walter's adventures, he feels like digging you up and beating you on the skull with your own tibia."

He found this vastly amusing too, and I felt an urgent need then to walk away and leave him standing there.

"If I ever meet him, I'll kill him," Sánchez said suddenly, his smile suddenly replaced by a very grim expression indeed.

I felt afraid.

"I'll kill him," he repeated.

That's when I considered going away, beginning my "escape in a nightshirt" right there and then. Leaving my home Petronius-style, with just a small leather satchel. Telling Carmen one last time that I was going downstairs to buy some cigarettes at Bar Tender and not coming back. Or else paying modest homage to the legendary suicide of Coyote's hero, José Mallorquí, the previous tenant of Sánchez's apartment, who left behind this simple note: "I can't go on. I'm going to kill myself. There are signed checks in the drawer in my desk. Papa."

But I've always had my doubts about suicide, because, whenever I think of it, I can't help remembering that the man who kicks away the chair he is standing on takes the leap into the void only to feel that the rope around his neck binds him ever closer to the very existence he wanted to leave.

"So, if I've understood you correctly," Sánchez said, interrupting my thoughts, "I now have two men who hate me, both called Pedro."

"Yes."

I was about to add:

"Two enemies, the rope and the void."

Instead I said something very different, about how certain stories appear in our lives and how the path they follow ends up merging with our own.

Another guffaw. A huge guffaw. It was almost painful to see how much he reveled in what I'd just said. Perhaps the most irritating thing of all was this: he was convinced that his "bogus nephew" was bogus and didn't exist.

48

Dusk was coming on, and, in the time it took me to walk down Rua do Sol, night fell as suddenly as it does in the tropics. But I wasn't in the tropics and one thing was certain: I was walking along, wide awake and alert to the dangers of that street; I was walking along thinking about myself—about my fate, to be exact—and I avoided smiling at all costs because whenever I smiled, I looked sad. I didn't want to give myself away to the other passersby. Then I realized that the harlequin's mask was covering my face. How could I have forgotten that? I looked like someone on his way to a fancy-dress party, and so my fears could not have been more absurd. Who could possibly recognize me? Who could possibly know of my sadness, still less my crimes? I was walking with a cane that I didn't actually need, but which was part of my camouflage. I was limping to give credibility to my role as an anonymous man going to a party in a small town somewhere south of Lisbon. I was shuffling down the cobbled street when, through an open window, I heard a Beatles song being sung in Portuguese by a young woman with a delicate voice. The song repeated these words several times: "Now I need a place to hide away."

&

A thought: do kids today still read Marco Polo?

49

Here in this village near Évora, where the hours pass in a slow but lively fashion, I think only about life. There's hardly anything in my room, and almost nothing in the village; some of the furniture stands out starkly against the whitewashed walls, and outside, the red earth is covered in a vast blanket of dry stubble. From here I can see an agricultural civilization, with people wearing pants and full skirts that seem to come from another age. They've already harvested the wheat and have nothing to do. Nor have I.

Setting off with just this notebook, without my computer, should have made me feel lighter, but, oddly, what I miss more and more is the patient editing on paper that I used to do at home, before writing it all out again, transferring it onto the computer, printing it out, rereading it, making more changes on paper and then on screen, at which stage, I would feel like a pianist seated at the piano, faithful to the score, but free now to interpret it.

Each day I took greater and greater pleasure in repetition, a pleasure closely bound up with my diary, which, from the very start, has taken repetition as its theme. Contrary to expectations, I soon realized that, for this new stage, traveling light has its disadvantages, because now all I do is yearn for that perfectionist system I'd instituted at home, the system of repeating over and over that particular day's words, to the point where I became an obsessive stalker of what I'd already written, and which I always believed could be improved. Now I see that, in Barcelona, when I repeated the words over and over, what I was seeking was physical and mental exhaustion. In Barcelona, I was beginning to resemble the painter with the big bushy beard who my grandfather used to invite to spend the summers at our family's vacation home in the country when I was a child. Over a period of three or four years, he painted the same tree more than one hundred times, perhaps because—as happened with me and my writing—he understood the appeal of constantly interrogating what he had already put down on paper.

&

As evening fell, I went to the village bar, fearing that not showing my face might arouse suspicions. The police would doubtless already be looking for me in Lisbon. As I crossed the square, I passed someone I took to be the local tailor; he had the air of a tailor who has just shut up shop and still has a few pins stuck somewhere on his clothing. Bowed head, melancholy, languorous. I wondered again what it is about the "repairers" of this world—as I would like to call them—who are always so taciturn; what a difference between their world and that of barbers, who take such an interest in life, an interest very hard to find in the sad world of tailors.

In the village bar, I couldn't quite catch what the customers were talking about, because they were speaking very softly, as they were in the final story in my neighbor's novel. Perhaps they were discussing the story of the dead horse and the young Jew. I was afraid someone might suddenly ask me for a light and ask if I was the ventriloquist they were looking for in Lisbon. Just then a woman came into the bar. She had broad hips and strangely tapered limbs, and was so terribly pale that, as she tottered up to the bar, she reminded me of nothing so much as a very reluctant ghost. I, for my part, was so dreadfully somber that I could have been mistaken for someone in a skeleton costume. This scene was a million miles from the beggars and other conspirators in my old Coyote neighborhood. In reality, everything was a million miles away, because mine was a journey with no return, a kind of one-way ticket to Mars.

I finished my glass of wine and, as I was about to leave the bar, I heard the woman asking another customer for a light, and she did so in a low voice and in a staccato language that sounded like Arabic. Things were clearly becoming far too complicated, and I reminded myself that it was time to continue on my way. I lingered for a few seconds longer, however, drawing little circles in the dark with my lit cigarette. And I recalled other times, when the profoundest idea in the world would suddenly pop into my head only to be lost, to vanish inside my brain, long before I could find something with which to write it down.

50

When I woke, I had the sense that I'd shifted into a kind of earthly writing, although I don't know why my friends in the dream called it earthly, presumably because, having been left with no study and no books to refer to, I'd sat down on the ground, alone with this notebook, just as I am right now: in this case, sitting on the beach in Algeciras, traveling, or, rather, fleeing to Morocco.

Writing at ground level, and, with each second that passes, feeling a joy that seems to be returning me to that pure substance of self, namely, a past impression, pure life preserved in its pure state (and which, as Proust says, we can only know in that preserved state, because, at the moment we actually experience it, it is too clouded by other sensations to be apparent), a past impression, an extraordinary return to the pure substance of self, to something that concerns only you, that is completely yours, and which, suddenly, more than half a century later, you recover: it's to do with a notebook, with the ground on which you are sitting, with a particular age—I would have been five years old on that day, in my maternal grandmother's house, the first time I formed letters into words in my drawing book, the first time in my entire life that I wrote a story, my first contact with a written narrative, and, of course, with no study, no computer, no book to call my own.

A return to myself. I thought about tourists, and about all those friends who travel to see the thing they've always dreamed of seeing: the Leaning Tower of Pisa, the Palacio de Cristal in Madrid, the Great Pyramids on the outskirts of Cairo, the seven hills of Rome, the *Mona Lisa* in Paris, the chair in Bar Melitón in Cadaqués where Duchamp would sit to play chess, the Musetta Caffé in the Palermo district in Buenos Aires.... One day, a friend suggested that it was actually better to discover all that hasn't already been seen, all that you weren't expecting to see, which, he said, was probably neither grand nor impressive nor alien, but was, on the contrary, the familiar regained.

It hurts to think this when I'm so far from my past and my city, but sitting here with Africa lying before me, at least this notebook and the act of setting down words beyond the safety of my study walls allow me to feel that something is restoring that pure substance to me, bringing me closer to the familiar things I've now lost, but which are perhaps recoverable beneath today's strangely ancient light, the light which, they say, always falls on these straits.

51

I had heard people talk about the voices of Marrakech, but had no idea what was so special about them. Perhaps they're different from all the other voices in the world, I thought as I sat down here, outside this bar, from which you can observe everything going on in Jemaa el-Fnaa, the square where, for centuries, and still today, storytelling is actively cultivated, and you can hear all kinds of stories told out loud, in the midst of all the haggling and the hubbub, the blinding North African light, and the faded awnings. On the square I can see storytellers, Berber musicians, and snake charmers. I realize that no one ever talks about the color of voices, but Marrakech is the perfect place to do so. A voice the color of Petrarch's Siena, a voice the color of a Hindu fakir's robes, the deep, dark voice of New Orleans. It was no surprise, then, that when the Moroccan waiter came over to me, I heard in his voice the sonorous depths of the muezzins when they issue the call to prayer from the minarets.

Then a lunatic suddenly appeared, his skin dark against his white djellaba. And I focused all my attention on him and his weightless voice. I had never seen such violent gestures: they seemed to reproduce, in the faltering air, a whole life story, doubtless his. The autobiography of a sad, solitary tree trunk standing like a mast in the middle of this huge square. I assumed that he spoke only about himself, about his solitary life and the days when he loved adventures and traveled to strange lands, and, on his wanderings, picked up fragments of stories from other fellow solitaries, and from those scraps pieced together an invented memoir. A very skeletal one, which, with the skill of a mime artiste, he could sell every day like a dream to an ever-faithful public, here in Jemaa el-Fnaa. I imagine him selling the partial story of his life, a trajectory that could be reduced to a few clamorous gestures and the acoustic, rhythmic tones of a voice the color of the white tailcoat worn by a black jazz musician in Chicago.

52

I imagined that as I fled to the south of Tunis, among the tall palm trees of the oasis of Douz, I enlisted in the Foreign Legion and went on to see images that came from my oldest memories of action movies, or adventure books set in Africa—as if they were being projected on to the white dunes of the Grand Erg Oriental. I conjured memories of the sun glinting on the enemy's swords, for example. And later, in the luminous desert night, I saw myself in the company of legionnaires and friendly Bedouins and a prisoner called Boj. And I watched this, with my veteran soldier's eyes, as my identity softly, slowly, marvelously dissolved into anonymity. A luminous night after the sandstorm that battered us, a profoundly still night turned in on itself. Beside me, the prisoner Boj keeps endlessly summoning up stories and the voices of all kinds of characters, who, as they recount episodes from their lives, parade past me as if they were the peaceful nomads of a slow desert caravan. Tonight, to the south of Tunis, among the tall palm trees of the oasis of Douz, I have the tender, but also bitter sense that I am I, but that I'm also Boj and all the members of that slow caravan of stories told by anonymous voices and of anonymous fates, which all seems to confirm that certain stories appear in our lives, and the path they follow ends up merging with our own.

53

When it came to bidding farewell to the kind, friendly inhabitants of this village near the ruins of Berenice, something happened that was very similar to Robert Louis Stevenson in his account of saying goodbye to the inhabitants of one of the Gilbert Islands, where he disembarked on his way from Honolulu en route to Apia in Samoa.

I had spent several days at Berenice, living alongside the fishermen and recounting to them, in a considerable variety of voices, the most important events of my life, or—what amounts to the same thing—the stories I'd heard others tell and which, during my travels, I'd gradually appropriated. When the time came to say farewell, having embraced all those dear people, I was obliged, because there was no wind, to wait for a few hours in the small port. During that time, the islanders remained hidden behind the trees and gave no sign of life, *because we had already said our farewells.*

54

I am one and many and yet I do not know who I am. I don't recognize this voice, I only know that I passed through Aden and organized a caravan of tireless, anonymous voices that I led to the Bab-el-Mandeb Strait. And I only know that yesterday, I set off again, retracing my steps from the other day. Beyond the devastated hills lay darkness and dust. From the road, I saw my own room with the light on. The faded light from the small window, next to which I've spent some hours writing. There is nothing quite like walking. Things happen, and sometimes there are coincidences and chance events you could die laughing about, and then there are coincidences and chance events you die as a result of. You get the feeling that, the more we travel the earth and plow it in every sense of the word, the more bound we become to the ghost of the familiar, which we hope one day to recover, because, in truth, that is the only thing we can truly claim to be ours. A glimpse of some unremarkable piece of writing, of a world we'd forgotten we had written. Along the way, you might recall or stumble over something you'd forgotten. For example, I've just remembered those Cherry Cokes.